THE GREAT
WRITERS
L I B R A R Y

"*I'm not ambitious for a splendid fortune, a fashionable position, or a great name for my girls . . . I know, by experience, how much genuine happiness can be had in a plain little house, where the daily bread is earned, and some privations give sweetness to the few pleasures.*"

LITTLE WOMEN

LOUISA MAY ALCOTT

Front cover: Little Women by M.E. Gray. Hodder & Stoughton/McMullen Collection

This edition is the copyright © 1987 of Marshall Cavendish Ltd.

Published in 1987 for The Great Writers library by
Marshall Cavendish Partworks Ltd, 58 Old Compton Street, London W1V 5PA.
Printed and bound in Spain by Printer Industria Gráfica, Barcelona. D.L.B. 20866-1987

ISBN 0-86307-679-3

This is a facsimile reproduction of an edition published by
Hutchinson & Co, London in the 1920s.

PREFACE

"Go then, my little Book, and show to all
That entertain, and bid thee welcome shall,
What thou dost keep close shut up in thy breast;
And wish what thou dost show them may be blest
To them for good, may make them choose to be
Pilgrims better, by far, than thee or me.
Tell them of Mercy; she is one
Who early hath her pilgrimage begun.
Yea, let young damsels learn of her to prize
The world which is to come, and so be wise;
For little tripping maids may follow God
Along the ways which saintly feet have trod."

Adapted from John Bunyan.

CONTENTS.

LITTLE WOMEN.

CHAPTER I.

PLAYING PILGRIMS.

"CHRISTMAS won't be Christmas without any presents," grumbled Jo, lying on the rug.

"It's so dreadful to be poor!" sighed Meg, looking down at her old dress.

"I don't think it's fair for some girls to have lots of pretty things, and other girls nothing at all," added little Amy, with an injured sniff.

"We've got father and mother, and each other, anyhow," said Beth, contentedly, from her corner.

The four young faces on which the firelight shone brightened at the cheerful words, but darkened again as Jo said sadly—

"We haven't got father, and shall not have him for a long time." She didn't say "perhaps never," but each silently added it, thinking of father far away, where the fighting was.

Nobody spoke for a minute; then Meg said in an altered tone—

"You know the reason mother proposed not having any presents this Christmas, was because it's going to be a hard winter for every one; and she thinks we ought not to spend money for pleasure, when our men are suffering so in the army.

We can't do much, but we can make our little sacrifices, and ought to do it gladly. But I am afraid I don't " ; and Meg shook her head, as she thought regretfully of all the pretty things she wanted.

" But I don't think the little we should spend would do any good. We've each got a dollar, and the army wouldn't be much helped by our giving that. I agree not to expect anything from mother or you, but I do want to buy Undine and Sintram for myself ; I've wanted it *so* long," said Jo, who was a bookworm.

" I planned to spend mine on new music," said Beth, with a little sigh, which no one heard but the hearth-brush and kettle-holder.

" I shall get a nice box of Faber's drawing pencils ; I really need them," said Amy, decidedly.

" Mother didn't say anything about our money, and she won't wish us to give up everything. Let's each buy what we want, and have a little fun ; I'm sure we grub hard enough to earn it," cried Jo, examining the heels of her boots in a gentlemanly manner.

" I know *I* do,—teaching those dreadful children nearly all day, when I'm longing to enjoy myself at home," began Meg, in the complaining tone again.

" You don't have half such a hard time as I do," said Jo. " How would you like to be shut up for hours with a nervous, fussy old lady, who keeps you trotting, is never satisfied, and worries you till you're ready to fly out of the window or box her ears ? "

" It's naughty to fret,—but I do think washing dishes and keeping things tidy is the worst work in the world. It makes me cross ; and my hands get so stiff, I can't practise good a bit." And Beth looked at her rough hands with a sigh that any one could hear that time.

"I don't believe any of you suffer as I do," cried Amy; "for you don't have to go to school with impertinent girls, who plague you if you don't know your lessons, and laugh at your dresses, and label your father if he isn't rich, and insult you when your nose isn't nice."

"If you mean *libel* I'd say so, and not talk about *labels*, as if pa was a pickle-bottle," advised Jo, laughing.

"I know what I mean, and you needn't be ' statirical ' about it. It's proper to use good words, and improve your *vocabilary*," returned Amy, with dignity.

"Don't peck at one another, children. Don't you wish we had the money papa lost when we were little, Jo? Dear me, how happy and good we'd be, if we had no worries," said Meg, who could remember better times.

"You said the other day you thought we were a deal happier than the King children, for they were fighting and fretting all the time, in spite of their money."

"So I did, Beth. Well, I guess we are; for though we do have to work, we make fun for ourselves, and are a pretty jolly set, as Jo would say."

"Jo does use such slang words," observed Amy, with a reproving look at the long figure stretched on the rug. Jo immediately sat up, put her hands in her apron pockets, and began to whistle.

"Don't Jo, it's so boyish."

"That's why I do it."

"I detest rude, unlady-like girls."

"I hate affected niminy piminy chits."

"Birds in their little nests agree," sang Beth the peacemaker, with such a funny face that both sharp voices softened to a laugh, and the "pecking" ended for that time.

"Really, girls, you are both to be blamed," said Meg, beginning to lecture in her elder-sisterly fashion. "You are old enough to leave off boyish tricks, and behave better, Josephine. It didn't matter so much when you were a little girl; but now you are so tall, and turn up your hair, you should remember that you are a young lady."

"I ain't! and if turning up my hair makes me one, I'll wear it in two tails till I'm twenty," cried Jo, pulling off her net, and shaking down a chestnut mane. "I hate to think I've got to grow up and be Miss March, and wear long gowns, and look as prim as a China-aster. It's bad enough to be a girl, any way; when I like boy's games, and work, and manners. I can't get over my disappointment in not being a boy, and it's worse than ever now, for I'm dying to go and fight with papa, and I can only stay at home and knit like a poky old woman"; and Jo shook the blue army-sock till the needles rattled like castanets, and her ball bounded across the room.

"Poor Jo; it's too bad! But it can't be helped, so you must try to be contented with making your name boyish, and playing brother to us girls," said Beth, stroking the rough head at her knee with a hand that all the dish-washing and dusting in the world could not make ungentle in its touch.

"As for you, Amy," continued Meg, "you are altogether too particular and prim. Your airs are funny now, but you'll grow up an affected little goose, if you don't take care. I like your nice manners and refined ways of speaking, when you don't try to be elegant ; but your absurd words are as bad as Jo's slang."

"If Jo is a tom-boy, and Amy a goose, what am I please ? " asked Beth, ready to share the lecture.

"You're a dear, and nothing else," answered Meg, warmly ; and no one contradicted her, for the "Mouse" was the pet of the family.

As young readers like to know "how people look," we will take this moment to give them a little sketch of the four sisters, who sat knitting away in the twilight, while the December snow fell quietly without, and the fire crackled cheerfully within. It was a comfortable old room, though the carpet was faded and the furniture very plain, for a good picture or two hung on the walls, books filled the recesses, chrysanthemums and Christmas roses bloomed in the windows, and a pleasant atmosphere of home-peace pervaded it.

Margaret, the eldest of the four, was sixteen, and very pretty, being plump and fair, with large eyes, plenty of soft brown hair, a sweet mouth, and white hands, of which she was rather vain. Fifteen-year-old Jo was very tall, thin and brown, and reminded one of a colt ; for she never seemed to know what to do with her long limbs, which were very much in her way. She had a decided mouth, a comical nose, and sharp gray eyes, which appeared to see everything, and were by turns fierce, funny, or thoughtful. Her long, thick hair was her one beauty ; but it was usually bundled into a net, to be out of her way. Round shoulders had Jo, big hands and feet, a fly-away look to her clothes, and the uncomfortable appearance of a girl who was rapidly shooting up into a woman, and didn't like it. Elizabeth—or Beth, as every one called her—was a rosy, smooth-haired, bright-eyed girl of thirteen, with a shy manner, a timid voice, and a peaceful expression, which was seldom disturbed. Her father called her "Little Tranquillity," and the name suited her excellently ; for she seemed to live in a happy world of her own, only venturing out to meet the few whom she trusted and loved. Amy, though the youngest, was a most important person, in her own opinion at least. A regular snow maiden, with blue eyes, and yellow hair curling on her shoulders ; pale and slender, and always carrying herself like a young lady mindful of her manners. What the characters of the four sisters were we will leave to be found out.

The clock struck six ; and, having swept up the hearth, Beth put a pair of slippers down to warm. Somehow the sight of the old shoes had a good effect upon the girls, for mother was coming, and every one brightened to welcome her. Meg stopped lecturing, and lit the lamp. Amy got out of the easy chair without being asked, and Jo forgot how tired she was as she sat up to hold the slippers nearer to the blaze.

"They are quite worn out ; Marmee must have a new pair."

"I thought I'd get her some with my dollar," said Beth.

" No, I shall ! " cried Amy.

" I'm the oldest," began Meg, but Jo cut in with a decided—

" I'm the man of the family now papa is away, and *I* shall provide the slippers, for he told me to take special care of mother while he was gone."

" I'll tell you what we'll do," said Beth ; " let's each get her something for Christmas, and not get anything for ourselves."

" That's like you, dear ! What will we get ? " exclaimed Jo.

Every one thought soberly for a minute ; then Meg announced, as if the idea was suggested by the sight of her own pretty hands, " I shall give her a nice pair of gloves."

" Army shoes, best to be had," cried Jo.

" Some handkerchiefs, all hemmed," said Beth.

" I'll get a little bottle of Cologne ; she likes it, and it won't cost much, so I'll have some left to buy something for me," added Amy.

" How will we give the things ? " asked Meg.

" Put 'em on the table, and bring her in and see her open the bundles. Don't you remember how we used to do on our birthdays ? " answered Jo.

" I used to be *so* frightened when it was my turn to sit in the big chair with the crown on, and see you all come marching round to give the presents, with a kiss. I liked the things and the kisses, but it was dreadful to have you sit looking at me while I opened the bundles," said Beth, toasting her face and the bread at the same time.

" Let Marmee think we are getting things for ourselves, and then surprise her. We must go shopping to-morrow afternoon, Meg ; there is lots to do about the play for Christmas night," said Jo, marching up and down with her hands behind her back.

"I don't mean to act any more after this time ; I'm getting too old for such things," observed Meg, who was as much a child as ever about "dressing up" frolics.

"You won't stop, I know, as long as you can trail round in a white gown with your hair down, and wear gold-paper jewellery. You are the best actress we've got, and there'll be an end of everything if you quit the boards," said Jo. "We ought to rehearse to-night. Come here, Amy, and do the fainting scene, for you are as stiff as a poker in that."

"I can't help it ; I never saw any one faint, and I don't choose to make myself all black and blue, tumbling flat as you do. If I can go down easily, I'll drop ; if I can't, I shall fall into a chair and be graceful. I don't care if Hugo does come at me with a pistol," returned Amy, who was not gifted with dramatic power, but was chosen because she was small enough to be borne out shrieking by the hero of the piece.

"Do it this way : clasp your hands so, and stagger across the room, crying frantically, 'Roderigo ! save me ! save me !'" and away went Jo, with a melo-dramatic scream which was truly thrilling.

Amy followed, but she poked her hands out stiffly before her, and jerked herself along as if she went by machinery ; and her "Ow !" was more suggestive of pins being run into her than of fear and anguish. Jo gave a despairing groan, and Meg laughed outright, while Beth let her bread burn as she watched the fun, with interest.

"It's no use ! do the best you can when the time comes, and if the audience shout, don't blame me. Come on, Meg."

Then things went smoothly ; for Don Pedro defied the world in a speech of two pages without a single break ; Hagar, the witch, chanted an awful incantation over her kettleful of simmering toads, with weird effect ; Roderigo rent his chains asunder manfully, and Hugo died in agonies of remorse and arsenic, with a wild " Ha ! ha ! "

" It's the best we've had yet," said Meg, as the dead villain sat up and rubbed his elbows.

" I don't see how you can write and act such splendid things, Jo. You're a regular Shakespeare ! " exclaimed Beth, who firmly believed that her sisters were gifted with wonderful genius in all things.

" Not quite," replied Jo, modestly. " I do think ' The Witch's Curse, an Operatic Tragedy,' is rather a nice thing ; but I'd like to try Macbeth, if we only had a trap door for Banquo. I always wanted to do the killing part. ' Is that a dagger that I see before me ? ' " muttered Jo, rolling her eyes and clutching at the air, as she had seen a famous tragedian do.

" No, it's the toasting fork, with ma's shoe on it instead of the bread. Beth's stage struck ! " cried Meg, and the rehearsal ended in a general burst of laughter.

" Glad to find you so merry, my girls," said a cheery voice at the door, and actors and audience turned to welcome a stout, motherly lady, with a

" can I help you " look about her which was truly delightful. She wasn't a particularly handsome person, but mothers are always lovely to their children, and the girls thought the gray cloak and the unfashionable bonnet covered the most splendid woman in the world.

"Well, dearies, how have you got on to-day? There was so much to do, getting the boxes ready to go to-morrow, that I didn't come home to dinner. Has any one called, Beth? How is your cold, Meg? Jo, you look tired to death. Come and kiss me, baby."

While making these maternal inquiries Mrs. March got her wet things off, her hot slippers on, and sitting down in the easy chair, drew Amy to her lap, preparing to enjoy the happiest hour of her busy day. The girls flew about, trying to make things comfortable, each in her own way. Meg arranged the tea-table ; Jo brought wood and set chairs dropping, overturning, and clattering everything she touched ; Beth trotted to and fro between parlour and kitchen, quiet and busy ; while Amy gave directions to every one, as she sat with her hands folded.

As they gathered about the table, Mrs. March said, with a particularly happy face, " I've got a treat for you after supper."

A quick, bright smile went round like a streak of sunshine. Beth clapped her hands, regardless of the hot biscuit she held, and Jo tossed up her napkin, crying, " A letter ! a letter ! Three cheers for father ! "

" Yes, a nice, long letter. He is well, and thinks he shall get through the cold season better than we feared. He sends all sorts of loving wishes for Christmas, and an especial message to you girls," said Mrs. March, patting her pocket as if she had got a treasure there.

" Hurry up and get done. Don't stop to quirk your little finger, and prink over your plate, Amy," cried Jo, choking in her tea, and dropping her bread, butter side down, on the carpet, in her haste to get at the treat.

Beth ate no more, but crept away, to sit in her shadowy corner and brood over the delight to come, till the others were ready.

" I think it was so splendid in father to go as a chaplain when he was too old to be drafted, and not strong enough for a soldier," said Meg, warmly.

" Dont I wish I could go as a drummer, a *vivan* —what's its name ? or a nurse, so I could be near him and help him," exclaimed Jo, with a groan.

" It must be very disagreeable to sleep in a tent, and eat all sorts of bad-tasting things, and drink out of a tin mug," sighed Amy.

" When will he come home, Marmee ? " asked Beth, with a little quiver in her voice.

" Not for many months, dear, unless he is sick. He will stay and do his work faithfully as long as he can, and we won't ask for him back a minute sooner than he can be spared. Now come and hear the letter."

They all drew to the fire, mother in the big chair with Beth at her feet, Meg and Amy perched on either arm of the chair, and Jo leaning on the back, where no one would see any sign of emotion if the letter should happen to be touching.

Very few letters were written in those hard

times that were not touching, especially those which fathers sent home. In this one little was said of the hardships endured, the dangers faced, or the homesickness conquered; it was a cheerful, hopeful letter, full of lively descriptions of camp life, marches, and military news; and only at the end did the writer's heart overflow with fatherly love and longing for the little girls at home.

"Give them all my dear love and a kiss. Tell them I think of them by day, pray for them by night, and find my best comfort in their affection at all times. A year seems very long to wait before I see them, but remind them that while we wait we may all work, so that these hard days need not be wasted. I know they will remember all I said to them, that they will be loving children to you, will do their duty faithfully, fight their bosom enemies bravely, and conquer themselves so beautifully that when I come back to them I may be fonder and prouder than ever of my little women."

Everybody sniffed when they came to that part; Jo wasn't ashamed of the great tear that dropped off the end of her nose, and Amy never minded the rumpling of her curls as she hid her face on her mother's shoulder and sobbed out, "I *am* a selfish pig! but I'll try truly to be better, so he mayn't be disappointed in me by and by."

"We all will!" cried Meg. "I think too much of my looks, and hate to work, but won't any more, if I can help it."

"I'll try to be what he loves to call me, 'a little woman,' and not be rough and wild; but do my duty here instead of wanting to be somewhere else," said Jo, thinking that keeping her temper at home was a much harder task than facing a rebel or two down South.

Beth said nothing, but wiped away her tears with the blue army-sock, and began to knit with all her might, losing no time in doing the duty that lay nearest her, while she resolved in her quiet little soul to be all that father hoped to find her when the year brought round the happy coming home.

Mrs. March broke the silence that followed Jo's words, by saying in her cheery voice, " Do you remember how you used to play Pilgrim's Progress when you were little things ? Nothing delighted you more than to have me tie my piece-bags on your backs for burdens, give you hats and sticks, and rolls of paper, and let you travel through the house from the cellar, which was the City of Destruction, up, up, to the house-top, where you had all the lovely things you could collect to make a Celestial City."

" What fun it was, especially going by the lions, fighting Apollyon, and passing through the Valley where the hobgoblins were," said Jo.

" I liked the place where the bundles fell off and tumbled down stairs," said Meg.

" My favourite part was when we came out on the flat roof where our flowers and arbours, and pretty things were, and all stood and sung for joy up there in the sunshine," said Beth, smiling, as if that pleasant moment had come back to her.

" I don't remember much about it, except that I was afraid of the cellar and the dark entry, and always liked the cake and milk we had up at the top. If I wasn't too old for such things, I'd rather like to play it over again," said Amy, who began to talk of renouncing childish things at the mature age of twelve.

"We never are too old for this, my dear, because it is a play we are playing all the time in one way or another. Our burdens are here, our road is before us, and the longing for goodness and happiness is the guide that leads us through many troubles and mistakes to the peace which is a true Celestial City. Now, my little pilgrims, suppose you begin again, not in play, but in earnest, and see how far on you can get before father comes home."

"Really, mother? Where are our bundles?" asked Amy, who was a very literal young lady.

"Each of you told what your burden was just now, except Beth; I rather think she hasn't got any," said her mother.

"Yes, I have; mine is dishes and dusters, and envying girls with nice pianos, and being afraid of people."

Beth's bundle was such a funny one that everybody wanted to laugh; but nobody did, for it would have hurt her feelings very much.

"Let us do it," said Meg, thoughtfully. "It is only another name for trying to be good, and the story may help us; for though we do want to be good, it's hard work, and we forget, and don't do our best."

"We were in the Slough of Despond to-night, and mother came and pulled us out, as Help did in the book. We ought to have our roll of directions, like Christian. What shall we do about that?" asked Jo, delighted with the fancy which lent a little romance to the very dull task of doing her duty.

"Look under your pillows, Christmas morning, and you will find your guide-book," replied Mrs. March.

They talked over the new plan while old Hannah cleared the table ; then out came the four little work-baskets, and the needles flew as the girls made sheets for Aunt March. It was uninteresting sewing, but to-night no one grumbled. They adopted Jo's plan of dividing the long seams into four parts, and calling the quarters Europe, Asia, Africa, and America, and in that way got on capitally, especially when they talked about the different countries as they stitched their way through them.

At nine they stopped work, and sang, as usual, before they went to bed. No one but Beth could get much music out of the old piano ; but she had a way of softly touching the yellow keys, and making a pleasant accompaniment to the simple songs they sang. Meg had a voice like a flute, and she and her mother led the little choir. Amy chirped like a cricket, and Jo wandered through the airs at her own sweet will, always coming out at the wrong place with a crook or a quaver that spoilt the most pensive tune. They had always done this from the time they could lisp

"Crinkle, crinkle, 'ittle 'tar,"

and it had become a household custom, for the mother was a born singer. The first sound in the morning was her voice, as she went about the house singing like a lark ; and the last sound at night was the same cheery sound, for the girls never grew too old for that familiar lullaby.

CHAPTER II.

A MERRY CHRISTMAS.

Jo was the first to wake in the grey dawn of Christmas morning. No stockings hung at the fireplace, and for a moment she felt as much disappointed as she did long ago, when her little sock fell down because it was so crammed with goodies. Then she remembered her mother's promise, and slipping her hand under her pillow, drew out a little crimson-covered book. She knew it very well, for it was that beautiful old story of the best life ever lived, and Jo felt that it was a true guide-book for any pilgrim going the long journey. She woke Meg with a " Merry Christmas," and bade her see what was under her pillow. A green-covered book appeared with the same picture inside, and a few words written by their mother, which made their one present very precious in their eyes. Presently Beth and Amy woke, to rummage and find their little books also—one dove-coloured, the other blue ; and all sat looking and talking about them, while the East grew rosy with the coming day.

In spite of her small vanities, Margaret had a sweet and pious nature, which unconsciously influenced her sisters, especially Jo, who loved her very tenderly, and obeyed her because her advice was so gently given.

" Girls," said Meg, seriously, looking from the

tumbled head beside her to the two little night-capped ones in the room beyond, " mother wants us to read and love and mind these books, and we must begin at once. We used to be faithful about it, but since father went away, and all this war trouble unsettled us, we have neglected many things. You can do as you please, but *I* shall keep my book on the table here, and read a little every morning as soon as I wake, for I know it will do me good and help me through the day."

Then she opened her book and began to read. Jo put her arm round her, and, leaning cheek to cheek, read also, with the quiet expression so seldom seen on her restless face.

" How good Meg is ! Come, Amy, let's do as they do. I'll help you with the hard words, and they'll explain things if we don't understand," whispered Beth, very much impressed by the pretty books and her sister's example.

" I'm glad mine is blue," said Amy ; and then the rooms were very still while the pages were softly turned, and the winter sunshine crept in to touch the bright heads and serious faces with a Christmas greeting.

" Where is mother ? " asked Meg, as she and Jo ran down to thank her for their gifts, half-an-hour later.

" Goodness only knows. Some poor creeter come a-beggin', and your ma went straight off to see what was needed. There never *was* such a woman for givin' away vittles and drink, clothes and firin'," replied Hannah, who had lived with the family since Meg was born, and was considered by them all more as a friend than a servant.

" She will be back soon, I guess ; so do your

cakes, and have everything ready," said Meg, looking over the presents which were collected in a basket and kept under the sofa, ready to be produced at the proper time. "Why, where is Amy's bottle of Cologne ? " she added, as the little flask did not appear.

"She took it out a minute ago, and went off with it to put a ribbon on it, or some such notion," replied Jo, dancing about the room to take the first stiffness off the new army-slippers.

"How nice my handkerchiefs look, don't they ? Hannah washed and ironed them for me, and I marked them all myself," said Beth, looking proudly at the somewhat uneven letters which had cost her such labour.

"Bless the child, she's gone and put ' Mother ' on them instead of ' M. March ' ; how funny ! " cried Jo, taking up one.

"Isn't it right ? I thought it was better to do so, because Meg's initals are ' M.M.,' and I don't want anyone to use these but Marmee," said Beth, looking troubled.

"It's all right, dear, and a very pretty idea ; quite sensible, too, for no one can ever mistake now. It will please her very much, I know," said Meg, with a frown for Jo, and a smile for Beth.

"There's mother ; hide the basket, quick ! " cried Jo, as a door slammed, and steps sounded in the hall.

Amy came in hastily, and looked rather abashed when she saw her sisters all waiting for her.

"Where have you been, and what are you hiding behind you ? " asked Meg, surprised to see, by her hood and cloak, that lazy Amy had been out so early.

"Don't laugh at me, Jo, I didn't mean anyone should know till the time came. I only meant to change the little bottle for a big one, and I gave *all* my money to get it, and I'm truly trying not to be selfish any more."

As she spoke, Amy showed the handsome flask which replaced the cheap one ; and looked so earnest and humble in her little effort to forget herself, that Meg hugged her on the spot, and Jo pronounced her "a trump," while Beth ran to the window, and picked her finest rose to ornament the stately bottle.

"You see I felt ashamed of my present, after reading and talking about being good this morning, so I ran round the corner and changed it the minute I was up ; and I'm *so* glad, for mine is the handsomest now."

Another bang at the street-door sent the basket under the sofa, and the girls to the table eager for for breakfast.

"Merry Christmas, Marmee ! Lots of them ! Thank you for our books ; we read some, and mean to every day," they cried, in chorus.

"Merry Christmas, little daughters ! I'm glad you began at once, and hope you will keep on. But I want to say one word before we sit down. Not far away from here lies a poor woman with a little new-born baby. Six children are huddled into one bed to keep from freezing, for they have no fire. There is nothing to eat over there ; and the eldest boy came to tell me they were suffering hunger and cold. My girls, will you give them your breakfast as a Christmas present ? "

They were all unusually hungry, having waited

nearly an hour, and for a minute no one spoke only a minute, for Jo exclaimed impetuously :—

" I'm so glad you came before we began ! "

" May I go and help carry the things to the poor little children ? " asked Beth, eagerly.

" *I* shall take the cream and muffins," added Amy, heroically giving up the articles she most liked.

Meg was already covering the buckwheats, and piling the bread into one big plate.

" I thought you'd do it," said Mrs. March, smiling as if satisfied. " You shall all go and help me, and when we come back we will have bread and milk for breakfast, and make it up at dinner time."

They were soon ready, and the procession set out. Fortunately it was early, and they went through back streets, so few people saw them, and ne one laughed at the funny party.

A poor, bare, miserable room it was, with broken windows, no fire, ragged bed-clothes, a sick mother, wailing baby, and a group of pale, hungry children cuddled under one old quilt, trying to keep warm. How the big eyes startled, and the blue lips smiled, as the girls went in !

" Ach, mein Gott ! it is good angels come to us ! " cried the poor woman, crying for joy.

" Funny angels in hoods and mittens," said Jo, and set them laughing.

In a few minutes it really did seem as if kind spirits had been at work there. Hannah, who had carried wood, made a fire, and stopped up the broken panes with old hats, and her own shawl. Mrs. March gave the mother tea and gruel, and comforted her with promises of help, while she dressed the little baby as tenderly as if it had been her own. The girls, meantime, spread the table, set the children round the fire, and fed them like so many hungry birds ; laughing, talking, and trying to understand the funny broken English.

" Das ist gut ! " " Die Angel-kinder ! " cried the poor things, as they ate, and warmed their purple hands at the comfortable blaze. The girls had never been called angel children before, and thought it very agreeable, especially Jo, who had been considered a " Sancho " ever since she was born. That was a very happy breakfast, though they didn't get any of it ; and when they went away, leaving comfort behind, I think there was not in all the city four merrier people than the hungry little girls who gave away their breakfasts, and contented themselves with bread and milk on Christmas morning.

" That's loving our neighbour better than ourselves, and I like it," said Meg, as they set out their presents, while their mother was upstairs collecting clothes for the poor Hummels.

Not a very splendid show, but there was a great deal of love done up in the few little bundles ; and the tall vase of red roses, white chrysanthemums, and trailing vines, which stood in the middle, gave quite an elegant air to the table.

" She's coming ! strike up, Beth ; open the door, Amy. Three cheers for Marmee ! " cried Jo, prancing about, while Meg went to conduct mother to the seat of honour.

Beth played her gayest march, Amy threw open the door, and Meg enacted escort with great dignity. Mrs. March was both surprised and touched, and smiled with her eyes full as she examined the presents and read the little notes which accompanied them. The slippers went on at once, a new handkerchief was slipped into her pocket, well scented with Amy's Cologne, the rose was fastened in her bosom, and the nice gloves were pronounced a " perfect fit."

There was a good deal of laughing, and kissing, and explaining, in the simple, loving fashion which makes these home-festivals so pleasant at the time, so sweet to remember long afterward, and then all fell to work.

The morning charities and ceremonies took so much time, that the rest of the day was devoted to preparations for the evening festivities. Being still too young to go often to the theatre, and not rich enough to afford any great outlay for private performances, the girls put their wits to work, and, necessity being the mother of invention, made whatever they needed. Very clever were some of their productions ; paste-board guitars, antique lamps made of old-fashioned butter-boats, covered with silver paper, gorgeous robes of old cotton, glittering with tin spangles from a pickle factory, and armour covered with the same useful diamond-shaped bits, left in sheets when the lids of tin preserve-pots were cut out. The furniture was used to being turned topsy-turvy, and the big chamber was the scene of many innocent revels.

No gentlemen were admitted ; so Jo played male parts to her heart's content, and took immense satisfaction in a pair of russet-leather boots given her by a friend, who knew a lady who knew an actor. These boots, an old foil, and a slashed doublet, once used by an artist for some picture, were Jo's chief treasures, and appeared on all occasions.

The smallness of the company made it necessary for the two principal actors to take several parts apiece ; and they certainly deserved some credit for the hard work they did in learning three or four different parts, whisking in and out of various costumes, and managing the stage besides. It was excellent drill for their memories, a harmless amusement, and employed many hours which otherwise would have been idle, lonely, or spent in less profitable society.

On Christmas night a dozen girls piled on to the bed, which was the dress circle, and sat before the blue and yellow chintz curtains in a most flattering state of expectancy. There was a good deal of rustling and whispering behind the curtain, a trifle of lamp smoke, and an occasional giggle from Amy, who was apt to get hysterical in the excitement of the moment. Presently a bell sounded, the curtain flew apart, and the Operatic Tragedy began.

" A gloomy wood," according to the one play-bill, was represented by a few shrubs in pots, a green baize on the floor, and a cave in the distance. This cave was made with a clothes-horse for a roof, bureaus for walls ; and in it was a small furnace in full blast, with a black pot on it, and an old witch bending over it. The stage was dark, and the glow of the furnace had a fine effect, especially as real steam issued from the kettle when the witch took off the cover. A moment was allowed for the first thrill to subside ; then Hugo, the villain, stalked in with a clanking sword at his side, a slouched hat, black beard, mysterious cloak, and the boots. After pacing to and fro in much agitation, he struck his forehead and burst out in a wild strain, singing of his hatred to Roderigo, his love for Zara, and his pleasing resolution to kill the one and win the other. The gruff tones of Hugo's voice, with an occasional shout when his feelings overcame him, were very impressive, and the audience applauded the moment he paused for breath. Bowing with the air of one accustomed to public praise, he stole to the cavern and ordered Hagar to come forth with a commanding "What ho! minion! I need thee!"

Out came Meg, with grey horse-hair hanging about her face, a red and black robe, a staff, and cabalistic signs upon her cloak. Hugo demanded a potion to make Zara adore him, and one to destroy Roderigo. Hagar, in a fine dramatic melody promised both, and proceeded to call up the spirit who would bring the love philter :—

> " Hither, hither, from thy home,
> Airy sprite, I bid thee come !
> Born of roses, fed on dew,
> Charms and potions canst thou brew ?
> Bring me here, with elfin speed,
> The fragrant philter which I need ;
> Make it sweet, and swift and strong ;
> Spirit, answer now my song ! "

A soft strain of music sounded, and then at the back of the cave appeared a little figure in cloudy white, with glittering wings, golden hair, and a garland of roses on its head. Waving a wand it sung :—

> " Hither I come,
> From my airy home,
> Afar in the silver moon ;
> Take the magic spell,
> Oh, use it well !
> Or its power will vanish soon ! "

and dropping a small gilded bottle at the witch's feet,

the spirit vanished. Another chant from Hagar produced another apparition—not a lovely one, for, with a bang, an ugly, black imp appeared, and having croaked a reply, tossed a dark bottle at Hugo, and disappeared with a mocking laugh. Having warbled his thanks, and put the potions in his boots, Hugo departed ; and Hagar informed the audience that, as he has killed a few of her friends in times past, she has cursed him, and intends to thwart his plans, and be revenged on him. Then the curtain fell, and the audience reposed and ate candy while discussing the merits of the play.

A good deal of hammering went on before the curtain rose again ! but when it became evident what a masterpiece of stage carpentering had been got up no one murmured at the delay. It was truly superb. A tower rose to the ceiling ; half-way up appeared a window, with a lamp burning in it, and behind the white curtain appeared Zara in a lovely blue and silver dress, waiting for Roderigo. He came, in gorgeous array, with plumed cap, red cloak, chestnut love-locks, a guitar, and the boots, of course. Kneeling at the foot of the tower, he sang a serenade in melting tones. Zara replied, and after a musical dialogue, consented to fly. Then came the grand effect of the play. Roderigo produced a rope ladder with five steps to it, threw up one end, and invited Zara to descend. Timidly she crept from her lattice, put her hand on Roderigo's shoulder, and was about to leap grace-fully down when, " alas, alas, for Zara ! " she forgot her train ; it caught in the window—the tower tottered, leaned forward, fell with a crash, and buried the unhappy lovers in the ruins !

A universal shriek arose as the russet boots waved wildly from the wreck, and a golden head emerged, exclaiming, " I told you so ! I told you so ! " With wonderful presence of mind, Don Pedro, the cruel sire, rushed in, dragged out his daughter with a hasty aside :—

" Don't laugh, act as if it was all right ! " and ordering Roderigo up, banished him from the kingdom with wrath and scorn. Though decidedly shaken by the fall of the tower upon him, Roderigo defied the old gentleman, and refused to stir. This dauntless example fired Zara ; she also defied her sire, and he ordered them both to the deepest dungeons of the castle. A stout little retainer came in with chains, and led them away, looking very much frightened, and evidently forgetting the speech he ought to have made.

Act third was the castle hall ; and here Hagar appeared, having come to free the lovers and finish Hugo. She hears him coming, and hides ; sees him put the potions into two cups of wine, and bid the timid little servant " Bear them to the captives in their cells, and tell them I shall come anon." The servant takes Hugo aside to tell him something, and Hagar changes the cups for two others, which are harmless. Ferdinando, the " minion," carries them away, and Hagar puts back the cup which holds the poison meant for Roderigo. Hugo, getting thirsty after a long warble, drinks it, loses his wits, and after a good deal of clutching and stamping, falls flat and dies ; while Hagar informs him what she has done in a song of exquisite power and melody.

This was a truly thrilling scene, though some

persons might have thought that the sudden tumbling down of a quantity of long hair rather marred the effect of the villain's death. He was called before the curtain, and with great propriety appeared leading Hagar, whose singing was considered more wonderful than all the rest of the performance put together.

Act fourth displayed the despairing Roderigo on the point of stabbing himself, because he has been told that Zara has deserted him. Just as the dagger is at his heart, a lovely song is sung under his window, informing him that Zara is true, but in danger, and he can save her if he will. A key is thrown in, which unlocks the door, and in a spasm of rapture he tears off his chains, and rushes away to find and rescue his lady-love.

Act fifth opened with a stormy scene between Zara and Don Pedro. He wishes her to go into a convent, but she won't hear of it ; and, after a touching appeal, is about to faint, when Roderigo dashes in and demands her hand. Don Pedro refuses because he is not rich. They shout and gesticulate tremendously, but cannot agree, and Roderigo is about to bear away the exhausted Zara, when the timid servant enters with a letter and a bag from Hagar, who has mysteriously disappeared. The letter informs the party that she bequeaths untold wealth to the young pair, and an awful doom to Don Pedro if he doesn't make them happy. The bag is opened, and several quarts of tin money shower down upon the stage, till it is quite glorified with the glitter. This entirely softens the " stern sire ; " he consents without a murmur, all join in a joyful chorus, and the curtain falls upon the lovers kneeling to receive

Don Pedro's blessing, in attitudes of the most romantic grace.

Tumultuous applause followed, but received an unexpected check, for the cot-bed on which the " dress circle " was built, suddenly shut up, and extinguished the enthusiastic audience. Roderigo and Don Pedro flew to the rescue, and all were taken out unhurt, though many were speechless with laughter. The excitement had hardly subsided when Hannah appeared, with " Mrs. March's compliments, and would the ladies walk down to supper."

This was a surprise, even to the actors ; and when they saw the table they looked at one another in rapturous amazement. It was like " Marmee " to get up a little treat for them, but anything so fine as this was unheard of since the departed days of plenty. There was ice cream, actually two dishes of it—pink and white—and cake, and fruit, and distracting French bon-bons, and in the middle of the table four great bouquets of hot-house flowers !

It quite took their breath away ; and they stared first at the table and then at their mother, who looked as if she enjoyed it immensely.

" Is it fairies ? " asked Amy.

" It's Santa Claus," said Beth.

" Mother did it," and Meg smiled her sweetest, in spite of her grey beard and white eyebrows.

" Aunt March had a good fit, and sent the supper," cried Jo, with a sudden inspiration.

" All wrong ; old Mr. Laurence sent it," replied Mrs. March.

" The Laurence boy's grandfather ! What in the world put such a thing into his head ? We don't know him," exclaimed Meg.

"Hannah told one of his servants about your breakfast party; he is an odd old gentleman, but that pleased him. He knew my father, years ago, and he sent me a polite note this afternoon, saying he hoped I would allow him to express his friendly feeling towards my children by sending them a few trifles in honour of the day. I could not refuse, and so you have a little feast at night to make up for the bread and milk breakfast."

"That boy put it into his head, I know he did! He's a capital fellow, and I wish we could get acquainted. He looks as if he'd like to know us; but he's bashful, and Meg is so prim she won't let me speak to him when we pass," said Jo, as the plates went round, and the ice began to melt out of sight, with ohs! and ahs! of satisfaction.

"You mean the people who live in the big house next door, don't you?" asked one of the girls. "My mother knows old Mr. Laurence, but says he's very proud, and don't like to mix with his neighbours. He keeps his grandson shut up when he isn't riding or walking with his tutor, and makes him study dreadfully hard. We invited him to our party, but he didn't come. Mother says he's very nice, though he never speaks to us girls."

"Our cat ran away once, and he brought her back, and we talked over the fence, and were getting on capitally, all about cricket, and so on, when he saw Meg coming and walked off. I mean to know him some day, for he needs fun, I'm sure he does," said Jo, decidedly.

"I like his manners and he looks like a little gentleman, so I've no objection to your knowing him if a proper opportunity comes. He brought the flowers himself, and I should have asked him in if I had been sure what was going on upstairs. He looked so wistful as he went away, hearing the frolic, and evidently having none of his own."

"It's a mercy you didn't, mother," laughed Jo, looking at her boots. "But we'll have another play some time, that he *can* see. Maybe he'll help act ; wouldn't that be jolly ? "

"I never had a bouquet before ; how pretty it is," and Meg examined her flowers with great interest.

"They *are* lovely, but Beth's roses are sweeter to me," said Mrs. March, sniffing at the half-dead posy in her belt.

Beth nestled up to her, and whispered, softly, "I wish I could send my bunch to father. I'm afraid he isn't having such a merry Christmas as we are."

CHAPTER III.

THE LAURENCE BOY.

"Jo ! Jo ! where are you ? " cried Meg, at the foot of the garret stairs.

"Here," answered a husky voice from above ; and running up, Meg found her sister eating apples and crying over the " Heir of Redcliffe," wrapped up in a comforter on an old three-legged sofa by the sunny window. This was Jo's favourite refuge ; and here she loved to retire with half a dozen russets and a nice book, to enjoy the quiet and the society of a pet rat who lived near by, and didn't mind her a particle. As Meg appeared, Scrabble whisked into his hole. Jo shook the tears off her cheeks and waited to hear the news.

"Such fun ! only see ! a regular note of invitation from Mrs. Gardiner for to-morrow night ! " cried Meg, waving the precious paper and then proceeding to read it, with girlish delight.

"'Mrs. Gardiner would be happy to see Miss March and Miss Josephine at a little dance on New Year's Eve.' Marmee is willing we should go ; now what *shall* we wear ? "

"What's the use of asking that, when you know we shall wear our poplins, because we haven't got anything else," answered Jo.

"If I only had a silk ! " sighed Meg ; "mother says I may when I'm eighteen, perhaps ; but two years is an everlasting time to wait."

"I'm sure our pops look like silk, and they are nice enough for us. Yours is as good as new, but I forgot the burn and tear in mine ; whatever shall I do ? the burn shows horridly, and I can't take any out."

"You must sit still all you can, and keep your back out of sight ; the front is all right. I shall have a new ribbon for my hair, and Marmee will lend me her little pearl pin, and my new slippers are lovely, and my gloves will do, though they aren't as nice as I'd like."

"Mine are spoilt with lemonade, and I can't get any new ones, so I shall have to go without," said Joe, who never troubled herself much about dress.

"You *must* have gloves, or I won't go," cried Meg, decidedly. "Gloves are more important than anything else ; you can't dance without them, and if you don't I should be *so* mortified."

"Then I'll stay still; I don't care much for company dancing; it's no fun to go sailing round, I like to fly about and cut capers."

"You can't ask mother for new ones, they are so expensive, and you are so careless. She said, when you spoilt the others, that she shouldn't get you any more this winter. Can't you fix them any way?" asked Meg anxiously.

"I can hold them scrunched up in my hand, so no one will know how stained they are. No! I'll tell you how we can manage—each wear one good one and carry a bad one; don't you see?"

"Your hands are bigger than mine, and you will stretch my glove dreadfully," began Meg, whose gloves were a tender point with her.

"Then I'll go without. I don't care what people say," cried Jo, taking up her book.

"You may have it, you may! only don't strain it, and do behave nicely; don't put your hands behind you, or stare, or say 'Christopher Columbus!' will you?"

"Don't worry about me; I'll be prim as a dish, and not get into any scrapes, if I can help it. Now go and answer your note, and let me finish this splendid story."

So Meg went away to "accept with thanks," look over her dress, and sing blithely as she did up her one real lace frill; while Jo finished her story, her four apples, and had a game of romps with Scrabble.

On New Year's Eve the parlour was deserted, for the two younger girls played dressing maids, and the two elder were absorbed in the all-important business of "getting ready for the party." Simple as the toilets were, there was a great deal of running up and down, laughing and talking, and at one time a strong smell of burnt hair pervaded the house. Meg wanted a few curls about her face, and Jo undertook to pinch the papered locks with a pair of hot tongs.

"Ought they to smoke like that?" asked Beth, from her perch on the bed.

"It's the dampness drying," replied Jo.

"What a queer smell! it's like burnt feathers," observed Amy, smoothing her own pretty curls with a superior air.

"There, now I'll take off the papers and you'll see a cloud of little ringlets," said Jo, putting down the tongs.

She did take off the papers, but no cloud of ringlets appeared, for the hair came with the papers, and the horrified hair-dresser laid a row of little scorched bundles on the bureau before her victim.

"Oh, oh, oh! what *have* you done? I'm spoilt! I can't go! my hair, oh, my hair!" wailed Meg, looking with despair at the uneven frizzle on her forehead.

"Just my luck! you shouldn't have asked me to do it; I always spoil everything. I'm no end sorry, but the tongs were too hot, and so I've made a mess," groaned poor Jo, regarding the black pancakes with tears of regret.

"It isn't spoilt; just frizzle it, and tie your ribbon so the ends come on your forehead a bit, and it will look like the last fashion. I've seen lots of girls do it so," said Amy, consolingly.

"Serves me right for trying to be fine. I wish I'd let my hair alone," cried Meg, petulantly.

"So do I, it was so smooth and pretty. But it will soon grow out again," said Beth, coming to kiss and comfort the shorn sheep.

After various lesser mishaps, Meg was finished at last, and by the united exertions of the family Jo's hair was got up, and her dress on. They looked very well in their simple suits, Meg in silvery drab, with a blue velvet snood, lace frills, and the pearl pin ; Jo in maroon, with a stiff, gentlemanly linen collar, and a white chrysanthemum or two for her only ornament. Each put on one nice light glove, and carried one soiled one, and all pronounced the effect "quite easy and nice." Meg's high-heeled slippers were dreadfully tight, and hurt her, though she would not own it, and Jo's nineteen hair pins all seemed stuck straight into her head, which was not exactly comfortable ; but, dear me, let us be elegant or die.

"Have a good time, dearies," said Mrs. March, as the sisters went daintily down the walk. "Don't eat much supper, and come away at eleven, when I send Hannah for you." As the gate clashed behind them, a voice cried from a window :

"Girls, girls ! *have* you both got nice pocket-handkerchiefs ? "

"Yes, yes, very nice, and Meg has Cologne on her's," cried Jo, adding, with a laugh, as they went on, " I do believe Marmee would ask that if we were all running away from an earthquake."

"It is one of her aristocratic tastes, and quite proper, for a real lady is always known by neat boots, gloves, and handkerchief," replied Meg, who had a good many little "aristocratic tastes" of her own.

" Now don't forget to keep the bad breadth out of sight, Jo. Is my sash right ? and does my hair look *very* bad ? " said Meg, as she turned from the glass in Mrs. Gardiner's dressing-room after a prolonged prink.

" I know I shall forget. If you see me doing anything wrong, you just remind me by a wink, will you ? " returned Jo, giving her collar a twitch, and her head a hasty brush.

" No, winking is not lady-like ; I'll lift my eyebrows if anything is wrong, and nod if you are all right. Now hold your shoulders straight, and take short steps, and don't shake hands if you are introduced to any one; it isn't the thing."

"How *do* you learn all the proper quirks ? I never can. Isn't that music gay ? "

Down they went, feeling a trifle timid, for they seldom went to parties, and, informal as this little gathering was, it was an event to them. Mrs. Gardiner, a stately old lady, greeted them kindly, and handed them over to the eldest of her six daughters. Meg knew Sallie and was at her ease very soon ; but Jo, who didn't care much for girls or girlish gossip, stood about with her back carefully against the wall, and felt as much out of place as a colt in a flower garden. Half-a-dozen jovial lads were talking about skates in another part of the room, and she longed to go and join them, for skating was one of the joys of her life. She telegraphed her wish to Meg, but the eyebrows went up so alarmingly that she dared not stir. No one came to talk to her, and one by one the group near her dwindled away, till she was left alone. She could not roam about and amuse herself, for the burnt breadth would show, so she stared at people rather forlornly till the dancing began. Meg was asked at once, and the tight slippers tripped about so briskly that none would have guessed the pain their wearer suffered smilingly. Jo saw a big, red-headed youth approaching her corner, and fearing he meant to engage her, she slipped into a curtained recess, intending to peep and enjoy herself in peace. Unfortunately, another bashful person had chosen the same refuge, for, as the curtain fell behind her, she found herself face to face with the "Laurence Boy."

"Dear me, I didn't know anyone was here!" stammered Jo, preparing to back out as speedily as she had bounced in.

But the boy laughed, and said, though he looked a little startled,—

"Don't mind me; stay if you like."

"Shan't I disturb you?"

"Not a bit; I only came here because I don't know many people, and felt rather strange at first, you know."

"So did I. Don't go away, please, unless you'd rather."

The boy sat down again and looked at his boots, till Jo said, trying to be polite and easy,—

"I think I've had the pleasure of seeing you before; you live near us, don't you?"

"Next door"; and he looked up and laughed outright, for Jo's prim manner was rather funny when he remembered how they had chatted about cricket when he brought the cat home.

That put Jo at her ease; and she laughed too, as she said, in her heartiest way,—

"We did have such a good time over your nice Christmas present."

"Grandpa sent it."

"But you put it into his head, didn't you, now?"

How is your cat, Miss March?" asked the boy, trying to look sober, while his black eyes shone with fun.

"Nicely, thank you, Mr. Laurence; but I ain't Miss March, I'm only Jo," returned the young lady.

"I'm not Mr. Laurence, I'm only Laurie."

"Laurie Laurence; what an odd name."

"My first name is Theodore, but I don't like it, for the fellows call me Dora, so I made them say Laurie instead."

"I hate my name, too—so sentimental! I wish every one would say Jo, instead of Josephine. How did you make the boys stop calling you Dora?"

"I thrashed 'em."

"I can't thrash Aunt March, so I suppose I shall have to bear it"; and Jo resigned herself with a sigh.

"Don't you like to dance, Miss Jo?" asked Laurie, looking as if he thought the name suited her.

"I like it well enough if there is plenty of room, and every one is lively. In a place like this I'm sure to upset something, tread on people's toes, or do something dreadful, so I keep out of mischief, and let Meg do the pretty. Don't you dance?"

"Sometimes; you see I've been abroad a good many years, and haven't been about enough yet to know how you do things here."

" Abroad ! " cried Jo, " oh, tell me about it ! I love dearly to hear people describe their travels."

Laurie didn't seem to know where to begin ; but Jo's eager questions soon set him going, and he told her how he had been at school in Vevay, where the boys never wore hats, and had a fleet of boats on the lake, and for holiday fun went walking trips about Switzerland with their teachers.

" Don't I wish I'd been there ! " cried Jo. " Did you go to Paris ? "

" We spent last winter there."

" Can you talk French ? "

" We were not allowed to speak anything else at Vevay."

" Do say some. I can read it, but can't pronounce."

" Quel nom à cette jeune demoiselle en les pantoufles jolis ? " said Laurie, good-naturedly.

" How nicely you do it ! Let me see—you said, ' Who is the young lady in the pretty slippers,' didn't you ? "

" Oui, mademoiselle."

" It's my sister Margaret, and you knew it was ! Do you think she is pretty ? "

" Yes ; she makes me think of the German girls, she looks so fresh and quiet, and dances like a lady."

Jo quite glowed with pleasure at this boyish praise of her sister, and stored it up to repeat to Meg. Both peeped, and criticised, and chatted, till they felt like old acquaintances. Laurie's bashfulness soon wore off, for Jo's gentlemanly demeanour amused and set him at his ease, and

Jo was her merry self again, because her dress was forgotten, and nobody lifted their eyebrows at her. She liked the " Laurence boy " better than ever, and took several good looks at him, so that she might describe him to the girls; for they had no brothers, very few male cousins, and boys were almost unknown creatures to them.

" Curly black hair, brown skin, big black eyes, long nose, nice teeth, little hands and feet, tall as I am; very polite for a boy, and altogether jolly. Wonder how old he is ! "

It was on the tip of Jo's tongue to ask, but she checked herself in time, and, with unusual tact, tried to find out in a roundabout way.

" I suppose you are going to college soon ? I see you are pegging away at your books—no, I mean studying hard "; and Jo blushed at the dreadful " pegging " which had escaped her.

Laurie smiled, but didn't seem shocked, and said, with a shrug,—

" Not for two or three years yet; not before seventeen, anyway."

" Aren't you but fifteen ? " asked Jo, looking at the tall lad, whom she had imagined seventeen already.

" Sixteen, next month."

" How I wish I was going to college ; you don't look as if you liked it."

" I hate it ! nothing but grinding or sky-larking ; and I don't like the way fellows do either, in this country."

" What do you like ? "

" To live in Italy, and to enjoy myself in my own way."

Jo wanted very much to ask what his own way was ; but his black brows looked rather threatening as he knit them, so she changed the subject by saying, as her foot kept time, " That's a splendid polka ; why don't you go and try it ? "

" If you will come too," he answered, with a queer little French bow.

I can't ; for I told Meg I wouldn't, because——" there Jo stopped, and looked undecided whether to tell or to laugh.

" Because what ? " asked Laurie, curiously.

" You won't tell ? "

" Never ! "

" Well, I have a bad trick of standing before the fire, and so I burn my frocks, and I scorched this one ; and, though it's nicely mended, it shows ; and Meg told me to keep still, so no one would see it. You may laugh if you want to ; it is funny, I know."

But Laurie didn't laugh ; he only looked down a minute, and the expression of his face puzzled Jo, when he said very gently,—

" Never mind that ; I'll tell you how we can manage : there's a long hall out there, and we can dance grandly, and no one will see us. Please come."

Jo thanked him, and gladly went, wishing she had two neat gloves, when she saw the nice pearl-coloured ones her partner put on. The hall was empty, and they had a grand polka, for Laurie danced well, and taught her the German step, which delighted Jo, being full of swing and spring. When the music stopped they sat down on the stairs to get their breath, and Laurie was in the midst of an account of a students' festival at

Heidelberg, when Meg appeared in search of her sister. She beckoned, and Jo reluctantly followed her into a side-room, where she found her on a sofa holding her foot, and looking pale.

" I've sprained my ankle. That stupid high heel turned, and gave me such a horrid wrench. It aches so, I can hardly stand, and I don't know how I'm ever going to get home," she said, rocking to and fro in pain.

" I knew you'd hurt your feet with those silly things. I'm sorry; but I don't see what you can do, except get a carriage, or stay here all night," answered Jo, softly rubbing the poor ankle as she spoke.

" I can't have a carriage without its costing ever so much; I dare say I can't get one at all, for most people come in their own, and it's a long way to the stable, and no one to send."

" I'll go."

" No, indeed; it's past ten, and dark as Egypt. I can't stop here, for the house is full; Sallie has some girls staying with her. I'll rest till Hannah comes, and then do the best I can."

" I'll ask Laurie; he will go," said Jo, looking relieved as the idea occurred to her.

" Mercy, no! don't ask or tell any one. Get me my rubbers, and put these slippers with our things. I can't dance any more; but as soon as supper is over, watch for Hannah, and tell me the minute she comes."

" They are going out to supper now. I'll stay with you; I'd rather."

" No, dear; run along, and bring me some coffee. I'm so tired, I can't stir."

So Meg reclined, with the rubbers well hidden, and Jo went blundering away to the dining-room, which she found after going into a china-closet and opening the door of a room where old Mr. Gardiner was taking a little private refreshment. Making a dive at the table, she secured the coffee, which she immediately spilt, thereby making the front of her dress as bad as the back.

"Oh dear! what a blunderbuss I am!" exclaimed Jo, finishing Meg's glove by scrubbing her gown with it.

"Can I help you?" said a friendly voice; and there was Laurie, with a full cup in one hand and a plate of ice in the other.

"I was trying to get something for Meg, who is very tired, and some one shook me, and here I am, in a nice state," answered Jo, glancing dismally from the stained skirt to the coffee-coloured glove.

"Too bad! I was looking for some one to give this to; may I take it to your sister?"

"Oh, thank you; I'll show you where she is. I don't offer to take it myself, for I should only get into another scrape if I did."

Jo led the way; and, as if used to waiting on ladies, Laurie drew up a little table, brought a second instalment of coffee and ice for Jo, and was so obliging that even particular Meg pronounced him a "nice boy." They had a merry time over the bonbons and mottoes, and were in the midst of a quiet game of "buzz" with two or three other young people who had strayed in, when Hannah appeared. Meg forgot her foot, and rose so quickly that she was forced to catch hold of Jo, with an exclamation of pain.

"Hush! don't say anything," she whispered; adding aloud, "it's nothing; I turned my foot a little, that's all," and limped upstairs to put her things on.

Hannah scolded, Meg cried, and Jo was at her wits' end, till she decided to take things into her own hands. Slipping out, she ran down, and finding a servant, asked if he could get her a carriage. It happened to be a hired waiter, who knew nothing about the neighbourhood; and Jo was looking round for help, when Laurie, who had heard what she said, came up and offered his grandfather's carriage, which had just come for him, he said.

"It's so early—you can't mean to go yet," began Jo, looking relieved, but hesitating to accept the offer.

"I always go early—I do, truly. Please let me take you home; it's all on my way, you know, and it rains, they say."

That settled it; and telling him of Meg's mishap, Jo gratefully accepted, and rushed up to bring down the rest of the party. Hannah hated rain as much as a cat does; so she made no trouble, and they rolled away in a luxurious closed carriage, feeling very festive and elegant. Laurie went on the box, so Meg could keep her foot up, and the girls talked over their party in freedom.

"I had a capital time; did you?" asked Jo, rumpling up her hair, and making herself comfortable.

"Yes, till I hurt myself. Sallie's friend, Annie Moffat, took a fancy to me, and asked me to come and spend a week with her when Sallie does. She is going in the spring, when the opera comes, and it will be perfectly splendid if mother only lets me go," answered Meg, cheering up at the thought.

"I saw you dancing with the red-headed man I ran away from; was he nice?"

"Oh, very! his hair is auburn, not red; and he was very polite, and I had a delicious redowa with him!"

"He looked like a grasshopper in a fit when he did the new step. Laurie and I couldn't help laughing; did you hear us?"

"No, but it was very rude. What *were* you about all that time hidden away there?"

Jo told her adventures, and by the time she had finished they were at home. With many thanks, they said "Good-night," and crept in, hoping to disturb no one; but the instant their door creaked, two little night-caps bobbed up, and two eager voices cried out—

"Tell about the party! tell about the party!"

With what Meg called "a great want of manners," Jo had saved some bonbons for the little girls, and they soon subsided, after hearing the most thrilling events of the evening.

"I declare it really seems like being a fine young lady, to come home from my party in my carriage, and sit in my dressing-gown with a maid to wait on me," said Meg, as Jo bound up her foot with arnica, and brushed her hair.

"I don't believe fine young ladies enjoy themselves a bit more than we do, in spite of our burnt hair, old gowns, one glove apiece, and tight slippers, that sprain our ankles when we are silly enough to wear them." And I think Jo was quite right.

CHAPTER IV.

BURDENS.

" Oh dear, how hard it seems to take up our packs and go on," sighed Meg, the morning after the party ; for now the holidays were over, the week of merry-making did not fit her for going on easily with the task she never liked.

" I wish it was Christmas or New Year all the time ; wouldn't it be fun ? " answered Jo, yawning dismally.

" We shouldn't enjoy ourselves half so much as we do now. But it does seem so nice to have little suppers and bouquets, and go to parties, and drive home in a carriage, and read and rest, and not grub. It's like other people, you know, and I always envy girls who do such things ; I'm so fond of luxury," said Meg, trying to decide which of two shabby gowns was the least shabby.

" Well, we can't have it, so don't let's grumble, but shoulder our bundles and trudge along as cheerfully as Marmee does. I'm sure Aunt March is a regular Old Man of the Sea to me, but I suppose when I've learnt to carry her without complaining, she will tumble off, or get so light that I shan't mind her."

This idea tickled Jo's fancy, and put her in good spirits ; but Meg didn't brighten, for her burden, consisting of four spoilt children, seemed heavier than ever. She hadn't heart enough even to make herself pretty, as usual, by putting on a blue neck-ribbon, and dressing her hair in the most becoming way.

"What's the use of looking nice, when no one sees me but those cross midgets, and no one cares whether I'm pretty or not," she muttered, shutting her drawer with a jerk. "I shall have to toil and moil all my days, with only little bits of fun now and then, and get old and ugly and sour, because I'm poor, and can't enjoy my life as other girls do. It's a shame!"

So Meg went down, wearing an injured look, and wasn't at all agreeable at breakfast-time. Everyone seemed rather out of sorts, and inclined to croak. Beth had a headache, and lay on the sofa trying to comfort herself with the cat and three kittens; Amy was fretting because her lessons were not learned, and she couldn't find her rubbers; Jo *would* whistle, and make a great racket getting ready; Mrs. March was trying to finish a letter, which must go at once; and Hannah was grumpy, for being up late didn't suit her.

'There never *was* such a cross family!" cried Jo, losing her temper when she had upset an inkstand, broken both boot-lacings, and sat down upon her hat.

"You're the crossest person in it!" returned Amy, washing out the sum that was all wrong with the tears that had fallen on her slate.

"Beth, if you don't keep these horrid cats down in the cellar I'll have them drowned," exclaimed Meg, angrily, as she tried to get rid of the kitten that had swarmed up her back, and stuck like a burr just out of reach.

Jo laughed, Meg scolded, Beth implored, and Amy wailed, because she couldn't remember how much nine times twelve was.

" Girls ! girls ! do be quiet one minute. I *must* get this off by the early mail, and you drive me distracted with your worry," cried Mrs. March, crossing out the third spoilt sentence in her letter.

There was a momentary lull, broken by Hannah, who bounced in, laid two hot turn-overs on the table, and bounced out again. These turn-overs were an institution ; and the girls called them " muffs," for they had no others, and found the hot pies very comforting to their hands on cold mornings. Hannah never forgot to make them, no matter how busy or grumpy she might be, for the walk was long and bleak ; the poor things got no other lunch, and were seldom home before three.

" Cuddle your cats and get over your headache, Bethy. Good-bye, Marmee ; we are a set of rascals this morning, but we'll come home regular angels. Now then, Meg," and Jo tramped away, feeling that the pilgrims were not setting out as they ought to do.

They always looked back before turning the corner, for their mother was always at the window, to nod, and smile, and wave her hand to them. Somehow it seemed as if they couldn't have got through the day without that, for, whatever their mood might be, the last glimpse of that face was sure to affect them like sunshine.

" If Marmee shook her fist instead of kissing her hand to us, it would serve us right, for more ungrateful minxes than we are were never seen," cried Jo, taking a remorseful satisfaction in the slushy road and bitter wind.

" Don't use such dreadful expressions," said Meg, from the depths of the veil in which she had shrouded herself like a nun sick of the world.

" I like good, strong words, that mean something," replied Jo, catching her hat as it took a leap off her head, preparatory to flying away altogether. " Call yourself any names you like ; but *I* am neither a rascal nor a minx, and I don't choose to be called so."

" You're a blighted being, and decidedly cross to-day, because you can't sit in the lap of luxury all the time. Poor dear ! just wait till I make my fortune, and you shall revel in carriages, and ice-cream, and high-heeled slippers, and posies, and red-headed boys to dance with."

" How ridiculous you are, Jo ! " but Meg laughed at the nonsense, and felt better in spite of herself.

" Lucky for you I am ; for if I put on crushed airs, and tried to be dismal, as you do, we should be in a nice state. Thank goodness, I can always find something funny to keep me up. Don't croak any more, but come home jolly, there's a dear."

Jo gave her sister an encouraging pat on the shoulder as. they parted for the day, each going a different way, each hugging her little warm turn-over, and each trying to be cheerful in spite of wintry weather, hard work, and the unsatisfied desires of pleasure-loving youth.

When Mr. March lost his property in trying to help an unfortunate friend, the two eldest girls begged to be allowed to do something towards their own support, at least. Believing that they could not begin too early to cultivate energy, industry, and independence, their parents consented, and both fell to work with the hearty good-will which, in spite of all obstacles, is sure to succeed at last. Margaret found a place as nursery governess, and felt rich with her small salary. As she said, she *was* "fond of luxury," and her chief trouble was poverty. She found it harder to bear than the others, because she could remember a time when home was beautiful, life full of ease and pleasure, and want of any kind unknown. She tried not to be envious or discontented, but it was very natural that the young girl should long for pretty things, gay friends, accomplishments, and a happy life. At the Kings' she daily saw all she wanted, for the children's older sisters were just out, and Meg caught frequent glimpses of dainty ball dresses and bouquets, heard lively gossip about theatres, concerts, sleighing parties and merry-makings of all kinds, and saw money lavished on trifles which would have been so precious to her. Poor Meg seldom complained, but a sense of injustice made her feel bitter towards everyone sometimes, for she had not yet learned to know how rich she was in the blessings which alone can make life happy.

Jo happened to suit Aunt March, who was lame, and needed an active person to wait upon her. The childless old lady had offered to adopt one of the girls when the troubles came, and was much offended because her offer was declined. Other friends told the Marches that they had lost all chance of being remembered in the rich old lady's will ; but the unworldly Marches only said :—

" We can't give up our girls for a dozen fortunes.

Rich or poor, we will keep together and be happy in one another."

The old lady wouldn't speak to them for a time, but, happening to meet Jo at a friend's, something in her comical face and blunt manners struck the old lady's fancy, and she proposed to take her for a companion. This did not suit Jo at all; but she accepted the place, since nothing better appeared, and, to everyone's surprise, got on remarkably well with her irascible relative. There was an occasional tempest, and once Jo had marched home, declaring she couldn't bear it any longer; but Aunt March always cleared up quickly, and sent for her back again with such urgency that she could not refuse, for in her heart she rather liked the peppery old lady.

I suspect that the real attraction was a large library of fine books, which was left to dust and spiders since Uncle March died. Jo remembered the kind old gentleman who used to let her build railroads and bridges with his big dictionaries, tell her stories about the queer pictures in his Latin books, and buy her cards of gingerbread whenever he met her in the street. The dim, dusty room, with the busts staring down from the tall book-cases, the cosy chairs, the globes, and, best of all, the wilderness of books, in which she could wander where she liked, made the library a region of bliss to her. The moment Aunt March took her nap, or was busy with company, Jo hurried to this quiet place, and, curling herself up in the big chair, devoured poetry, romance, history, travels, and pictures, like a regular bookworm. But, like all happiness, it did not last long; for as sure as she had just reached the heart of the story, the sweetest verse of the song, or the most perilous adventure of her traveller, a shrill voice called, "Josy-phine! Josy-phine!" and she had to leave her paradise to wind yarn, wash the poodle, or read Belsham's Essays, by the hour together.

Jo's ambition was to do something very splendid; what it was she had no idea, but left it for time to tell her; and, meanwhile, found her greatest affliction in the fact that she couldn't read, run, and ride as much as she liked. A quick temper, sharp tongue, and restless spirit were always getting her into scrapes, and her life was a series of ups and downs, which were both comic and pathetic. But the training she received at Aunt March's was just what she needed; and the thought that she was doing something to support herself made her happy, in spite of the perpetual "Josy-phine!"

Beth was too bashful to go to school; it had been tried, but she suffered so much that it was given up, and she did her lessons at home, with her father. Even when he went away, and her mother was called to devote her skill and energy to Soldiers' Aid Societies, Beth went faithfully on by herself, and did the best she could. She was a housewifely little creature, and helped Hannah keep home neat and comfortable for the workers, never thinking of any reward but to be loved. Long, quiet days she spent, not lonely nor idle, for her little world was peopled with imaginary friends, and she was by nature a busy bee. There were six dolls to be taken up and dressed every morning, for Beth was a child still, and loved her pets as well as ever; not one whole or handsome one among them; all were outcasts till

Beth took them in ; for, when her sisters outgrew these idols, they passed to her, because Amy would have nothing old or ugly. Beth cherished them all the more tenderly for that very reason, and set up a hospital for infirm dolls. No pins were ever stuck into their cotton vitals ; no harsh words or blows were ever given them ; no neglect ever saddened the heart of the most repulsive, but all were fed and clothed, nursed and caressed, with an affection which never failed. One forlorn fragment of *dollanity* had belonged to Jo ; and, having led a tempestuous life, was left a wreck in the rag-bag, from which dreary poor-house it was rescued by Beth, and taken to her refuge. Having no top to its head, she tied on a neat little cap, and, as both arms and legs were gone, she hid these deficiencies by folding it in a blanket, and devoting her best bed to this chronic invalid. If anyone had known the care lavished on that dolly, I think it would have touched their hearts, even while they laughed. She brought it bits of bouquets ; she read to it, took it out to breathe the air, hidden under her coat ; she sung it lullabies, and never went to bed without kissing its dirty face, and whispering tenderly, " I hope you'll have a good night, my poor dear."

Beth had her troubles as well as the others ; and not being an angel, but a very humane little girl, she often " wept a little weep," as Jo said, because she couldn't take music lessons and have a fine piano. She loved music so dearly, tried so hard to learn, and practised away so patiently at the jingling old instrument, that it did seem as if some one (not to hint Aunt March) ought to help her. Nobody did, however, and nobody saw Beth wipe the tears off the yellow keys, that wouldn't keep in tune, when she was all alone. She sang like a little lark about her work, never was too tired to play for Marmee and the girls, and day after day said hopefully to herself, " I know I'll get my music some time, if I'm good."

There are many Beths in the world, shy and quiet, sitting in corners till needed, and living for others so cheerfully, that no one sees the sacrifices till the little cricket on the hearth stops chirping, and the sweet, sunshiny presence vanishes, leaving silence and shadow behind.

If anybody had asked Amy what the greatest trial of her life was, she would have answered at once, " My nose." When she was a baby, Jo had accidentally dropped her into the coal-hod, and Amy insisted that the fall had ruined her nose for ever. It was not big, nor red, like poor " Petrea's " ; it was only rather flat, and all the pinching in the world could not give it an aristocratic point. No one minded it but herself, and it was doing its best to grow, but Amy felt deeply the want of a Grecian nose, and drew whole sheets of handsome ones to console herself.

" Little Raphael," as her sisters called her, had a decided talent for drawing, and was never so happy as when copying flowers, designing fairies, or illustrating stories with queer specimens of art. Her teachers complained that instead of doing her sums, she covered her slate with animals ; the blank pages of her atlas were used to copy maps on, and caricatures of the most ludicrous description came fluttering out of her books at unlucky moments.

She got through her lessons as well as she could, and managed to escape reprimands by being a model of deportment. She was a great favourite with her mates, being good-tempered, and possessing the happy art of pleasing without effort. Her little airs and graces were much admired, so were her accomplishments ; for besides her drawing she could play twelve tunes, crochet, and read French without mispronouncing more than two-thirds of the words. She had a plaintive way of saying, " When papa was rich we did so-and-so," which was very touching ; and her long words were considered " perfectly elegant " by the girls.

Amy was in a fair way to be spoilt ; for every one petted her, and her small vanities and selfish-nesses were growing nicely. One thing, however, rather quenched the vanities ; she had to wear her cousin's clothes. Now Florence's mother hadn't a particle of taste, and Amy suffered deeply at having to wear a red instead of a blue bonnet, unbecoming gowns, and fussy aprons that did not fit. Every-thing was good, well made, and little worn ; but Amy's artistic eyes were much afflicted, especially this winter, when her school dress was a dull purple, with yellow dots, and no trimming.

" My only comfort," she said to Meg, with tears in her eyes, " is, that mother don't take tucks in my dresses whenever I'm naughty, as Maria Parks' mother does. My dear, it's really dreadful ; for sometimes she is so bad, her frock is up to her knees, and she can't come to school. When I think of this *deggerredation*, I fear that I can bear even my flat nose and purple gown, with yellow sky-rockets on it."

Meg was Amy's confidant and monitor, and, by some strange attraction of opposites, Jo was gentle Beth's. To Jo alone did the shy child tell her thoughts ; and over her big, harum-scarum sister, Beth unconsciously exercised more influence than any one in the family. The two older girls were a great deal to each other, but both took one of the younger into their keeping, and watched over them in their own way ; "playing mother" they called it, and put their sisters in the places of discarded dolls, with the maternal instincts of little women.

"Has anybody got anything to tell ? It's been such a dismal day I'm really dying for some amusement," said Meg, as they sat sewing together that evening.

"I had a queer time with Aunt to-day, and as I got the best of it, I'll tell you about it," began Jo, who dearly loved to tell stories. "I was reading that everlasting Belsham, and droning away as I always do, for aunt soon drops off, and then I take out some nice book, and read like fury, till she wakes up. I actually made myself sleepy ; and, before she began to nod, I gave such a gape that she asked me what I meant by opening my mouth wide enough to take the whole book in at once.

" 'I wish I could, and be done with it,' said I, trying not to be saucy.

"Then she gave me a long lecture on my sins, and told me to sit and think them over while she just 'lost' herself for a moment. She never finds herself very soon ; so the minute her cap began to bob, like a top-heavy dahlia, I whipped the 'Vicar of Wakefield' out of my pocket, and read away, with one eye on him and one on aunt. I'd just got to where they all tumbled into the water, when I forgot, and laughed out aloud. Aunt woke up ; and, being more good-natured after her nap, told me to read a bit, and show what frivolous work I preferred to the worthy and instructive Belsham. I did my very best, and she liked it, though she only said :—

" ' I don't understand what it's all about ; go back, and begin it, child.'

" Back I went, and made the Primroses as interesting as ever I could. Once I was wicked enough to stop in a thrilling place, and say meekly, ' I'm afraid it tires you, ma'am ; shan't I stop now ? '

" She caught up her knitting which had dropped out of her hands, gave a sharp look through her specs, and said in her short way :—

" ' Finish the chapter, and don't be impertinent, miss.' "

" Did she own she liked it ? " asked Meg.

" Oh, bless you, no ! but she let old Belsham rest ; and when I ran back after my gloves this afternoon, there she was, so hard at the Vicar, that she didn't hear me laugh as I danced a jig in the hall, because of the good time coming. What a pleasant life she might have, if she only chose. I don't envy her much, in spite of her money, for after all rich people have about as many worries as poor ones, I guess," added Jo.

" That reminds me," said Meg, " that I've got something to tell. It isn't funny, like Jo's story, but I thought about it a good deal as I came home. At the Kings' to-day I found everybody in a flurry, and one of the children said that her oldest brother had done something dreadful, and papa had sent him away. I heard Mrs. King crying, and Mr. King talking very loud, and Grace and Ellen turned away their faces when they passed me, so I shouldn't see how red their eyes were. I didn't ask any questions, of course ; but I felt so sorry for them, and was rather glad I hadn't any wild brothers to do wicked things, and disgrace the family."

" I think being disgraced in school is a great deal try*inger* than anything bad boys can do," said Amy, shaking her head, as if her experience of life had been a deep one. " Susie Perkins came to school to-day with a lovely red carnelian ring ; I wanted it dreadfully, and wished I was her with all my might. Well, she drew a picture of Mr. Davis, with a monstrous nose and a hump, and the words, ' Young ladies, my eye is upon you ! ' coming out of his mouth in a balloon thing. We were laughing over it, when all of a sudden his eye *was* on us, and he ordered Susie to bring up her slate. She was *parry*lised with fright, but she went, and oh ! what do you think he did ? He took her by the ear ! just fancy how horrid ! and led her to the recitation platform, and made her stand there half an hour, holding that slate so that every one could see."

" Didn't the girls shout at the picture ? " asked Jo, who relished the scrape.

" Laugh ! not a one ; they sat as still as mice, and Susie cried quarts, I know she did. I didn't envy her then, for I felt that millions of carnelian rings wouldn't have made me happy after that. I never, never should have got over such an agonising mortification ; " and Amy went on with her work, in the proud consciousness of virtue, and the successful utterance of two long words in a breath.

"I saw something that I liked this morning, and I meant to tell it at dinner, but I forgot," said Beth, putting Jo's topsy-turvy basket in order as she talked. "When I went to get some oysters for Hannah, Mr. Laurence was in the fish shop, but he didn't see me, for I kept behind a barrel, and he was busy with Mr. Cutter, the fish-man. A poor woman came in with a pail and a mop, and asked Mr. Cutter if he would let her do some scrubbing for a bit of fish, because she hadn't any dinner for her children, and had been disappointed of a day's work. Mr. Cutter was in a hurry, and said 'No,' rather crossly ; so she was going away, looking hungry and sorry, when Mr. Laurence hooked up a big fish with the crooked end of his cane, and held it out to her. She was so glad and surprised she took it right in her arms, and thanked him over and over. He told her to ' go along and cook it,' and she hurried off, so happy! wasn't it nice of him ? Oh, she did look so funny, hugging the big, slippery fish, and hoping Mr. Laurence's bed in heaven would be ' aisy.'"

When they had laughed at Beth's story, they asked their mother for one ; and, after a moment's thought, she said soberly :—

"As I sat cutting out blue flannel jackets to-day, at the rooms, I felt very anxious about father, and thought how lonely and helpless we should be if anything happened to him. It was not a wise thing to do, but I kept on worrying, till an old man came in with an order for some things. He sat down near me, and I began to talk to him, for he looked poor, and tired, and anxious.

"'Have you sons in the Army?' I asked, for the note he brought was not to me.

" ' Yes, ma'am ; I had four, but two were killed ; one is a prisoner, and I'm going to the other, who is very sick in a Washington hospital,' he answered, quietly.

" ' You have done a great deal for your country, sir,' I said, feeling respect now, instead of pity.

" ' Not a mite more than I ought, ma'am. I'd go myself, if I was any use ; as I ain't, I give my boys, and give 'em free.'

" He spoke so cheerfully, looked so sincere, and seemed so glad to give his all, that I was ashamed of myself. I'd given one man, and thought it too much, while he gave four, without grudging them ; I had all my girls to comfort me at home, and his last son was waiting, miles away, to say ' good-bye ' to him, perhaps. I felt so rich, so happy, thinking of my blessings, that I made him a nice bundle, gave him some money, and thanked him heartily for the lesson he had taught me."

" Tell another story, mother ; one with a moral to it, like this. I like to think about them afterwards, if they are real, and not too preachy," said Jo, after a minute's silence.

Mrs. March smiled, and began at once ; for she had told stories to this little audience for many years, and knew how to please them.

" Once upon a time there were four girls, who had enough to eat, and drink, and wear ; a good many comforts and pleasures, kind friends and parents, who loved them dearly, and yet they were not contented." (Here the listeners stole sly looks at one another, and began to sew diligently.) " These girls were anxious to be good, and made many excellent resolutions, but somehow they did

not keep them very well, and were constantly saying, ' If only we had this,' or ' if we could only do
that,' quite forgetting how much they already had,
and how many pleasant things they actually could
do ; so they asked an old woman what spell they
could use to make them happy, and she said,
' When you feel discontented, think over your
blessings, and be grateful.' " (Here Jo looked up
quickly, as if about to speak, but changed her mind,
seeing that the story was not done yet.)

" Being sensible girls, they decided to try her
advice, and soon were surprised to see how well off
they were. One discovered that money couldn't
keep shame and sorrow out of rich people's houses ;
another that though she was poor, she was a great
deal happier with her youth, health, and good spirits
than a certain fretful, feeble old lady, who couldn't
enjoy her comforts ; a third, that, disagreeable as
it was to help get dinner, it was harder still to have
to go begging for it ; and the fourth, that even
carnelian rings were not so valuable as good behaviour. So they agreed to stop complaining,
to enjoy the blessings already possessed, and try to
deserve them, lest they should be taken away
entirely, instead of increased ; and I believe they
were never disappointed, or sorry that they took
the old woman's advice."

" Now, Marmee, that is very cunning of you to
turn our own stories against us, and give us a
sermon instead of a ' spin,' " cried Meg.

" I like that kind of sermon ; it's the sort father
used to tell us," said Beth, thoughtfully, putting
the needles straight on Joe's cushion.

" I don't complain near as much as the others do,

and I shall be more careful than ever now, for I've had warning from Susie's downfall," said Amy, morally.

"We needed that lesson, and we won't forget it. If we do, you just say to us as Old Chloe did in Uncle Tom—'Tink ob yer marcies, chillen, tink ob yer marcies,'" added Jo, who could not for the life of her help getting a morsel of fun out of the little sermon, though she took it to heart as much as any of them.

CHAPTER V.

BEING NEIGHBOURLY.

"WHAT in the world are you going to do now, Jo?" asked Meg, one snowy afternoon, as her sister came clumping through the hall, in rubber boots, old sack and hood, with a broom in one hand and a shovel in the other.

"Going out for exercise," answered Jo, with a mischievous twinkle in her eyes.

"I should think two long walks this morning would have been enough. It's cold and dull out, and I advise you to stay, warm and dry, by the fire, as I do," said Meg, with a shiver.

"Never take advice; can't keep still all day, and, not being a pussy-cat, I don't like to doze by the fire. I like adventures, and I'm going to find some."

Meg went back to toast her feet, and read "Ivanhoe," and Jo began to dig paths with great energy. The snow was light : and with her broom she soon swept a path all round the garden for Beth to walk in when the sun came out; and the invalid dolls needed air. Now the garden separated the Marches' house from that of Mr. Laurence; both stood in a suburb of the city, which was still country-like, with groves and lawns, large gardens and quiet streets. A low hedge parted the two estates. On one side was an old brown house, looking rather bare and shabby, robbed of the vines that in summer covered its walls, and the flowers which then surrounded it. On the other side was a stately stone mansion, plainly betokening every sort of comfort and luxury, from the big coach-house and well-kept grounds to the conservatory, and the glimpses of lovely things one caught between the rich curtains. Yet it seemed a lonely, lifeless sort of house; for no children frolicked on the lawn, no motherly face ever smiled at the windows, and few people went in and out, except the old gentleman and his grandson.

To Jo's lively fancy this fine house seemed a kind of enchanted palace, full of splendours and delights, which no one enjoyed. She had long wanted to behold these hidden glories, and to know the " Laurence boy," who looked as if he would like to be known, if he only knew how to begin. Since the party she had been more eager than ever, and had planned many ways of making friends with him ; but he had not been lately seen, and Jo began to think he had gone away, when one day she spied a brown face at an upper window, looking wistfully down into their garden, where Beth and Amy were snowballing one another.

" That boy is suffering for society and fun," she said to herself. " His grandpa doesn't know what's good for him, and keeps him shut up all alone. He needs a lot of jolly boys to play with, or somebody young and lively. I've a great mind to go over and tell the old gentleman so."

The idea amused Jo, who liked to do daring things, and was always scandalizing Meg by her queer performances. The plan of " going over " was not forgotten ; and, when the snowy afternoon came, Jo resolved to try what could be done. She saw Mr. Laurence drive off, and then sallied out to dig her way down to the hedge, where she paused, and took a survey. All quiet ; curtains down at the lower windows ; servants out of sight, and nothing human visible but a curly black head leaning on a thin hand, at the upper window.

" There he is," thought Jo ; " poor boy ! all alone, and sick, this dismal day ! It's a shame ! I'll toss up a snowball, and make him look out, and then say a kind word to him."

Up went a handful of soft snow, and the head turned at once, showing a face which lost its listless look in a minute, as the big eyes brightened, and the mouth began to smile. Jo nodded, and laughed, and flourished her broom as she called out—

" How do you do ? Are you sick ? "

Laurie opened the window and croaked out as hoarsely as a raven :

" Better, thank you. I've had a horrid cold, and been shut up a week."

" I'm sorry. What do you amuse yourself with ? "

"Nothing; it's as dull as tombs up here."

"Don't you read?"

"Not much; they won't let me."

"Can't somebody read to you?"

"Grandpa does, sometimes; but my books don't interest him, and I hate to ask Brooke all the time."

"Have some one come and see you, then."

"There isn't any one I'd like to see. Boys make such a row, and my head is weak."

"Isn't there some nice girl who'd read and amuse you? Girls are quiet, and like to play nurse."

"Don't know any."

"You know me," began Jo, then laughed, and stopped.

"So I do. Will you come, please?" cried Laurie.

"I'm not quiet and nice; but I'll come, if mother will let me. I'll go ask her. Shut that window, like a good boy, and wait till I come."

With that, Jo shouldered her broom and marched into the house, wondering what they would all say to her. Laurie was in a little flutter of excitement at the idea of having company, and flew about to get ready; for, as Mrs. March said, he was "a little gentleman," and did honour to the coming guest by brushing his curly pate, putting on a fresh collar, and trying to tidy up the room, which, in spite of half-a-dozen servants, was anything but neat. Presently there came a loud ring, then a decided voice, asking for "Mr. Laurie," and a surprised-looking servant came running up to announce a young lady.

"All right, show her up, it's Miss Jo," said

Laurie, going to the door of his little parlour to meet Jo, who appeared, looking rosy and kind, and quite at her ease, with a covered dish in one hand, and Beth's three kittens in the other.

" Here I am, bag and baggage," she said briskly. " Mother sent her love, and was glad if I could do anything for you. Meg wanted me to bring some of her blanc-mange, she makes it very nice, and Beth thought her cats would be comforting. I knew you'd shout at them, but I couldn't refuse, she was so anxious to do something."

It so happened that Beth's funny loan was just the thing ; for, in laughing over the kits, Laurie forgot his bashfulness, and grew sociable at once.

" That looks too pretty to eat," he said, smiling with pleasure, as Jo uncovered the dish, and showed the blanc-mange, surrounded by a garland of green leaves, and the scarlet flowers of Amy's pet geranium.

" It isn't anything, only they all felt kindly, and wanted to show it. Tell the girl to put it away for your tea ; it's so simple, you can eat it ; and, being soft, it will slip down without hurting your sore throat. What a cosy room this is."

" It might be, if it was kept nice ; but the maids are lazy, and I don't know how to make them mind. It worries me, though."

" I'll right it up in two minutes ; for it only needs to have the hearth brushed, so—and the things stood straight on the mantelpiece, so—and the books put here, and the bottles there, and your sofa turned from the light, and the pillows plumped up a bit. Now, then, you're fixed."

And so he was ; for, as she laughed and talked,

Jo had whisked things into place, and given quite a different air to the room. Laurie watched her in respectful silence ; and when she beckoned him to his sofa, he sat down with a sigh of satisfaction, saying gratefully—

"How kind you are! Yes, that's what it wanted. Now please take the big chair, and let me do something to amuse my company."

"No; I came to amuse you. Shall I read aloud?" and Jo looked affectionately toward some inviting books near by.

"Thank you; I've read all those, and if you don't mind, I'd rather talk," answered Laurie.

"Not a bit; I'll talk all day if you'll only set me going. Beth says I never know when to stop."

"Is Beth the rosy one, who stays at home a good deal, and sometimes goes out with a little basket?" asked Laurie, with interest.

"Yes, that's Beth; she's my girl, and a regular good one she is, too."

"The pretty one is Meg, and the curly-haired one is Amy, I believe?"

"How did you find that out?"

Laurie coloured up, but answered frankly, "Why, you see, I often hear you calling to one another, and when I'm alone up here, I can't help looking over at your house, you always seem to be having such good times. I beg your pardon for being so rude, but sometimes you forget to put down the curtain at the window where the flowers are ; and, when the lamps are lighted, it's like looking at a picture to see the fire, and you all round the table with your mother ; her face is right opposite, and it looks so sweet behind the flowers, I can't help watching it. I haven't got any mother, you know"; and Laurie poked the fire to hide a little twitching of the lips that he could not control.

The solitary, hungry look in his eyes went straight to Jo's warm heart. She had been so simply taught that there was no nonsense in her head, and at fifteen she was as frank and innocent as any child. Laurie was sick and lonely; and, feeling how rich she was in home-love and happiness, she gladly tried to share it with him. Her brown face was very friendly, and her sharp voice unusually gentle, as she said—

"We'll never draw that curtain any more, and I give you leave to look as much as you like. I just wish, though, instead of peeping, you'd come over and see us. Mother is so splendid, she'd do you heaps of good, and Beth would sing to you, if *I* begged her to, and Amy would dance; Meg and I would make you laugh over our funny stage properties, and we'd have jolly times. Wouldn't your grandpa let you?"

"I think he would, if your mother asked him. He's very kind, though he don't look it; and he lets me do what I like pretty much, only he's afraid I might be a bother to strangers," began Laurie, brightening more and more.

"We ain't strangers, we are neighbours, and you needn't think you'd be a bother. We *want* to know you, and I've been trying to do it this ever so long. We haven't been here a great while, you know, but we have got acquainted with all our neighbours but you."

"You see grandpa lives among his books, and don't mind much what happens outside. Mr.

Brooke, my tutor, don't stay here, you know, and I have no one to go round with me, so I just stop at home, and get on as I can!"

"That's bad; you ought to make a dive, and go visiting everywhere you're asked; then you'll have lots of friends, and pleasant places to go to. Never mind being bashful, it won't last long if you keep going."

Laurie turned red again, but wasn't offended at being accused of bashfulness, for there was so much good-will in Jo, it was impossible not to take her blunt speeches as kindly as they were meant.

"Do you like your school?" asked the boy, changing the subject, after a little pause, during which he stared at the fire, and Jo looked about her well pleased.

"Don't go to school; I'm a business man—girl I mean. I go to wait on my aunt, and a dear, cross old soul she is, too," answered Jo.

Laurie opened his mouth to ask another question; but remembering just in time that it wasn't manners to make too many inquiries into people's affairs, he shut it again, and looked uncomfortable. Jo liked his good breeding, and didn't mind having a laugh at Aunt March, so she gave him a lively description of the fidgety old lady, her fat poodle, the parrot that talked Spanish, and the library where she revelled. Laurie enjoyed that immensely; and when she told about the prim old gentleman who came once to woo Aunt March, and, in the middle of a fine speech, how Poll had tweaked his wig off to his great dismay, the boy lay back and laughed till the tears ran down his cheeks, and a maid popped her head in to see what was the matter.

"Oh ! that does me lots of good ; tell on, please," he said, taking his face out of the sofa-cushion, red and shining with merriment.

Much elated with her success, Jo did "tell on," all about their plays and plans, their hopes and fears for father, and the most interesting events of the little world in which the sisters lived. Then they got to talking about books ; and to Jo's delight she found that Laurie loved them as well as she did, and had read even more than herself.

"If you like them so much, come down and see ours. Grandpa is out, so you needn't be afraid," said Laurie, getting up.

"I'm not afraid of anything," returned Jo, with a toss of the head.

"I don't believe you are !" exclaimed the boy, looking at her with much admiration, though he privately thought she would have good reason to be a trifle afraid of the old gentleman if she met him in some of his moods.

The atmosphere of the whole house being summer-like, Laurie led the way from room to room, letting Jo stop to examine whatever struck her fancy ; and so at last they came to the library, where she clapped her hands, and pranced, as she always did when especially delighted. It was lined with books, and there were pictures and statues, and distracting little cabinets full of coins and curiosities, and Sleepy - Hollow chairs, and queer tables, and bronzes ; and, best of all, a great, open fireplace, with quaint tiles all round it.

"What richness !" sighed Jo, sinking into the

depths of a velvet chair, and gazing about her with an air of intense satisfaction. "Theodore Laurence, you ought to be the happiest boy in the world," she added, impressively.

"A fellow can't live on books," said Laurie, shaking his head, as he perched on a table opposite.

Before he could say more, a bell rung, and Jo flew up, exclaiming with alarm, "Mercy me! it's your grandpa!"

"Well, what if it is? You are not afraid of anything, you know," returned the boy, looking wicked.

"I think I am a little bit afraid of him, but I don't know why I should be. Marmee said I might come, and I don't think you're any the worse for it," said Jo, composing herself, though she kept her eyes on the door.

"I'm a great deal better for it, and ever so much obliged. I'm only afraid you are very tired talking to me; it was *so* pleasant, I couldn't bear to stop," said Laurie, gratefully.

"The doctor to see you, sir," and the maid beckoned as she spoke.

"Would you mind if I left you for a minute? I suppose I must see him," said Laurie.

"Don't mind me. I'm happy enough here," answered Jo.

Laurie went away, and his guest amused herself in her own way. She was standing before a fine portrait of the old gentleman, when the door opened again, and, without turning, she said, decidedly, "I'm sure now that I shouldn't be afraid of him, for he's got kind eyes, though his mouth is grim, and he looks as if he had a tre-

mendous will of his own. He isn't as handsome
as *my* grandfather, but I like him."

"Thank you, madam," said a gruff voice behind
her; and there, to her great dismay, stood old Mr.
Laurence.

Poor Jo blushed till she couldn't blush any
redder, and her heart began to beat uncomfortably
fast as she thought of what she had said. For a
minute a wild desire to run away possessed her;
but that was cowardly, and the girls would laugh
at her; so she resolved to stay, and get out of the
scrape as she could. A second look showed her
that the living eyes, under the bushy grey eyebrows,
were kinder even than the painted ones; and
there was a sly twinkle in them, which lessened
her fear a good deal. The gruff voice was gruffer
than ever, as the old gentleman said abruptly,
after that dreadful pause, "So you're not much
afraid of me, hey?"

"Not much, sir."

"And you don't think me as handsome as your
grandfather?"

"Not quite, sir."

"And I've got a tremendous will, have I?"

"I only said I thought so."

"But you like me in spite of it?"

"Yes, I do, sir."

That answer pleased the old gentleman; he
gave a short laugh, shook hands with her, and
putting his finger under her chin, turned up her
face, examined it gravely, and let it go, saying,
with a nod, "You've got your grandfather's spirit,
if you haven't his face. He *was* a fine man,
my dear; but, what is better, he was a brave

and an honest one, and I was proud to be his friend."

"Thank you, sir"; and Jo was quite comfortable after that, for it suited her exactly.

"What have you been doing to this boy of mine, hey?" was the next question, sharply put.

"Only trying to be neighbourly, sir"; and Jo told how her visit came about.

"You think he needs cheering up a bit, do you?"

"Yes, sir; he seems a bit lonely, and young folks would do him good, perhaps. We are only girls, but we should be glad to help if we could, for we don't forget the splendid Christmas present you sent us," said Jo, eagerly.

"Tut, tut, tut; that was the boy's affair. How is the poor woman?"

"Doing nicely, sir"; and off went Jo, talking very fast, as she told all about the Hummels, in whom her mother had interested richer friends than they were.

"Just her father's way of doing good. I shall come and see your mother some fine day. Tell her so. There's the tea-bell; we have it early, on the boy's account. Come down, and go on being neighbourly."

"If you'd like to have me, sir."

"Shouldn't ask you, if I didn't"; and Mr. Laurence offered her his arm with old-fashioned courtesy.

"What *would* Meg say to this?" thought Jo, as she was marched away, while her eyes danced with fun as she imagined herself telling the story at home.

"Hey! what the dickens has come to the

fellow ? " said the old gentleman, as Laurie came running down stairs, and brought up with a start of surprise at the astonishing sight of Jo arm-in-arm with his redoubtable grandfather.

" I didn't know you'd come, sir," he began, as Jo gave him a triumphant little glance.

" That's evident, by the way you racket down-stairs. Come to your tea, sir, and behave like a gentleman " ; and having pulled the boy's hair by way of a caress, Mr. Laurence walked on, while Laurie went through a series of comic evolutions behind their backs, which nearly produced an explosion of laughter from Jo.

The old gentleman did not say much as he drank his four cups of tea, but he watched the young people, who soon chatted away like old friends, and the change in his grandson did not escape him. There was colour, light and life in the boy's face now, vivacity in his manner, and genuine merriment in his laugh.

" She's right ; the lad *is* lonely. I'll see what these little girls can do for him," thought Mr. Laurence, as he looked and listened. He liked Jo, for her odd, blunt ways suited him ; and she seemed to understand the boy almost as well as if she had been one herself.

If the Laurences had been what Jo called " prim and poky," she would not have gone at all, for such people always made her shy and awkward ; but finding them free and easy, she was so herself, and made a good impression. When they rose she proposed to go, but Laurie said he had something more to show her, and took her away to the con-servatory, which had been lighted for her benefit.

It seemed quite fairy-like to Jo, as she went up and down the walks, enjoying the blooming walls on either side,—the soft light, the damp, sweet air, and the wonderful vines and trees that hung above her,—while her new friend cut the finest flowers till his hands were full; then he tied them up, saying, with the happy look Jo liked to see, " Please give these to your mother, and tell her I like the medicine she sent very much."

They found Mr. Laurence standing before the fire in the great drawing-room, but Jo's attention was entirely absorbed by a grand piano which stood open.

" Do you play ? " she asked, turning to Laurie with a respectful expression.

" Sometimes," he answered modestly.

" Please do, now ; I want to hear it, so I can tell Beth."

" Won't you first ? "

" Don't know how ; too stupid to learn, but I love music dearly."

So Laurie played, and Jo listened, with her nose luxuriously buried in tea roses and heliotrope. Her respect and regard for the " Laurence boy " increased very much, for he played remarkably well, and didn't put on any airs. She wished Beth could hear him, but she did not say so ; only praised him till he was quite abashed, and his grandfather came to the rescue. " That will do, that will do, young lady ; too many sugar-plums are not good for him. His music isn't bad, but I hope he will do as well in more important things. Going ? Well, I'm much obliged to you, and I hope you'll come again. My respects to your mother ; good-night Doctor Jo."

He shook hands kindly, but looked as if something did not please him. When they got into the hall Jo asked Laurie if she had done anything amiss; he shook his head.

"No, it was me; he don't like to hear me play."

"Why not?"

"I'll tell you some day. John is going home with you, as I can't."

"No need of that; I ain't a young lady, and it's only a step. Take care of yourself, won't you?"

"Yes, but you will come again, I hope."

"If you promise to come and see us after you are well."

"I will."

"Good-night, Laurie."

"Good-night, Jo, good-night."

When all the afternoon's adventures had been told, the family felt inclined to go visiting in a body, for each found something very attractive in the big house on the other side of the hedge. Mrs. March wanted to tal' of her father with the old man who had not forgotten him; Meg longed to walk in the conservatory; Beth sighed for the grand piano, and Amy was eager to see the fine pictures and statues.

"Mother, why didn't Mr. Laurence like to have Laurie play?" asked Jo, who was of an inquiring disposition.

"I am not sure, but I think it was because his son, Laurie's father, married an Italian lady, a musician, which displeased the old man, who is very proud. The lady was good and lovely and accomplished, but he did not like her, and never saw his son after he married. They both died when Laurie was a little child, and then his grandfather took him home. I fancy the boy, who was born in Italy, is not very strong, and the old man is afraid of losing him, which makes him so careful. Laurie comes naturally by his love of music, for he is like his mother, and I daresay his grandfather fears that he may want to be a musician; at any rate, his skill reminds him of the woman he did not like, and so he 'glowered' as Jo said."

"Dear me, how romantic!" exclaimed Meg.

"How silly," said Jo; "let him be a musician, if he wants to, and not plague his life out sending him to college, when he hates to go."

"That's why he has such handsome black eyes and pretty manners, I suppose; Italians are always nice," said Meg, who was a little sentimental.

"What do you know about his eyes and his manners? You never spoke to him hardly," cried Jo, who was *not* sentimental.

"I saw him at the party, and what you tell shows that he knows how to behave. That was a nice little speech about the medicine mother sent him."

"He meant the blanc-mange, I suppose."

"How stupid you are, child; he meant you, of course."

"Did he?" and Jo opened her eyes as if it had never occurred to her before.

"I never saw such a girl! You don't know a compliment when you get it," said Meg, with the air of a young lady who knew all about the matter.

"I think they are great nonsense, and I'll thank you not to be silly, and spoil my fun. Laurie's

a nice boy, and I like him, and I won't have any
sentimental stuff about compliments and such
rubbish.   We'll all be good to him, because he
hasn't got any mother, and he *may* come over and
see us, mayn't he, Marmee ? "

"Yes, Jo ; your little friend is very welcome,
and I hope Meg will remember that children should
be children as long as they can."

"I don't call myself a child, and I'm not in my
teens yet," observed Amy. "What do you say,
Beth ? "

"I was thinking about our ' Pilgrim's Progress,' "
answered Beth, who had not heard a word. "How
we got out of the Slough and through the Wicket
Gate by resolving to be good, and up the steep hill,
by trying ; and that maybe the house over there,
full of splendid things, is going to be our Palace
Beautiful."

"We have got to get by the lions first," said Jo,
as if she rather liked the prospect.

CHAPTER VI.

BETH FINDS THE PALACE BEAUTIFUL.

THE big house did prove a Palace Beautiful, though
it took some time for all to get in, and Beth found it
very hard to pass the lions. Old Mr. Laurence was
the biggest one ; but, after he had called, said something funny or kind to each one of the girls, and
talked over old times with their mother, nobody
felt much afraid of him, except timid Beth. The
other lion was that they were poor and Laurie rich ;

for this made them shy of accepting favours which they could not return. But after a while they found that he considered them the benefactors, and could not do enough to show how grateful he was for Mrs. March's motherly welcome, their cheerful society, and the comfort he took in that humble home of theirs ; so they soon forgot their pride, and interchanged kindnesses without stopping to think which was the greater.

All sorts of pleasant things happened about that time, for the new friendship flourished like grass in spring. Every one liked Laurie, and he privately informed his tutor that " the Marches were regularly splendid girls." With the delightful enthusiasm of youth, they took the solitary boy into their midst, and made much of him, and he found something very charming in the innocent companionship of these simple-hearted girls. Never having known mother or sisters, he was quick to feel the influences they brought about him ; and their busy, lively ways made him ashamed of the indolent life he led. He was tired of books, and found people so interesting now, that Mr. Brooke was obliged to make very unsatisfactory reports ; for Laurie was always playing truant, and running over to the Marches.

" Never mind, let him take a holiday, and make it up afterwards," said the old gentleman. " The good lady next door says he is studying too hard, and needs young society, amusement, and exercise. I suspect she is right, and that I've been coddling the fellow as if I'd been his grandmother. Let him do what he likes, as long as he is happy ; he can't get into mischief in that little nunnery over there, and Mrs. March is doing more than we can."

What good times they had, to be sure! Such plays and tableaux; such sleigh rides and skating frolics; such pleasant evenings in the old parlour, and now and then such gay little parties at the great house. Meg could walk in the conservatory whenever she liked, and revel in bouquets; Jo browsed over the new library voraciously, and convulsed the old gentleman with her criticisms; Amy copied pictures and enjoyed beauty to her heart's content, and Laurie played lord of the manor in the most delightful style.

But Beth, though yearning for the grand piano, could not pluck up courage to go to the " mansion of bliss," as Meg called it. She went once with Jo, but the old gentleman, not being aware of her infirmity, stared at her so hard from under his heavy eyebrows, and said " hey ! " so loud, that he frightened her so much her " feet chattered on the floor," she told her mother; and she ran away, declaring she would never go there any more, not even for the dear piano. No persuasions or enticements could overcome her fear, till the fact coming to Mr. Laurence's ear, in some mysterious way, he set about mending matters. During one of the brief calls he made, he artfully led the conversation to music, and talked away about great singers whom he had seen, fine organs he had heard, and told such charming anecdotes, that Beth found it impossible to stay in her distant corner, but crept nearer and nearer, as if fascinated. At the back of his chair she stopped, and stood listening with her great eyes wide open, and her cheeks red with the excitement of this unusual performance. Taking no more notice of her than if she had been a fly, Mr.

Laurence talked on about Laurie's lessons and teachers; and presently, as if the idea had just occurred to him, he said to Mrs. March—

"The boy neglects his music now, and I am glad of it, for he was getting too fond of it. But the piano suffers for want of use; wouldn't some of your girls like to run over, and practise on it now and then, just to keep it in tune, you know, ma'am?"

Beth took a step forward, and pressed her hands tightly together, to keep from clapping them, for this was an irresistible temptation; and the thought of practising on that splendid instrument quite took her breath away. Before Mrs. March could reply, Mr. Laurence went on with an odd little nod and smile—

"They needn't see or speak to any one, but run in at any time, for I am shut up in my study at the other end of the house. Laurie is out a great deal, and the servants are never near the drawing-room after nine o'clock." Here he rose, as if going, and Beth made up her mind to speak, for that last arrangement left nothing to be desired. "Please tell the young ladies what I say, and if they don't care to come, why, never mind;" here a little hand slipped into his, and Beth looked up at him with a face full of gratitude, as she said, in her earnest, yet timid, way—

"Oh, sir! they do care, very, very much!"

"Are you the musical girl?" he asked, without any startling "hey!" as he looked down at her very kindly.

"I'm Beth; I love it dearly, and I'll come if you are quite sure nobody will hear me—and be disturbed," she added, fearing to be rude, and trembling at her own boldness as she spoke.

" Not a soul, my dear ; the house is empty half the day, so come and drum away as much as you like, and I shall be obliged to you."

" How kind you are, sir."

Beth blushed like a rose under the friendly look he wore, but she was not frightened now, and gave the big hand a grateful squeeze, because she had no words to thank him for the precious gift he had given her. The old gentleman softly stroked the hair off her forehead, and, stooping down, he kissed her, saying, in a tone few people ever heard—

" I had a little girl once with eyes like these ; God bless you, my dear ; good-day, ma'am," and away he went, in a great hurry.

Beth had a rapture with her mother, and then rushed up to impart the glorious news to her family of invalids, as the girls were not at home. How blithely she sang that evening, and how they all laughed at her, because she awoke Amy in the night, by playing the piano on her face in her sleep. Next day, having seen both the old and the young gentleman out of the house, Beth, after two or three retreats, fairly got in at the side door, and made her way as noiselessly as any mouse to the drawing-room, where her idol stood. Quite by accident, of course, some pretty, easy music lay on the piano ; and, with trembling fingers, and frequent stops to listen and look about, Beth at last touched the great instrument, and straightway forgot her fear, herself, and everything else but the unspeakable delight which the music gave her, for it was like the voice of a beloved friend.

She stayed till Hannah came to take her home to dinner ; but she had no appetite, and could only sit and smile upon every one in a general state of beatitude.

After that, the little brown hood slipped through the hedge nearly every day, and the great drawing-room was haunted by a tuneful spirit that came and went unseen. She never knew that Mr. Laurence often opened his study door to hear the old-fashioned airs he liked ; she never saw Laurie mount guard in the hall, to warn the servants away ; she never suspected that the exercise books and new songs which she found in the rack were put there for her especial benefit ; and when he talked to her about music at home, she only thought how kind he was to tell things that helped her so much. So she enjoyed herself heartily, and found, what isn't always the case, that her granted wish was all she had hoped. Perhaps it was because she was so grateful for this blessing that a greater was given her ; at any rate she deserved both.

" Mother, I'm going to work Mr. Laurence a pair of slippers. He is so kind to me I must thank him, and I don't know any other way. Can I do it ? " asked Beth, a few weeks after that eventful call of his.

" Yes, dear ; it will please him very much, and be a nice way of thanking him. The girls will help you about them, and I will pay for the making up," replied Mrs. March, who took peculiar pleasure in granting Beth's requests, because she so seldom asked anything for herself.

After many serious discussions with Meg and Jo, the pattern was chosen, the materials bought, and the slippers begun. A cluster of grave yet cheerful pansies, on a deeper purple ground, was pronounced very appropriate and pretty, and Beth worked away early and late, with occasional lifts over hard parts. She was a nimble little needle-woman, and they were finished before anyone got tired of them. Then she wrote a very short, simple note, and, with Laurie's help, got them smuggled on to the study table one morning before the old gentleman was up.

When this excitement was over, Beth waited to see what would happen. All that day passed, and a part of the next, before any acknowledgment arrived, and she was beginning to fear she had offended her crotchety friend. On the afternoon of the second day she went out to do an errand, and give poor Joanna, the invalid doll, her daily exercise. As she came up the street on her return she saw three—yes, four heads popping in and out of the parlour windows ; and the moment they saw her several hands were waved, and several joyful voices screamed—

" Here's a letter from the old gentleman ; come quick and read it ! "

" Oh, Beth ! he's sent you—" began Amy, gesticulating with unseemly energy ; but she got no further, for Jo quenched her by slamming down the window.

Beth hurried on in a twitter of suspense ; at the door her sisters seized and bore her to the parlour in a triumphal procession, all pointing, and all saying at once, " Look there ! look there ! " Beth did look, and turned pale with delight and surprise ; for there stood a little cabinet piano, with a letter lying on the glossy lid, directed like a signboard to " Miss Elizabeth March."

"For me ? " gasped Beth, holding on to Jo, and feeling as if she should tumble down, it was such an overwhelming thing altogether.

"Yes, all for you, my precious Isn't it splendid of him ? Don't you think he's the dearest old man in the world ? Here's the key in the letter ; we didn't open it, but we are dying to know what he says," cried Jo, hugging her sister, and offering the note.

"You read it ; I can't, I feel so queer. Oh, it is too lovely," and Beth hid her face in Jo's apron, quite upset by her present.

Jo opened the paper, and read aloud the kind-hearted old gentleman's note, which was as follows—

" ' MISS MARCH :

" ' *Dear Madam*—

" ' I have had many pairs of slippers in my life, but I never had any that suited me so well as yours. Heart's-ease is my favourite flower, and these will always remind me of the gentle giver. I like to pay my debts, so I know you will allow " the old gentle-man " to send you something which once belonged to a little granddaughter he lost. With hearty thanks, and best wishes, I remain,

" ' Your grateful friend and humble servant,

" ' JAMES LAURENCE.' "

"There, Beth, that's an honour to be proud of, I'm sure ! Laurie told me how fond Mr. Laurence used to be of the child who died, and how he kept all her little things carefully. Just think; he's given you her piano! That comes of having big blue eyes and loving music," said Jo, trying to soothe Beth, who trembled, and looked more excited than she had ever been before.

"See the cunning brackets to hold candles, and the nice green silk, puckered up with a gold rose in the middle, and the pretty rack and stool, all complete," added Meg, opening the instrument, and displaying its beauties.

"'Your humble servant, James Laurence;' only think of his writing that to you. I'll tell the girls; they'll think it's killing," said Amy, much impressed by the note.

"Try it, honey; let's hear the sound of the baby pianny," said Hannah, who always took a share in the family joys and sorrows.

So Beth tried it, and every one pronounced it the most remarkable piano ever heard. It had evidently been newly tuned, and put in apple-pie order; but, perfect as it was, I think the real charm of it lay in the happiest of all happy faces which leaned over it, as Beth lovingly touched the beautiful black and white keys, and pressed the shiny pedals.

"You'll have to go and thank him," said Jo, by way of a joke; for the idea of the child's really going never entered her head.

"Yes, I mean to; I think I'll go now, before I get frightened thinking about it," and, to the utter amazement of the assembled family, Beth walked deliberately down the garden, through the hedge and in at the Laurences' door.

"Well, I wish I may die, if it ain't the queerest

thing I ever see! The pianny has turned her head; she'd never have gone in her right mind," cried Hannah, staring after her, while the girls were rendered quite speechless by the miracle.

They would have been still more amazed, if they had seen what Beth did afterwards. If you will believe me, she went and knocked at the study door, before she gave herself time to think; and when a gruff voice called out "Come in!" she did go in, right up to Mr. Laurence, who looked quite taken aback, and held out her hand, saying, with only a small quaver in her voice, "I came to thank you, sir, for—" but she didn't finish, for he looked so friendly that she forgot her speech; and, only remembering that he had lost the little girl he loved, she put both arms round his neck, and kissed him.

If the roof of the house had suddenly flown off, the old gentleman wouldn't have been more astonished; but he liked it—oh dear, yes! he liked it amazingly; and was so touched and pleased by that confiding little kiss, that all his crustiness vanished; and he just set her on his knee, and laid his wrinkled cheek against her rosy one, feeling as if he had got his own little granddaughter back again. Beth ceased to fear him from that moment, and sat there talking to him as cosily as if she had known him all her life; for love casts out fear, and gratitude can conquer pride. When she went home, he walked with her to her own gate, shook hands cordially, and touched his hat as he marched back again, looking very stately and erect, like a handsome, soldierly old gentleman, as he was.

When the girls saw that performance, Jo began to dance a jig, by way of expressing her satisfaction;

Amy nearly fell out of the window in her surprise, and Meg exclaimed, with uplifted hands, "Well, I do believe the world is coming to an end!"

CHAPTER VII.

AMY'S VALLEY OF HUMILIATION.

"THAT boy is a perfect Cyclops, isn't he?" said Amy, one day, as Laurie clattered by on horseback, with a flourish of his whip as he passed.

"How dare you say so, when he's got both his eyes? and very handsome ones they are, too," cried Jo, who resented any slighting remarks about her friend.

"I didn't say anything about his eyes, and I don't see why you need fire up when I admire his riding."

"Oh, my goodness! that little goose positively means a centaur, and she called him a Cyclops," exclaimed Jo, with a burst of laughter.

"You needn't be so rude, it's only a 'lapse of lingy,' as Mr. Davis says," retorted Amy, finishing Jo with her Latin. "I just wish I had a little of the money Laurie spends on that horse," she added, as if to herself, yet hoping her sisters would hear.

"Why?" asked Meg, kindly, for Jo had gone off in another laugh at Amy's second blunder.

"I need it so much; I'm dreadfully in debt, and it won't be my turn to have the rag-money for a month."

"In debt, Amy; what do you mean?" and Meg looked sober.

"Why, I owe at least a dozen pickled limes, and

I can't pay them, you know, till I have money, for Marmee forbid my having anything charged at the shop."

"Tell me all about it. Are limes the fashion now? It used to be pricking bits of rubber to make balls"; and Meg tried to keep her countenance, Amy looked so grave and important.

"Why, you see, the girls are always buying them, and unless you want to be thought mean, you must do it too. It's nothing but limes now, for every one is sucking them in their desks in school-time, and trading them off for pencils, bead-rings, paper dolls, or something else, at recess. If one girl likes another, she gives her a lime; if she's mad with her, she eats one before her face, and don't offer even a suck. They treat by turns; and I've had ever so many, but haven't returned them, and I ought, for they are debts of honour, you know."

"How much will pay them off, and restore your credit?" asked Meg, taking out her purse.

"A quarter would more than do it, and leave a few cents over for a treat for you. Don't you like limes?"

"Not much; you may have my share. Here's the money—make it last as long as you can, for it isn't very plenty with us, as you know."

"Oh thank you! it must be so nice to have pocket-money. I'll have a grand feast, for I haven't tasted a lime this week. I felt delicate about taking any, as I couldn't return them, and I'm actually suffering for one."

Next day Amy was rather late at school; but could not resist the temptation of displaying, with pardonable pride, a moist brown paper parcel, before she consigned it to the inmost recesses of her desk. During the next few minutes the rumour that Amy March had got twenty-four delicious limes (she ate one on the way), and was going to treat, circulated through her " set," and the attentions of her friends became quite overwhelming. Katy Brown invited her to her next party on the spot ; Mary Kingsley insisted on lending her her watch till recess, and Jenny Snow, a satirical young lady who had basely twitted Amy upon her limeless state, promptly buried the hatchet, and offered to furnish answers to certain appalling sums. But Amy had not forgotten Miss Snow's cutting remarks about " some persons whose noses were not too flat to smell other people's limes, and stuck-up people, who were not too proud to ask for them " ; and she instantly crushed " that Snow girl's " hopes by the withering telegram, " You needn't be so polite all of a sudden, for you won't get any."

A distinguished personage happened to visit the school that morning, and Amy's beautifully drawn maps received praise, which honour to her foe rankled in the soul of Miss Snow, and caused Miss March to assume the airs of a studious young peacock. But, alas, alas ! pride goes before a fall, and the revengeful Snow turned the tables with disastrous success. No sooner had the guest paid the usual stale compliments, and bowed himself out, than Jenny, under pretence of asking an important question, informed Mr. Davis, the teacher, that Amy March had actually got some pickled limes in her desk.

Now Mr. Davis had declared limes a contraband article, and solemnly vowed to publicly ferule the first person who was found breaking the law. This much enduring man had succeeded in banishing gum after a long and stormy war, had made a bonfire of the confiscated novels and newspapers, had suppressed a private post-office, had forbidden distortions of the face, nicknames and caricatures, and done all that one man could do to keep half a hundred rebellious girls in order. Boys are trying enough to human patience, goodness knows! but girls are infinitely more so, especially to nervous gentlemen with tyrannical tempers, and no more talent for teaching than " Dr. Blimber." Mr. Davis knew any quantity of Greek, Latin, Algebra, and ologies of all sorts, so he was called a fine teacher ; and manners, morals, feelings, and examples were not considered of any particular importance. It was a most unfortunate moment for denouncing Amy, and Jenny knew it. Mr. Davis had evidently taken his coffee too strong that morning ; there was an east wind, which always affected his neuralgia, and his pupils had not done him the credit which he felt he deserved ; therefore, to use the expressive, if not elegant, language of a school-girl, " he was as nervous as a witch and as cross as a bear." The word " limes " was like fire to powder ; his yellow face flushed, and he rapped on his desk with an energy which made Jenny skip to her seat with unusual rapidity.

" Young ladies, attention, if you please ! "

At the stern order the buzz ceased, and fifty pairs of blue, black, grey, and brown eyes were obediently fixed upon his awful countenance.

" Miss Marsh, come to the desk."

Amy rose to comply, with outward composure, but a secret fear oppressed her, for the limes weighed far too heavily upon her conscience.

" Bring with you the limes you have in your desk," was the unexpected command which arrested her before she got out of her seat.

" Don't take all," whispered her neighbour, a young lady of great presence of mind.

Amy hastily shook out half a dozen, and laid the rest down before Mr. Davis, feeling that any man possessing a human heart would relent when that delicious perfume met his nose. Unfortunately Mr. Davis particularly detested the odour of the fashionable pickle, and disgust added to his wrath.

" Is that all ? "

" Not quite," stammered Amy.

" Bring the rest, immediately."

With a despairing glance at her set she obeyed.

" You are sure there are no more ? "

" I never lie, sir."

" So I see. Now take these disgusting things, two by two, and throw them out of the window."

There was a simultaneous sigh, which created quite a little gust as the last hope fled, and the treat was ravished from their longing lips. Scarlet with shame and anger, Amy went to and fro twelve mortal times ; and as each doomed couple looking, oh, so plump and juicy ! fell from her reluctant hands, a shout from the street completed the anguish of the girls, for it told them that their feast was being exulted over by the little Irish children, who were their sworn foes. This—this was too much ; all flashed indignant or appealing glances at the inexorable Davis, and one passionate lime-lover burst into tears.

As Amy returned from her last trip, Mr. Davis gave a portentous "hem," and said, in his most impressive manner,—

"Young ladies, you remember what I said to you a week ago. I am sorry this has happened; but I never allow my rules to be infringed, and I *never* break my word. Miss March, hold out your hand."

Amy started, and put both hands behind her, turning upon him an imploring look, which pleaded for her better than the words she could not utter. She was rather a favourite with "old Davis," as, of course, he was called, and it's my private belief that he *would* have broken his word if the indignation of one irrepressible young lady had not found vent in a hiss. That hiss, faint as it was, irritated the irascible gentleman, and sealed the culprit's fate.

"Your hand, Miss March!" was the only answer her mute appeal received; and, too proud to cry or beseech, Amy set her teeth, threw back her head defiantly, and bore without flinching several tingling blows on her little palm. They were neither many nor heavy, but that made no difference to her. For the first time in her life she had been struck; and the disgrace, in her eyes, was as deep as if he had knocked her down.

"You will now stand on the platform till recess, Miss March," said Mr. Davis, sternly, resolved to do the thing thoroughly, since he had begun.

That was dreadful; it would have been bad enough to go to her seat and see the pitying faces of her friends, or the satisfied ones of her few enemies;

but to face the whole school, with that shame fresh upon her, seemed impossible, and for a second she felt as if she could only drop down where she stood, and break her heart with crying. A bitter sense of wrong, and the thought of Jenny Snow, helped her to bear it ; and, taking the ignominious place, she fixed her eyes on the stove-funnel above what now seemed a sea of faces, and stood there so motionless and white, that the girls found it very hard to study, with that pathetic little figure before them.

During the fifteen minutes that followed, the proud and sensitive little girl suffered a shame and pain which she never forgot. To others it might seem a ludicrous or trivial affair, but to her it was a hard experience ; for during the twelve years of her life she had been governed by love alone, and a blow of that sort had never touched her before. The smart of her hand, and the ache of her heart, were forgotten in the sting of the thought,—

" I shall have to tell at home, and they will be so disappointed in me ! "

The fifteen minutes seemed an hour ; but they came to an end at last, and the word " recess ! " had never seemed so welcome to her before.

" You can go, Miss March," said Mr. Davis, looking, as he felt, uncomfortable.

He did not soon forget the reproachful look Amy gave him, as she went, without a word to any one, straight into the ante-room, snatched her things, and left the place " for ever," as she passionately declared to herself. She was in a sad state when she got home ; and when the older girls arrived, some time later, an indignation meeting was held at once. Mrs. March did not say much, but looked disturbed, and comforted her afflicted little daughter in her tenderest manner. Meg bathed the insulted hand with glycerine and tears; Beth felt that even her beloved kittens would fail as a balm for griefs like this, and Jo wrathfully proposed that Mr. Davis should be arrested without delay, while Hannah shook her fist at the "villain," and pounded potatoes for dinner as if she had him under her pestle.

No notice was taken of Amy's flight, except by her mates; but the sharp-eyed demoiselles discovered that Mr. Davis was quite benignant in the afternoon, also unusually nervous. Just before school closed, Jo appeared, wearing a grim expression, as she stalked up to the desk, and delivered a letter from her mother; then collected Amy's property and departed, carefully scraping the mud from her boots on the door-mat, as if she shook the dust of the place off her feet.

"Yes, you can have a vacation from school, but I want you to study a little every day, with Beth," said Mrs. March, that evening. "I don't approve of corporal punishment, especially for girls. I dislike Mr. Davis's manner of teaching, and don't think the girls you associate with are doing you any good, so I shall ask your father's advice before I send you anywhere else."

"That's good! I wish all the girls would leave, and spoil his old school. It's perfectly maddening to think of those lovely limes," sighed Amy, with the air of a martyr.

"I am not sorry you lost them, for you broke the rules, and deserved some punishment for disobedience," was the severe reply, which rather disappointed the young lady, who expected nothing but sympathy.

"Do you mean you are glad I was disgraced before the whole school?" cried Amy.

"I should not have chosen that way of mending a fault," replied her mother, "but I'm not sure that it won't do you more good than a milder method. You are getting to be altogether too conceited and important, my dear, and it is quite time you set about correcting it. You have a good many little gifts and virtues, but there is no need of parading them, for conceit spoils the finest genius. There is not much danger that real talent or goodness will be overlooked long; even if it is, the consciousness of possessing and using it well should satisfy one, and the great charm of all power is modesty."

"So it is," cried Laurie, who was playing chess in a corner with Jo. "I knew a girl, once, who had a really remarkable talent for music, and she didn't know it; never guessed what sweet little things she composed when she was alone, and wouldn't have believed if any one had told her."

"I wish I'd known that nice girl, maybe she would have helped me, I'm so stupid," said Beth, who stood beside him, listening eagerly.

"You do know her, and she helps you better than any one else could," answered Laurie, looking at her with such mischievous meaning in his merry black eyes, that Beth suddenly turned very red, and hid her face in the sofa-cushion, overcome by such an unexpected discovery.

Jo let Laurie win the game, to pay for that

praise of her Beth, who could not be prevailed upon to play for them after her compliment. So Laurie did his best, and sang delightfully, being in a particularly lively humour, for to the Marches he seldom showed the moody side of his character. When he was gone, Amy, who had been pensive all the evening, said, suddenly, as if busy with some new idea,—

"Is Laurie an accomplished boy?"

"Yes; he has an excellent education, and has much talent; he will make a fine man, if not spoilt by petting," replied her mother.

"And he isn't conceited, is he?" asked Amy.

"Not in the least; that is why he is so charming, and we all like him so much."

"I see; it's nice to have accomplishments, and be elegant; but not to show off, or get perked up," said Amy, thoughtfully.

"These things are always seen and felt in a person's manner and conversation, if modestly used; but it is not necessary to display them," said Mrs. March.

"Any more than it's proper to wear all your bonnets, and gowns, and ribbons, at once, that folks may know you've got 'em," added Jo; and the lecture ended in a laugh.

CHAPTER VIII.

JO MEETS APOLLYON.

"GIRLS, where are you going?" asked Amy, coming into their room one Saturday afternoon, and finding them getting ready to go out, with an air of secrecy which excited her curiosity.

"Never mind; little girls shouldn't ask questions," returned Jo, sharply.

Now if there *is* anything mortifying to our feelings, when we are young, it is to be told that; and to be bidden to "run away, dear," is still more trying to us. Amy bridled up at this insult, and determined to find out the secret, if she teased for an hour. Turning to Meg, who never refused her anything very long, she said, coaxingly, "Do tell me! I should think you might let me go, too; for Beth is fussing over her dolls, and I haven't got anything to do, and am *so* lonely."

"I can't, dear, because you aren't invited," began Meg; but Jo broke in impatiently, "Now, Meg, be quiet, or you will spoil it all. You can't go, Amy; so don't be a baby, and whine about it."

"You are going somewhere with Laurie, I know you are; you were whispering and laughing together on the sofa, last night, and you stopped when I came in. Aren't you going with him?"

" Yes, we are ; now do be still, and stop bothering."

Amy held her tongue, but used her eyes, and saw Meg slip a fan into her pocket.

" I know ! I know ! you're going to the theatre to see the ' Seven Castles ! ' " she cried ; adding, resolutely, " and I *shall* go, for mother said I might see it ; and I've got my rag-money, and it was mean not to tell me in time."

" Just listen to me a minute, and be a good child," said Meg, soothingly. " Mother doesn't wish you to go this week, because your eyes are not well enough yet to bear the light of this fairy piece. Next week you can go with Beth and Hannah, and have a nice time."

" I don't like that half as well as going with you and Laurie. Please let me go ; I've been sick with this cold so long, and shut up, I'm dying for some fun. Do, Meg ! I'll be ever so good," pleaded Amy, looking as pathetic as she could.

" Suppose we take her. I don't believe mother would mind, if we bundle her up well," began Meg.

" If *she* goes *I* shan't ; and if I don't, Laurie won't like it ; and it will be very rude, after he invited only us, to go and drag in Amy. I should think she'd hate to poke herself where she isn't wanted," said Jo, crossly, for she disliked the trouble of overseeing a fidgety child, when she wanted to enjoy herself.

Her tone and manner angered Amy, who began to put her boots on, saying, in her most aggravating way, " I *shall* go ; Meg says I may ; and if I pay for myself, Laurie hasn't anything to do with it."

" You can't sit with us, for our seats are reserved,

and you mustn't sit alone ; so Laurie will give you his place, and that will spoil our pleasure ; or he'll get another seat for you, and that isn't proper, when you weren't asked. You shan't stir a step ; so you must just stay where you are," scolded Jo, crosser than ever, having just pricked her finger in her hurry.

Sitting on the floor, with one boot on, Amy began to cry, and Meg to reason with her, when Laurie called from below, and the two girls hurried down, leaving their sister wailing ; for now and then she forgot her grown-up ways, and acted like a spoilt child. Just as the party was setting out Amy called over the banisters, in a threatening tone, " You'll be sorry for this, Jo March ! see if you ain't."

" Fiddlesticks ! " returned Jo, slamming the door.

They had a charming time, for " The Seven Castles of the Diamond Lake " were as brilliant and wonderful as heart could wish. But, in spite of the comical red imps, sparkling elves, and gorgeous princes and princesses, Jo's pleasure had a drop of bitterness in it ; the fairy queen's yellow curls reminded her of Amy ; and between the acts she amused herself with wondering what her sister would do to make her " sorry for it." She and Amy had had many lively skirmishes in the course of their lives, for both had quick tempers, and were apt to be violent when fairly roused. Amy teased Jo, and Jo irritated Amy, and semi-occasional explosions occurred, of which both were much ashamed afterwards. Although the oldest, Jo had the least self-control, and had hard times trying to curb the fiery spirit which was continually getting her into trouble; her anger never lasted long, and having humbly confessed her fault, she sincerely repented, and tried to do better. Her sisters used to say that they rather liked to get Jo into a fury, because she was such an angel afterwards. Poor Jo tried desperately to be good, but her bosom enemy was always ready to flame up and defeat her; and it took years of patient effort to subdue it.

When they got home, they found Amy reading in the parlour. She assumed an injured air as they came in, and never lifted her eyes from her book, or asked a single question. Perhaps curiosity might have conquered resentment, if Beth had not been there to inquire, and receive a glowing description of the play. On going up to put away her best hat, Jo's first look was towards the bureau; for, in their last quarrel, Amy had soothed her feelings by turning Jo's top drawer upside down, on the floor. Everything was in its place, however; and after a hasty glance into her various closets, bags and boxes, Jo decided that Amy had forgiven and forgotten her wrongs.

There Jo was mistaken; for next day she made a discovery which produced a tempest. Meg, Beth and Amy were sitting together, late in the afternoon, when Jo burst into the room, looking excited, and demanding, breathlessly, " Has any one taken my story ? "

Meg and Beth said " No," at once, and looked surprised; Amy poked the fire, and said nothing. Jo saw her colour rise, and was down upon her in a minute.

" Amy, you've got it ! "

" No, I haven't."

" You know where it is, then ! "

" No, I don't."

" That's a fib ! " cried Jo, taking her by the shoulders, and looking fierce enough to frighten a much braver child than Amy.

" It isn't. I haven't got it, don't know where it is now, and don't care."

" You know something about it, and you'd better tell at once, or I'll make you," and Jo gave her a slight shake.

" Scold as much as ever you like, you'll never get your silly old story again," cried Amy, getting excited in her turn.

" Why not ? "

" I burnt it up."

" What ! my little book I was so fond of, and worked over, and meant to finish before father got home ? Have you really burnt it ? " said Jo, turning very pale, while her eyes kindled and her hands clutched Amy nervously.

" Yes, I did ! I told you I'd make you pay for being so cross yesterday, and I have, so——"

Amy got no farther, for Jo's hot temper mastered her, and she shook Amy till her teeth chattered in her head ; crying, in a passion of grief and anger—

" You wicked, wicked girl ! I never can write it again, and I'll never forgive you as long I live."

Meg flew to rescue Amy, and Beth to pacify Jo, but Jo was quite beside herself ; and, with a parting box on her sister's ear, she rushed out of the room up to the old sofa in the garret, and finished her fight alone.

The storm cleared up below, for Mrs. March came home, and, having heard the story, soon brought Amy to a sense of the wrong she had done her sister. Jo's book was the pride of her heart, and was regarded by her family as a literary sprout of great promise. It was only half a dozen little fairy tales, but Jo had worked over them patiently, putting her whole heart into her work, hoping to make something good enough to print. She had just copied them with great care, and had destroyed the old manuscript, so that Amy's bonfire had consumed the loving work of several years. It seemed a small loss to others, but to Jo it was a dreadful calamity, and she felt that it could never be made up to her. Beth mourned as for a departed kitten, and Meg refused to defend her pet ; Mrs. March looked grave and grieved, and Amy felt that no one would love her till she had asked pardon for the act which she now regretted more than any of them.

When the tea-bell rang, Jo appeared, looking so grim and unapproachable, that it took all Amy's courage to say meekly—

" Please forgive me, Jo ; I'm very, very sorry."

" I never shall forgive you," was Jo's stern answer, and, from that moment, she ignored Amy entirely.

No one spoke of the great trouble,—not even Mrs. March,—for all had learned by experience that when Jo was in that mood words were wasted ; and the wisest course was to wait till some little accident, or her own generous nature, softened Jo's resentment, and healed the breach. It was not a happy evening ; for, though they sewed as usual, while their mother read aloud from Bremer, Scott, or Edgeworth, something was wanting, and the sweet home-peace was disturbed. They felt this most when singing-time came ; for Beth could only play, Jo stood dumb as a stone, and Amy broke down, so Meg and mother sung alone. But, in spite of their efforts to be as cheery as larks, the flute-like voices did not seem to chord as well as usual, and all felt out of tune.

As Jo received her good-night kiss, Mrs. March whispered gently—

" My dear, don't let the sun go down upon your anger ; forgive each other, help each other, and begin again to-morrow."

Jo wanted to lay her head down on that motherly bosom, and cry her grief and anger all away ; but tears were an unmanly weakness, and she felt so deeply injured that she really *couldn't* quite for-give yet. So she winked hard, shook her head, and said, gruffly, because Amy was listening—

" It was an abominable thing, and she don't deserve to be forgiven."

With that she marched off to bed, and there was no merry or confidential gossip that night.

Amy was much offended that her overtures of peace had been repulsed, and began to wish she had not humbled herself, to feel more injured than ever, and to plume herself on her superior virtue in a way which was particularly exasperating. Jo still looked like a thunder-cloud, and nothing went well all day. It was bitter cold in the morning ; she dropped her precious turn-over in the gutter. Aunt March had an attack of fidgets, Meg was pensive, Beth *would* look grieved and wistful when she got home, and Amy kept making remarks about people who were always talking about being good, and yet wouldn't try, when other people set them a virtuous example.

"Everybody is so hateful, I'll ask Laurie to go skating. He is always kind and jolly, and will put me to rights, I know," said Jo to herself, and off she went.

Amy heard the clash of skates, and looked out with an impatient exclamation—

"There! she promised I should go next time, for this is the last ice we shall have. But it's no use to ask such a cross patch to take me."

"Don't say that; you *were* very naughty, and it *is* hard to forgive the loss of her precious little book; but I think she might do it now, and I guess she will, if you try her at the right minute," said Meg. "Go after them; don't say anything till Jo has got good-natured with Laurie, then take a quiet minute, and just kiss her, or do some kind thing, and I'm sure she'll be friends again, with all her heart."

"I'll try," said Amy, for the advice suited her; and, after a flurry to get ready, she ran after her friends, who were just disappearing over the hill.

It was not far to the river, but both were ready before Amy reached them. Jo saw her coming, and turned her back; Laurie did not see her, for he was carefully skating along the shore, sounding the ice, for a warm spell had preceded the cold snap.

"I'll go on to the first bend, and see if it's all right, before we begin to race," Amy heard him say, as he shot away, looking like a young Russian, in his fur-trimmed coat and cap.

Jo heard Amy panting after her run, stamping her feet, and blowing her fingers, as she tried to put her skates on ; but Jo never turned, and went slowly zigzagging down the river, taking a bitter unhappy sort of satisfaction in her sister's troubles. She had cherished her anger till it grew strong and took possession of her, as evil thoughts and feelings always do, unless cast out at once. As Laurie turned the bend, he shouted back—

" Keep near the shore ; it isn't safe in the middle."

Jo heard, but Amy was just struggling to her feet, and did not catch a word. Jo glanced over her shoulder, and the little demon she was harbouring said in her ear—

" No matter whether she heard or not, let her take care of herself."

Laurie had vanished round the bend ; Jo was just at the turn, and Amy, far behind, striking out towards the smoother ice in the middle of the river. For a moment Jo stood still, with a strange feeling at her heart ; then she resolved to go on, but something held and turned her round, just in time to see Amy throw up her hands and go down, with the sudden crash of rotten ice, the splash of water, and a cry that made Jo's heart stand still with fear. She tried to call Laurie, but her voice was gone ; she tried to rush forward, but her feet seemed to have no strength in them ; and, for a second, she could only stand motionless, staring, with a terror-stricken face, at the little blue hood above the black water. Something rushed swiftly by her, and Laurie's voice cried out—

" Bring a rail ; quick, quick ! "

How she did it, she never knew; but for the next few minutes she worked as if possessed, blindly obeying Laurie, who was quite self-possessed; and, lying flat, held Amy up by his arm and stick, till Jo dragged a rail from the fence, and together they got the child out, more frightened than hurt.

"Now then, we must walk her home as fast as we can; pile our things on her, while I get off these confounded skates," cried Laurie, wrapping his coat round Amy, and tugging away at the straps, which never seemed so intricate before.

Shivering, dripping, and crying, they got Amy home; and after an exciting time of it, she fell asleep, rolled in blankets, before a hot fire. During the bustle Jo had scarcely spoken; but flown about, looking pale and wild, with her things half off, her dress torn, and her hands cut and bruised by ice and nails, and refractory buckles. When Amy was comfortably asleep, the house quiet, and Mrs. March sitting by the bed, she called Jo up to her, and began to bind up the hurt hands.

"Are you sure she is safe?" whispered Jo, looking remorsefully at the golden head, which might have been swept away from her sight for ever, under the treacherous ice.

"Quite safe, dear; she is not hurt, and won't even take cold, I think, you were so sensible in covering and getting her home quickly," replied her mother cheerfully.

"Laurie did it all; I only let her go. Mother, if she *should* die, it would be my fault"; and Jo dropped down beside the bed, in a passion of penitent tears, telling all that had happened, bitterly condemning her hardness of heart, and sobbing out her gratitude for being spared the heavy punishment which might have come upon her.

"It's my dreadful temper! I try to cure it; I think I have, and then it breaks out worse than ever. Oh, mother! what shall I do! what shall I do?" cried poor Jo in despair.

"Watch and pray, dear; never get tired of trying, and never think it impossible to conquer your fault," said Mrs. March, drawing the blowzy head to her shoulder, and kissing the wet cheek so tenderly, that Jo cried harder than ever.

"You don't know; you can't guess how bad it is! It seems as if I could do anything when I'm in a passion; I get so savage, I could hurt any one, and enjoy it. I'm afraid I *shall* do something dreadful some day, and spoil my life, and make everybody hate me. Oh, mother! help me, do help me!"

"I will, my child; I will. Don't cry so bitterly, but remember this day, and resolve, with all your soul, that you will never know another like it. Jo, dear, we all have our temptations, some far greater than yours, and it often takes us all our lives to conquer them. You think your temper is the worst in the world; but mine used to be just like it."

"Yours, mother? Why, you are never angry!" and for the moment Jo forgot remorse in surprise.

"I've been trying to cure it for forty years, and have only succeeded in controlling it. I am angry nearly every day of my life, Jo; but I have learned not to show it ; and I still hope to learn not to feel it, though it may take me another forty years to do so."

The patience and the humility of the face she loved so well was a better lesson to Jo than the wisest lecture, the sharpest reproof. She felt comforted at once by the sympathy and confidence given her ; the knowledge that her mother had a fault like hers, and tried to mend it, made her own easier to bear, and strengthened her resolution to cure it ; though forty years seemed rather a long time to watch and pray, to a girl of fifteen.

" Mother, are you angry when you fold your lips tight together, and go out of the room sometimes, when Aunt March scolds, or people worry you ? " asked Jo, feeling nearer and dearer to her mother than ever before.

" Yes, I've learned to check the hasty words that rise to my lips ; and when I feel that they mean to break out against my will, I just go away a minute, and give myself a little shake, for being so weak and wicked," answered Mrs. March with a sigh and a smile, as she tenderly smoothed and fastened up Jo's dishevelled hair.

" How did you learn to keep still ? That is what troubles me—for the sharp words fly out before I know what I'm about ; and the more I say the worse I get, till it's a pleasure to hurt people's feelings, and say dreadful things. Tell me how you do it," Marmee dear."

" My good mother used to help me——"

" As you do us— " interrupted Jo, with a grateful kiss, and smiling through her tears.

" But I lost her when I was a little older than

you are, and for years had to struggle on alone,
for I was too proud to confess my weakness to any
one else. I had a hard time, Jo, and shed a good
many bitter tears over my failures; for, in spite
of my efforts, I never seemed to get on. Then
your father came, and I was so happy that I found
it easy to be good. But by-and-by, when I had
four little daughters round me, and we were poor,
then the old trouble began again; for I am not
patient by nature, and it tried me very much to
see my children wanting anything."

"Poor mother! what helped you then?"

"Your father, Jo. He never loses patience—
never doubts or complains—but always hopes, and
works, and waits so cheerfully, that one is ashamed
to do otherwise before him. He helped and comforted me, and showed me that I must try to practise all the virtues I would have my little girls
possess, for I was their example. It was easier to
try for your sakes than for my own; a startled
or surprised look from one of you, when I spoke
sharply, rebuked me more than any words could
have done; and the love, respect, and confidence
of my children was the best and sweetest reward
I could receive for my efforts to be the woman I
would have my darlings try to copy."

"Oh, mother! if I'm ever half as good as you
I shall be satisfied," cried Jo, much touched.

"I hope you will be a great deal better, dear;
but you must keep watch over your 'bosom
enemy,' as father calls it, or it may sadden, if not
spoil, your life. You have had a warning; remember it, and try with heart and soul to master
this quick and rebellious temper, before it brings

you greater sorrow and regret than you have known to-day."

"I will try, mother: I truly will. But you must help me, remind me, and keep me from flying out. I used to see father sometimes put his finger on his lips, and look at you with a very kind, but sober face; and you always folded your lips tight, or went away; was he reminding you then?" asked Jo, softly.

"Yes; I asked him to help me so, and he never forgot it, but saved me from many a sharp word by that little gesture and kind look."

Jo saw that her mother's eyes filled, and her lips trembled, as she spoke; and, fearing that she had said too much, she whispered anxiously, "Was it wrong to watch you, and to speak of it? I didn't mean to be rude, but it's so comfortable to say all I think to you, and feel so safe and happy here."

"My Jo, you may say anything to your mother, for it is my greatest happiness and pride to feel that my girls confide in me, and know how much I love them."

"I thought I'd grieved you."

"No, dear; but speaking of father reminded me how much I miss him, how much I owe him, and how faithfully I should watch and work to keep his little daughters safe and good for him."

"Yet you told him to go, mother, and didn't cry when he went, and never complain now, or seem as if you needed any help," said Jo, wondering.

"I gave my best to the country I love, and kept my tears till he was gone. Why should I

complain, when we both have merely done our
duty, and will surely be the happier for it in the
end? If I don't seem to need help, it is because
I have a better friend even than father to comfort
and sustain me. My child, the troubles and temptations of your life are beginning, and may be
many; but you can overcome and outlive them
all if you learn to feel the strength and tenderness
of your Heavenly Father as you do that of your
earthly one. The more you love and trust Him,
the nearer you will feel to Him, and the less you
will depend on human power and wisdom. His
love and care never tire or change, can never be
taken from you, but may become the source of
life-long peace, happiness, and strength. Believe
this heartily, and go to God with all your little
cares, and hopes, and sins, and sorrows, as freely
and confidingly as you come to your mother."

Jo's only answer was to hold her mother close,
and, in the silence which followed, the sincerest
prayer she had ever prayed left her heart, without
words; for in that sad, yet happy hour, she had
learned not only the bitterness of remorse and
despair, but the sweetness of self-denial and self-
control; and, led by her mother's hand, she had
drawn nearer to the Friend who welcomes every
child with a love stronger than that of any father,
tenderer than that of any mother.

Amy stirred, and sighed in her sleep; and, as
if eager to begin at once to mend her fault, Jo
looked up with an expression on her face which
it had never worn before.

" I let the sun go down on my anger; I wouldn't
forgive her, and to-day, if it hadn't been for Laurie,

it might have been too late! How could I be so wicked?" said Jo, half aloud, as she leaned over her sister, softly stroking the wet hair scattered on the pillow.

As if she heard, Amy opened her eyes, and held out her arms, with a smile that went straight to Jo's heart. Neither said a word, but they hugged one another close, in spite of the blankets, and everything was forgotten and forgiven in one hearty kiss.

CHAPTER IX.

MEG GOES TO VANITY FAIR.

"I DO think it was the most fortunate thing in the world that those children should have the measles just now," said Meg, one April day, as she stood packing the "go abroady" trunk in her room, surrounded by her sisters.

"And so nice of Annie Moffat, not to forget her promise. A whole fortnight of fun will be regularly splendid," replied Jo, looking like a windmill, as she folded skirts with her long arms.

"And such lovely weather; I'm so glad of that," added Beth, tidily sorting neck and hair ribbons in her best box, lent for the great occasion.

"I wish I was going to have a fine time, and wear all these nice things," said Amy, with her mouth full of pins, as she artistically replenished her sister's cushion.

"I wish you were all going; but, as you can't, I shall keep my adventures to tell you when I come back. I'm sure it's the least I can do, when you have been so kind, lending me things, and helping me get ready," said Meg, glancing round the room at the very simple outfit, which seemed nearly perfect in their eyes.

"What did mother give you out of the treasure-box?" asked Amy, who had not been present at the opening of a certain cedar chest, in which Mrs. March kept a few relics of past splendour, as gifts for her girls when the proper time came.

"A pair of silk stockings, that pretty carved fan, and a lovely blue sash. I wanted the violet silk; but there isn't time to make it over, so I must be contented with my old tarlatan."

"It will look nicely over my new muslin skirt, and the sash will set it off beautifully. I wish I hadn't smashed my coral bracelet, for you might have had it," said Jo, who loved to give and lend, but whose possessions were usually too dilapidated to be of much use.

"There is a lovely old-fashioned pearl set in the treasure-box; but mother said real flowers were the prettiest ornament for a young girl, and Laurie promised to send me all I want," replied Meg. "Now, let me see; there's my new grey walking suit—just curl up the feather in my hat, Beth— then my poplin, for Sunday, and the small party— it looks heavy for spring, don't it? the violet silk would be so nice; oh, dear!"

"Never mind; you've got the tarlatan for the big party, and you always look like an angel in white," said Amy, brooding over the little store of finery in which her soul delighted.

"It isn't low-necked, and it don't sweep enough,

but it will have to do. My blue house-dress looks so well, turned and freshly trimmed, that I feel as if I'd got a new one. My silk sacque isn't a bit the fashion, and my bonnet don't look like Sallie's ; I didn't like to say anything, but I was dreadfully disappointed in my umbrella. I told mother black, with a white handle, but she forgot, and bought a green one, with an ugly yellowish handle. It's strong and neat, so I ought not to complain, but I know I shall feel ashamed of it beside Annie's silk one, with a gold top," sighed Meg, surveying the little umbrella with great disfavour.

"Change it," advised Jo.

"I won't be so silly, or hurt Marmee's feelings, when she took so much pains to get my things. It's a nonsensical notion of mine, and I'm not going to give up to it. My silk stockings and two pairs of spandy gloves are my comfort. You are a dear, to lend me yours, Jo ; I feel so rich, and sort of elegant, with two new pairs, and the old ones cleaned up for common ; " and Meg took a refreshing peep at her glove-box.

"Annie Moffat has blue and pink bows on her nightcaps ; would you put some on mine ? " she asked, as Beth brought up a pile of snowy muslins, fresh from Hannah's hands.

"No, I wouldn't ; for the smart caps won't match the plain gowns, without any trimming on them. Poor folks shouldn't rig," said Jo, decidedly.

"I wonder if I shall *ever* be happy enough to have real lace on my clothes, and bows on my caps ? " said Meg, impatiently.

"You said the other day that you'd be perfectly

happy if you could only go to Annie Moffat's," observed Beth, in her quiet way.

" So I did ! Well, I *am* happy, and *won't* fret ; but it does seem as if the more one gets the more one wants, don't it ? There, now, the trays are ready, and everything in but my ball-dress, which I shall leave for mother," said Meg, cheering up, as she glanced from the half-filled trunk to the many times pressed and mended tarlatan, which she called her " ball-dress," with an important air.

* * * * * *

The next day was fine, and Meg departed in style, for a fortnight of novelty and pleasure. Mrs. March had consented to the visit rather reluctantly, fearing that Margaret would come back more discontented than she went. But she had begged so hard, and Sallie had promised to take good care of her, and a little pleasure seemed so delightful after a winter of hard work, that the mother yielded, and the daughter went to take her first taste of fashionable life.

The Moffats *were* very fashionable, and simple Meg was rather daunted, at first, by the splendour of the house, and the elegance of its occupants. But they were kindly people in spite of the frivolous life they led, and soon put their guest at her ease. Perhaps Meg felt, without understanding why, that they were not particularly cultivated or intelligent people, and that all their gilding could not quite conceal the ordinary material of which they were made. It certainly was agreeable to fare sumptuously, drive in a fine carriage, wear her best frock every day, and do nothing else but enjoy herself. It suited her exactly ; and soon she began to imitate the manners and conversation of those about her ; to put on little airs and graces, use French phrases, crimp her hair, take in her dresses, and talk about the fashions, as well as she could. The more she saw of Annie Moffat's pretty things, the more she envied her, and sighed to be rich. Home now looked bare and dismal as she thought of it, work grew harder than ever, and she felt that she was a very destitute and much injured girl, in spite of the new gloves and silk stockings.

She had not much time for repining, however, for the three young girls were busily engaged in " having a good time." They shopped, walked, rode, and called all day ; went to theatres and operas, or frolicked at home in the evening ; for Annie had many friends, and knew how to entertain them. Her older sisters were very fine young ladies, and one was engaged, which was extremely interesting and romantic, Meg thought. Mr. Moffat was a fat, jolly old gentleman, who knew her father ; and Mrs. Moffat, a fat, jolly old lady, who took as great a fancy to Meg as her daughter had done. Everyone petted her ; and " Daisy," as they called her, was in a fair way to have her head turned.

When the evening for the " small party " came, she found that the poplin wouldn't do at all, for the other girls were putting on thin dresses, and making themselves very fine indeed ; so out came the tarlatan, looking older, limper, and shabbier than ever, beside Sallie's crisp new one. Meg saw the girls glance at it, and then at one another, and her cheeks began to burn ; for with all her gentleness, she was very proud. No one said a word about it, but Sallie offered to do her hair, and Annie to tie her sash, and Belle, the engaged sister, praised her white arms ; but, in their kindness, Meg saw only pity for her poverty, and her heart felt very heavy as she stood by herself, while the others laughed and chatted, prinked, and flew about like gauzy butterflies. The hard, bitter feeling was getting pretty bad, when the maid brought in a box of flowers. Before she could speak, Annie had the cover off, and all were exclaiming at the lovely roses, heath, and ferns within.

"It's for Belle, of course ; George always sends her some, but these are altogether ravishing," cried Annie, with a great sniff.

"They are for Miss March," the man said. "And here's a note," put in the maid, holding it to Meg.

"What fun ! Who are they from ? Didn't know you had a lover," cried the girls, fluttering about Meg in a high state of curiosity and surprise.

"The note is from mother, and the flowers from Laurie," said Meg, simply, yet much gratified that he had not forgotten her.

"Oh, indeed ! " said Annie, with a funny look, as Meg slipped the note into her pocket, as a sort of talisman against envy, vanity, and false pride ; for the few loving words had done her good, and the flowers cheered her up by their beauty.

Feeling almost happy again, she laid by a few ferns and roses for herself, and quickly made up the rest into dainty bouquets for the breasts, hair, or skirts of her friends, offering them so prettily, that Clara, the elder sister, told her she was " the sweetest little thing she ever saw ; " and they looked quite charmed with her small attention. Somehow the kind act finished her despondency ; and when all the rest went to show themselves to Mrs. Moffat, she saw a happy, bright-eyed face in the mirror, as she laid her ferns against her rippling hair, and fastened the roses in the dress that didn't strike her as so *very* shabby now.

She enjoyed herself very much that evening, for she danced to her heart's content ; every one was very kind, and she had three compliments. Annie made her sing, and someone said she had a remarkably fine voice ; Major Lincoln asked who " the fresh little girl, with the beautiful eyes, was ; " and Mr. Moffat insisted on dancing with her, because she " didn't dawdle, but had some spring in her," as he gracefully expressed it. So, alto-gether, she had a very nice time, till she overheard a bit of conversation, which disturbed her ex-tremely. She was sitting just inside the con-servatory, waiting for her partner to bring her an ice, when she heard a voice ask, on the other side of the flowery wall—

" How old is he ? "

" Sixteen or seventeen, I should say," replied another voice.

" It would be a grand thing for one of those girls, wouldn't it ? Sallie says they are very in-timate now, and the old man quite dotes on them."

" Mrs. M. has laid her plans, I daresay, and will play her cards well, early as it is. The girl evidently doesn't think of it yet," said Mrs. Moffat.

" She told that fib about her mamma, as if she did know, and coloured up when the flowers came, quite prettily. Poor thing She'd be so nice

if she was only got up in style. Do you think she'd
be offended if we offered to lend her a dress for
Thursday ? " asked another voice.

" She's proud, but I don't believe she'd mind,
for that dowdy tarlatan is all she has got. She
may tear it to-night, and that will be a good
excuse for offering a decent one."

" We'll see ; I shall ask that Laurence, as a
compliment to her, and we'll have fun about it
afterwards."

Here Meg's partner appeared, to find her looking
much flushed, and rather agitated. She was
proud, and her pride was useful just then, for it
helped her to hide her mortification, anger, and
disgust, at what she had just heard ; for, innocent
and unsuspicious as she was, she could not help
understanding the gossip of her friends. She tried
to forget it, but could not, and kept repeating to
herself, "Mrs. M. has her plans," " that fib about her
mamma," and " dowdy tarlatan," till she was
ready to cry, and rush home to tell her troubles,
and ask for advice. As that was impossible,
she did her best to seem gay ; and, being rather
excited, she succeeded so well, that no one dreamed
what an effort she was making. She was very glad
when it was all over, and she was quiet in her bed,
where she could think and wonder and fume till
her head ached, and her hot cheeks were cooled
by a few natural tears. Those foolish, yet well
meant words, had opened a new world to Meg,
and much disturbed the peace of the old one,
in which, till now, she had lived as happily as a
child. Her innocent friendship with Laurie was
spoilt by the silly speeches she had overheard ;

her faith in her mother was a little shaken by the worldly plans attributed to her by Mrs. Moffat, who judged others by herself ; and the sensible resolution to be contented with the simple wardrobe which suited a poor man's daughter was weakened by the unnecessary pity of girls, who thought a shabby dress one of the greatest calamities under heaven.

Poor Meg had a restless night, and got up heavy-eyed, unhappy, half resentful towards her friends, and half ashamed of herself for not speaking out frankly, and setting everything right. Everybody dawdled that morning, and it was noon before the girls found energy enough even to take up their worsted work. Something in the manner of her friends struck Meg at once ; they treated her with more respect, she thought ; took quite a tender interest in what she said, and looked at her with eyes that plainly betrayed curiosity. All this surprised and flattered her, though she did not understand it till Miss Belle looked up from her writing and said, with a sentimental air—

" Daisy, dear, I've sent an invitation to your friend, Mr. Laurence, for Thursday. We should like to know him, and it's only a proper compliment to you."

Meg coloured, but a mischievous fancy to tease the girls made her reply, demurely—

" You are very kind, but I'm afraid he won't come."

" Why not, chérie ? " asked Miss Belle.

" He's too old."

" My child, what do you mean ? What is his age, I beg to know ! " cried Miss Clara.

"Nearly seventy, I believe," answered Meg, counting stitches, to hide the merriment in her eyes.

"You sly creature! of course we meant the young man," exclaimed Miss Belle, laughing.

"There isn't any; Laurie is only a little boy," and Meg laughed also at the queer look which the sisters exchanged as she thus described her supposed lover.

"About your age?" Nan said.

"Nearer my sister Jo's; *I* am seventeen in August," returned Meg, tossing her head.

"It's very nice of him to send you flowers, isn't it?" said Annie, looking wise about nothing.

"Yes, he often does, to all of us; for their house is full, and we are so fond of them. My mother and old Mr. Laurence are friends, you know, so it is quite natural that we children should play together," and Meg hoped they would say no more.

"It's evident Daisy isn't out yet," said Miss Clara to Belle, with a nod.

"Quite a pastoral state of innocence all round," returned Miss Belle with a shrug.

"I'm going out to get some little matters for my girls; can I do anything for you, young ladies?" asked Mrs. Moffat, lumbering in, like an elephant, in silk and lace.

"No, thank you, ma'am," replied Sallie; "I've got my new pink silk for Thursday, and don't want a thing."

"Nor I—" began Meg, but stopped, because it occurred to her that she *did* want several things, and could not have them.

"What shall you wear?" asked Sallie.

"My old white one again, if I can mend it fit to be seen ; it got sadly torn last night," said Meg, trying to speak quite easily, but feeling very uncomfortable.

"Why don't you send home for another ? " said Sallie, who was not an observing young lady.

"I haven't got any other." It cost Meg an effort to say that, but Sallie did not see it, and exclaimed in amiable surprise—

"Only that ? how funny—" She did not finish her speech, for Belle shook her head at her, and broke in, saying, kindly—

"Not at all ; where is the use of having a lot of dresses when she isn't out ? There's no need of sending home, Daisy, even if you had a dozen, for I've got a sweet blue silk laid away, which I've outgrown, and you shall wear it, to please me ; won't you dear ? "

"You are very kind, but I don't mind my old dress, if you don't ; it does well enough for a little girl like me," said Meg.

"Now do let me please myself by dressing you up in style. I admire to do it, and you'd be a regular little beauty, with a touch here and there. I shan't let any one see you till you are done, and then we'll burst upon them like Cinderella and her godmother, going to the ball," said Belle, in her persuasive tone.

Meg couldn't refuse the offer so kindly made, for a desire to see if she would be " a little beauty " after touching up caused her to accept, and forget all her former uncomfortable feelings towards the Moffats.

On the Thursday evening Belle shut herself up with her maid ; and between them they turned

Meg into a fine lady. They crimped and curled her hair, they polished her neck and arms with some fragrant powder, touched her lips with coral-line salve, to make them redder, and Hortense would have added a "*soupçon* of rouge," if Meg had not rebelled. They laced her into a sky-blue dress, which was so tight she could hardly breathe, and so low in the neck that modest Meg blushed at herself in the mirror. A set of silver filagree was added, bracelets, necklace, brooch, and even ear-rings, for Hortense tied them on, with a bit of pink silk, which did not show. A cluster of tea-rose buds at the bosom, and a *ruche*, reconciled Meg to the display of her pretty white shoulders, and a pair of high-heeled blue silk boots satisfied the last wish of her heart. A laced handkerchief, a plumy fan, and a bouquet in a silver holder, finished her off; and Miss Belle surveyed her with the satisfaction of a little girl with a newly dressed doll.

"Mademoiselle is charmante, tres jolie, is she not?" cried Hortense, clasping her hands in an affected rapture.

"Come and show yourself," said Miss Belle, leading the way to the room where the others were waiting.

As Meg went rustling after, with her long skirts trailing, her ear-rings tinkling, her curls waving, and her heart beating, she felt as if her "fun" had really begun at last, for the mirror had plainly told that she *was* "a little beauty." Her friends repeated the pleasing phrase enthusiastically, and, for several minutes, she stood, like the jackdaw in the fable, enjoying her borrowed plumes, while the rest chattered like a party of magpies.

"While I dress, do you drill her, Nan, in the management of her skirt, and those French heels, or she will trip herself up. Put your silver butterfly in the middle of that white barbe, and catch up that long curl on the left side of her head, Clara, and don't any of you disturb the charming work of my hands," said Belle, as she hurried away, looking well pleased with her success.

"I'm afraid to go down, I feel so queer and stiff, and half dressed," said Meg to Sallie, as the bell rang, and Mrs. Moffat sent to ask the young ladies to appear at once.

"You don't look a bit like yourself, but you are very nice. I'm nowhere beside you, for Belle has heaps of taste, and you're quite French, I assure you. Let your flowers hang; don't be so careful of them, and be sure you don't trip," returned Sallie, trying not to care that Meg was prettier than herself.

Keeping that warning carefully in mind, Margaret got safely down stairs, and sailed into the drawing-rooms, where the Moffats and a few early guests were assembled. She very soon discovered that there is a charm about fine clothes which attract a certain class of people, and secures their respect. Several young ladies, who had taken no notice of her before, were very affectionate all of a sudden ; several young gentlemen, who had only stared at her at the other party, now not only stared, but asked to be introduced, and said all manner of foolish but agreeable things to her ; and several old ladies, who sat on sofas, and criticised the rest of the party, inquired who she was, with an air of interest. She heard Mrs. Moffat reply to one of them :—

" Daisy March—father a colonel in the army—one of our first families, but reverses of fortune, you know ; intimate friends of the Laurences ; sweet creature, I assure you ; my Ned is quite wild about her."

" Dear me ! " said the old lady, putting up her glass for another observation of Meg, who tried to look as if she had not heard, and been rather shocked at Mrs. Moffat's fibs.

The " queer feeling " did not pass away, but she imagined herself acting the new part of fine lady, and so got on pretty well, though the tight dress gave her a side-ache, the train kept getting under her feet, and she was in constant fear lest her ear-rings should fly off, and get lost or broken. She was flirting her fan, and laughing at the feeble jokes of a young gentleman who tried to be witty, when she suddenly stopped laughing, and looked confused ; for, just opposite, she saw Laurie. He was staring at her with undisguised surprise, and disapproval also, she thought ; for, though he bowed and smiled, yet something in his honest eyes made her blush, and wish she had her old dress on. To complete her confusion, she saw Belle nudge Annie, and both glance from her to Laurie, who, she was happy to see, looked unusually boyish and shy.

" Silly creatures, to put such thoughts into my head ! I won't care for it, or let it change me a bit," thought Meg, and rustled across the room to shake hands with her friend.

" I'm glad you came, for I was afraid you wouldn't," she said, with her most grown-up air.

" Jo wanted me to come and tell her how you looked, so I did ; " answered Laurie, without turning his eyes upon her, though he half smiled at her maternal tone.

"What shall you tell her?" asked Meg, full of curiosity to know his opinion of her, yet feeling ill at ease with him, for the first time.

"I shall say I didn't know you; for you look so grown-up, and unlike yourself, I'm quite afraid of you," he said, fumbling at his glove-button.

"How absurd of you! the girls dressed me up for fun, and I rather like it. Wouldn't Jo stare if she saw me?" said Meg, bent on making him say whether he thought her improved or not.

"Yes, I think she would," returned Laurie, gravely.

"Don't you like me so?" asked Meg.

"No, I don't," was the blunt reply.

"Why not?" in an anxious tone.

He glanced at her frizzled head, bare shoulders, and fantastically trimmed dress, with an expression that abashed her more than his answer, which had not a particle of his usual politeness about it.

"I don't like fuss and feathers."

That was altogether too much from a lad younger than herself; and Meg walked away, saying, petulantly—

"You are the rudest boy I ever saw."

Feeling very much ruffled, she went and stood at a quiet window, to cool her cheeks, for the tight dress gave her an uncomfortably brilliant colour. As she stood there, Major Lincoln passed by; and, a minute after, she heard him saying to his mother—

"They are making a fool of that little girl; I

wanted you to see her, but they have spoilt her entirely ; she's nothing but a doll to-night."

"Oh, dear ! " sighed Meg ; " I wish I'd been sensible, and worn my own things ; then I should not have disgusted other people, or felt so uncomfortable and ashamed of myself."

She leaned her forehead on the cool pane, and stood half hidden by the curtains, never minding that her favourite waltz had begun, till some one touched her ; and, turning, she saw Laurie looking penitent, as he said, with his very best bow, and his hand out—

" Please forgive my rudeness, and come and dance with me."

" I'm afraid it will be too disagreeable to you," said Meg, trying to look offended, and failing entirely.

"Not a bit of it ; I'm dying to do it. Come, I'll be good, I don't like your gown, but I do think you are—just splendid ; " and he waved his hands, as if words failed to express his admiration.

Meg smiled and relented, and whispered, as they stood waiting to catch the time—

"Take care my skirt don't trip you up ; it's the plague of my life, and I was a goose to wear it."

" Pin it round your neck, and then it will be useful," said Laurie, looking down at the little blue boots, which he evidently approved of.

Away they went, fleetly and gracefully ; for, having practised at home, they were well matched, and the blithe young couple were a pleasant sight to see, as they twirled merrily round and round, feeling more friendly than ever after their small tiff.

"Laurie, I want you to do me a favour; will you?" said Meg, as he stood fanning her, when her breath gave out, which it did, very soon, though she would not own why.

"Won't I!" said Laurie, with alacrity.

"Please don't tell them at home about my dress to-night. They won't understand the joke, and it will worry mother."

"Then why did you do it?" said Laurie's eyes so plainly, that Meg hastily added—

"I shall tell them myself all about it, and ' 'fess ' to mother how silly I've been. But I'd rather do it myself; so you'll not tell, will you?"

"I give you my word I won't; only what shall I say when they ask me?"

"Just say I looked nice, and was having a good time."

"I say the first, with all my heart; but how about the other? You don't look as if you were having a good time; are you?" and Laurie looked at her with an expression which made her answer, in a whisper—

"No; not just now. Don't think I'm horrid; I only wanted a little fun, but this sort don't pay, I find, and I'm getting tired of it."

"Here comes Ned Moffat; what does he want?" asked Laurie, knitting his black brows, as if he did not regard his young host in the light of a pleasant addition to the party.

"He put his name down for three dances, and I suppose he's coming for them; what a bore!" said Meg, assuming a languid air, which amused Laurie immensely.

He did not speak to her again till supper-time,

when he saw her drinking champagne with Ned, and his friend Fisher, who were behaving "like a pair of fools," as Laurie said to himself, for he felt a brotherly sort of right to watch over the Marches, and fight their battles, whenever a defender was needed.

"You'll have a splitting headache to-morrow, if you drink much of that. I wouldn't, Meg; your mother don't like it, you know," he whispered, leaning over her chair, as Ned turned to refill her glass, and Fisher stooped to pick up her fan.

"I'm not Meg, to-night; I'm 'a doll,' who does all sorts of crazy things. To-morrow I shall put away my 'fuss and feathers,' and be desperately good again," she answered, with an affected little laugh.

"Wish to-morrow was here, then," muttered Laurie, walking off, ill pleased at the change that he saw in her.

Meg danced and flirted, chattered and giggled, as the other girls did; after supper she undertook the German, and blundered through it, nearly upsetting her partner with her long skirt, and romping in a way that scandalised Laurie, who looked on and meditated a lecture. But he got no chance to deliver it, for Meg kept away from him till he came to say good-night.

"Remember!" she said, trying to smile, for the splitting headache had already begun.

"Silence à la mort," replied Laurie, with a melo-dramatic flourish as he went away.

This little bit of by-play excited Annie's curiosity; but Meg was too tired for gossip, and went to bed, feeling as if she had been to a masquerade, and hadn't enjoyed herself as much as she had expected. She was sick all the next day, and on Saturday went home, quite used up with her fortnight's fun, and feeling that she had sat in the lap of luxury long enough.

"It does seem pleasant to be quiet, and not have company manners on all the time. Home is a nice place, though it isn't splendid," said Meg, looking about her with a restful expression, as she sat with her mother and Jo on the Sunday evening.

"I'm glad to hear you say so, dear, for I was afraid home would seem dull and poor to you, after your fine quarters," replied her mother, who had given her many anxious looks that day; for motherly eyes are quick to see any change in children's faces.

Meg had told her adventures gaily, and said over and over what a charming time she had had; but something still seemed to weigh upon her spirits, and, when the younger girls were gone to bed, she sat thoughtfully staring at the fire, saying little and looking worried. As the clock struck nine, and Jo proposed bed, Meg suddenly left her chair, and, taking Beth's stool, leaned her elbows on her mother's knees, saying, bravely—

"Marmee, I want to ' 'fess,' "

"I thought so; what is it, dear?"

"Shall I go away?" asked Jo, discreetly.

"Of course not; don't I always tell you everything? I was ashamed to speak of it before the children, but I want you to know all the dreadful things I did at the Moffats'."

"We are prepared," said Mrs. March, smiling, but looking a little anxious.

" I told you they rigged me up, but I didn't tell you that they powdered and squeezed, and frizzled, and made me look like a fashion-plate. Laurie thought I wasn't proper ; I know he did, though he didn't say so, and one man called me ' a doll.' I knew it was silly, but they flattered me, and said I was a beauty, and quantities of nonsense, so I let them make a fool of me."

" Is that all ? " asked Jo, as Mrs. March looked silently at the downcast face of her pretty daughter, and could not find it in her heart to blame her little follies.

" No ; I drank champagne, and romped, and tried to flirt, and was altogether abominable," said Meg, self-reproachfully.

" There is something more, I think ; " and Mrs. March smoothed the soft cheek, which suddenly grew rosy, as Meg answered, slowly—

" Yes ; it's very silly, but I want to tell it, because I hate to have people say and think such things about us and Laurie."

Then she told the various bits of gossip she had heard at the Moffats' ; and, as she spoke, Jo saw her mother fold her lips tightly, as if ill pleased that such ideas should be put into Meg's innocent mind.

" Well, if that isn't the greatest rubbish I ever heard," cried Jo, indignantly. " Why didn't you pop out and tell them so on the spot ? "

" I couldn't, it was so embarrassing for me. I couldn't help hearing, at first, and then I was so angry and ashamed, I didn't remember that I ought to go away."

" Just wait till *I* see Annie Moffat, and I'll show

you how to settle such ridiculous stuff. The idea of having ' plans,' and being kind to Laurie, because he's rich, and may marry us by and by! Won't he shout when I tell him what these silly things say about us poor children ? " and Jo laughed, as if, on second thoughts, the thing struck her as a good joke.

"If you tell Laurie, I'll never forgive you! She mustn't, must she, mother ? " said Meg, looking distressed.

" No ; never repeat that foolish gossip, and forget it as soon as you can," said Mrs. March, gravely. " I was very unwise to let you go among people of whom I know so little ; kind, I dare say, but worldly, ill-bred, and full of these vulgar ideas about young people. I am more sorry than I can express, for the mischief this visit may have done you, Meg."

"Don't be sorry, I won't let it hurt me ; I'll forget all the bad, and remember only the good ; for I did enjoy a great deal, and thank you very much for letting me go. I'll not be sentimental or dissatisfied, mother ; I know I'm a silly little girl, and I'll stay with you till I'm fit to take care of myself. But it *is* nice to be praised and admired, and I can't help saying I like it," said Meg, looking half ashamed of the confession.

" That is perfectly natural, and quite harmless, if the liking does not become a passion, and lead one to do foolish or unmaidenly things. Learn to know and value the praise which is worth having, and to excite the admiration of excellent people, by being modest as well as pretty, Meg."

Margaret sat thinking a moment, while Jo stood

with her hands behind her, looking both interested and a little perplexed ; for it was a new thing to see Meg blushing and talking about admiration, lovers, and things of that sort, and Jo felt as if during that fortnight her sister had grown up amazingly, and was drifting away from her into a world where she could not follow.

"Mother, do you have 'plans,' as Mrs. Moffat said ? " asked Meg, bashfully.

"Yes, my dear, I have a great many ; all mothers do, but mine differ somewhat from Mrs. Moffat's, I suspect. I will tell you some of them, for the time has come when a word may set this romantic little head and heart of yours right on a very serious subject. You are young, Meg ; but not too young to understand me, and mothers' lips are the fittest to speak of such things to girls like you. Jo, your turn will come in time, perhaps, so listen to my 'plans,' and help me to carry them out, if they are good."

Jo went and sat on one arm of the chair, looking as if she thought they were about to join in some very solemn affair. Holding a hand of each, and watching the two young faces wistfully, Mrs. March said, in her serious yet cheery way—

"I want my daughters to be beautiful, accomplished, and good ; to be admired, loved, and respected, to have a happy youth, to be well and wisely married, and to lead useful, pleasant lives, with as little care and sorrow to try them as God sees fit to send. To be loved and chosen by a good man is the best and sweetest thing which can happen to a woman, and I sincerely hope my girls may know this beautiful experience. It is natural to think of it, Meg ; right to hope and wait for it, and wise to prepare for it ; so that, when the happy times comes, you may feel ready for the duties, and worthy of the joy. My dear girls, I *am* ambitious for you, but not to have you make a dash in the world—marry rich men merely because they are rich, or have splendid houses, which are not homes, because love is wanting. Money is a needful and precious thing—and, when well used, a noble thing—but I never want you to think it is the first or only prize to strive for. I'd rather see you poor men's wives, if you were happy, beloved, contented, than queens on thrones, without self-respect and peace."

" Poor girls don't stand any chance, Bella says, unless they put themselves forward," sighed Meg.

" Then we'll be old maids," said Jo, stoutly.

" Right, Jo ; better be happy old maids than un-happy wives, or unmaidenly girls, running about to find husbands," said Mrs. March, decidedly. " Don't be troubled, Meg ; poverty seldom daunts a sincere lover. Some of the best and most honoured women I know were poor girls, but so love-worthy that they were not allowed to be old maids. Leave these things to time ; make this home happy, so that you may be fit for homes of your own, if they are offered you, and contented here if they are not. One thing remember, my girls, mother is always ready to be your confidant, father to be your friend ; and both of us trust and hope that our daughters, whether married or single, will be the pride and comfort of our lives."

" We will, Marmee, we will ! " cried both, with all their hearts, as she bade them good-night.

CHAPTER X.

THE P. C. AND P. O.

As spring came on, a new set of amusements became the fashion, and the lengthened days gave long afternoons for work and play of all sorts. The garden had to be put in order, and each sister had a quarter of the little plot to do what she liked with. Hannah used to say, " I'd know which of them gardings belonged to, ef I see 'em in Chiny " ; and so she might, for the girls' tastes differed as much as their characters. Meg's had roses and heliotrope, myrtle, and a little orange-tree in it. Jo's bed was never alike two seasons, for she was always trying experiments ; this year it was to be a plantation of sun-flowers, the seeds of which cheerful and aspiring plant was to feed " Aunt Cockle-top " and her family of chicks. Beth had old-fashioned, fragrant flowers in her garden ; sweet peas and mignonette, larkspur, pinks, pansies, and southernwood, with chickweed for the bird and catnip for the pussies. Amy had a bower in hers—rather small and earwiggy, but very pretty to look at—with honeysuckles and morning glories hanging their coloured horns and bells in graceful wreaths all over it ; tall white lilies, delicate ferns, and as many brilliant, picturesque plants as would consent to blossom there.

Gardening, walks, rows on the river, and flower hunts employed the fine days ; and for the rainy ones, they had house diversions—some old, some new—all more or less original. One of these was the " P. C." ; for, as secret societies were the fashion, it was thought proper to have one ; and, as all of the girls admired Dickens, they called themselves the Pickwick Club. With a few interruptions, they had kept this up for a year, and met every Saturday evening in the big garret, on which occasion the ceremonies were as follows :—

Three chairs were arranged in a row before a table, on which was a lamp, also four white badges, with a big " P. C." in different colours on each, and the weekly newspaper, called " The Pickwick Portfolio," to which all contributed something ; while Jo, who revelled in pens and ink, was the editor. At seven o'clock, the four members ascended to the club-room, tied the badges round their heads, and took their seats with great solemnity. Meg, as the eldest, was Samuel Pickwick ; Jo, being of a literary turn, Augustus Snodgrass ; Beth, because she was round and rosy, Tracy Tupman ; and Amy, who was always trying to do what she couldn't, was Nathaniel Winkle. Pickwick, the President, read the paper, which was filled with original tales, poetry, local news, funny advertisements, and hints, in which they good-naturedly reminded each other of their faults and shortcomings. On one occasion, Mr. Pickwick put on a pair of spectacles without any glasses, rapped upon the table, hemmed, and, having stared hard at Mr. Snodgrass, who was tilting back in his chair, till he arranged himself properly, began to read—

"The Pickwick Portfolio."

MAY 20, 18—.

Poet's Corner.

ANNIVERSARY ODE.

Again we meet to celebrate
With badge and solemn rite,
Our fifty-second anniversary,
In Pickwick Hall, to-night.

We all are here in perfect health,
None gone from our small band;
Again we see each well-known face,
And press each friendly hand.

Our Pickwick always at his post,
With reverence we greet,
As, spectacles on nose, he reads
Our well-filled weekly sheet.

Although he suffers from a cold,
We joy to hear him speak,
For words of wisdom from him fall,
In spite of croak or squeak.

Old six-foot Snodgrass looms on high,
With elephantine grace,
And beams upon the company,
With brown and jovial face.

Poetic fire lights up his eye,
He struggles 'gainst his lot;
Behold ambition on his brow,
And on his nose a blot!

Next our peaceful Tupman comes,
So rosy, plump and sweet,
Who chokes with laughter at the puns
And tumbles off his seat.

Prim little Winkle too is here,
With every hair in place,
A model of propriety,
Though he hates to wash his face.

The year is gone, we still unite
To joke and laugh and read,
And tread the path of literature
That doth to glory lead.

Long may our paper prosper well,
Our club unbroken be,
And coming years their blessings pour
On the useful, gay "P. C."
                                    A. SNODGRASS.

THE MASKED MARRIAGE.
A TALE OF VENICE.

Gondola after gondola swept up to the marble steps, and left its lovely load to swell the brilliant throng that filled the stately halls of Count de Adelon. Knights and ladies, elves and pages, monks and flower girls, all mingled gaily in the dance. Sweet voices and rich melody filled the air; and so with mirth and music the masquerade went on.

"Has your Highness seen the Lady Viola to-night?" asked a gallant troubadour of the fairy queen who floated down the hall upon his arm.

"Yes; is she not lovely, though so sad! Her dress is well-chosen, too, for in a week she weds Count Antonio, whom she passionately hates."

"By my faith I envy him. Yonder he comes, arrayed like a bridegroom, except the black mask. When that is off we shall see how he regards the fair maid whose heart he cannot win, though her stern father bestows her hand," returned the troubadour.

"'Tis whispered that she loves the young English artist who haunts her steps, and is spurned by the old count," said the lady, as they joined the dance.

The revel was at its height when a priest appeared, and, withdrawing the young pair to an alcove hung with purple velvet, he motioned them to kneel. Instant silence fell upon the gay throng; and not a sound, but the dash of fountains or the rustle of orange groves sleeping in the moonlight, broke the hush, as Count de Adelon spoke thus:—

"My lords and ladies; pardon the ruse by which I have gathered you here to witness the marriage of my daughter. Father, we wait your services."

All eyes turned towards the bridal party, and a low murmur of amazement went through the throng, for neither bride nor groom removed their masks. Curiosity and wonder possessed all hearts, but respect restrained all tongues till the holy rite was over. Then the eager spectators gathered round the count, demanding an explanation.

"Gladly would I give it if I could; but I only know that it was the whim of my timid Viola, and I yielded to it. Now, my children, let the play end. Unmask, and receive my blessing."

But neither bent the knee; for the young bridegroom replied, in a tone that startled all listeners, as the mask fell, disclosing the noble face of Ferdinand Devereux, the artist lover, and, leaning on the breast where now flashed the star of an English earl, was the lovely Viola, radiant with joy and beauty.

"My lord, you scornfully bade me claim your daughter when I could boast as high a name and vast a fortune as the Count Antonio. I can do more; for even your ambitious soul cannot refuse the Earl of Devereux and De Vere, when he gives his ancient name and boundless wealth in return for the beloved hand of this fair lady, now my wife."

The count stood like one changed to stone; and, turning to the bewildered crowd, Ferdinand added, with a gay smile of triumph, "To you, my gallant friends, I can only wish that your wooing may prosper as mine has done; and that you may all win as fair a bride as I have, by this masked marriage."

S. PICKWICK.

Why is the P. C. like the Tower of Babel? It is full of unruly members.

THE HISTORY OF A SQUASH.

Once upon a time a farmer planted a little seed in his garden, and after a while it sprouted and became a vine, and bore many squashes. One day in October, when they were ripe, he picked one and took it to market. A grocer man bought and put it in his shop. That same morning, a little girl, in a brown hat and blue dress, with a round face and snubby nose, went and bought it for her mother. She lugged it home, cut it up, and boiled it in the big pot; mashed some of it, with salt and butter, for dinner; and to the rest she added a pint of milk, two eggs, four spoons of sugar, nutmeg, and some crackers; put it in a deep dish and baked it till it was brown and nice; and next day it was eaten by a family named March.

T. TUPMAN.

MR. PICKWICK. *Sir:*—

I address you upon the subject of sin the sinner I mean is a man named Winkle who makes trouble in his club by laughing and sometimes won't write his piece in this fine paper I hope you will pardon his badness and let him send a French cable because he can't write out of his head as he has so many lessons to do and no brains in future I will try to take time by the fetlock and prepare some work which will be all *commy la fo* that means all right I am in haste as it is nearly school time

Yours respectably N. WINKLE.

[The above is a manly and handsome acknowledgment of past misdemeanours. If our young friend studied punctuation, it would be well.]

A SAD ACCIDENT.

On Friday last, we were startled by a violent shock in our basement, followed by cries of distress. On rushing, in a body, to the cellar, we discovered our beloved president prostrate upon the floor, having tripped and fallen while getting wood for domestic purposes. A perfect scene of ruin met our eyes; for in his fall Mr. Pickwick had plunged his head and shoulders into a tub of water, upset a keg of soft soap upon his manly form, and torn his garments badly. On being removed from his perilous situation it was discovered that he had suffered no injury but several bruises; and, we are happy to add, is now doing well.

ED.

THE PUBLIC BEREAVEMENT.

It is our painful duty to record the sudden and mysterious disappearance of our cherished friend, Mrs. Snowball Pat Paw. This lovely and beloved cat was the pet of a large circle of warm and admiring friends; for her beauty attracted all eyes, her graces and virtues endeared her to all hearts, and her loss is deeply felt by the whole community.

When last seen, she was sitting at the gate, watching the butcher's cart; and it is feared that some villain, tempted by her charms, basely stole her. Weeks have passed, but no trace of her has been discovered; and we relinquish all hope, tie a black ribbon to her basket, set aside her dish, and weep for her as one lost to us for ever.

A sympathising friend sends the following gem :—

A LAMENT

FOR S. B. PAT PAW.

We mourn the loss of our little pet,
  And sigh o'er her hapless fate,
For never more by the fire she'll sit
  Nor play by the old green gate.

The little grave where her infant sleeps,
  Is 'neath the chestnut tree ;
But o'er *her* grave we may not weep,
  We know not where it may be.

Her empty bed, her idle ball,
  Will never see her more ;
No gentle tap, no loving purr
  Is heard at the parlour door.

Another cat comes after her mice,
  A cat with a dirty face ;
But she does not hunt as our darling did,
  Nor play with her airy grace.

Her stealthy paws tread the very hall
  Where Snowball used to play,
But she only spits at the dogs our pet
  So gallantly drove away.

She is useful and mild, and does her best,
  But she is not fair to see ;
And we cannot give her your place, dear,
  Nor worship her as we worship thee.

                 A. S.

ADVERTISEMENTS.

MISS ORANTHY BLUGGAGE, the accomplished Strong-Minded Lecturer, will deliver her famous Lecture on "WOMAN AND HER POSITION," at Pickwick Hall, next Saturday Evening, after the usual performances.

A WEEKLY MEETING will be held at Kitchen Place, to teach young ladies how to cook. Hannah Brown will preside; and all are invited to attend.

THE DUSTPAN SOCIETY will meet on Wednesday next, and parade in the upper story of the Club House. All members to appear in uniform, and shoulder their brooms at nine precisely.

MRS. BETH BOUNCER will open her new assortment of Dolls' Millinery next week. The latest Paris Fashions have arrived, and orders are respectfully solicited.

A NEW PLAY will appear at the Barnville Theatre, in the course of a few weeks, which will surpass anything ever seen on the American stage. "THE GREEK SLAVE, or Constantine the Avenger," is the name of this thrilling drama !!!

HINTS.

If S. P. didn't use so much soap on his hands, he wouldn't always be late at breakfast. A. S. is requested not to whistle in the street. T. T. please don't forget Amy's napkin. N. W. must not fret because his dress has not nine tucks.

WEEKLY REPORT.

Meg—Good.
Jo— Bad.
Beth—Very good.
Amy—Middling.

As the President finished reading the paper (which I beg leave to assure my readers is a *bonâ fide* copy of one written by *bonâ fide* girls once upon a time), a round of applause followed, and then Mr. Snodgrass rose to make a proposition.

"Mr. President and gentlemen," he began, assuming a parliamentary attitude and tone, "I wish to propose the admission of a new member ; one who highly deserves the honour, would be deeply grateful for it, and would add immensely to the spirit of the club, the literary value of the paper, and be no end jolly and nice. I propose Mr. Theodore Laurence as an honorary member of the P. C. Come now, do have him."

Jo's sudden change of tone made the girls laugh ; but all looked anxious, and no one said a word as Snodgrass took his seat.

"We'll put it to the vote," said the President. "All in favour of this motion please to manifest it by saying 'Aye.'"

A loud response from Snodgrass, followed, to everybody's surprise, by a timid one from Beth.

"Contrary minded say 'No.'"

Meg and Amy were contrary minded ; and Mr. Winkle rose to say, with great elegance, "We don't wish any boys, they only joke and bounce about. This is a lady's club, and we wish to be private and proper."

"I'm afraid he'll laugh at our paper, and make fun of us afterwards," observed Pickwick, pulling the little curl on her forehead, as she always did when doubtful.

Up bounced Snodgrass, very much in earnest. "Sir ! I give you my word as a gentleman, Laurie won't do anything of the sort. He likes to write, and he'll give a tone to our contributions, and keep us from being sentimental, don't you see ? We can do so little for him, and he does so much for us, I think the least we can do is to offer him a place here, and make him welcome if he comes."

This artful allusion to benefits conferred brought Tupman to his feet, looking as if he had quite made up his mind.

"Yes, we ought to do it, even if we *are* afraid.

I say he *may* come, and his grandpa, **too,** if he likes."

This spirited burst from Beth electrified the club, and Jo left her seat to shake hands approvingly.

"Now then, vote again. Everybody remember it's our Laurie, and say 'Aye!'" cried Snodgrass, excitedly.

"Aye! aye! aye!" replied three voices at once.

"Good! bless you! now, as there's nothing like 'taking time by the *fetlock*,' as Winkle characteristically observes, allow me to present the new member"; and, to the dismay of the rest of the club, Jo threw open the door of the closet, and displayed Laurie sitting on a rag-bag, flushed and twinkling with suppressed laughter.

"You rogue! you traitor! Jo, how could you?" cried the three girls, as Snodgrass led her friend triumphantly forth; and, producing both a chair and a badge, installed him in a jiffy.

"The coolness of you two rascals is amazing," began Mr. Pickwick, trying to get up an awful frown, and only succeeding in producing an amiable smile. But the new member was equal to the occasion; and, rising with a graceful salutation to the chair, said, in the most engaging manner—"Mr. President and ladies—I beg pardon, gentlemen—allow me to introduce myself as Sam Weller, the very humble servant of the club."

"Good, good!" cried Jo, pounding with the handle of the old warming-pan on which she leaned.

"My faithful friend and noble patron," continued Laurie, with a wave of the hand, "who has

so flatteringly presented me, is not to be blamed
for the base stratagem of to-night. I planned it,
and she only gave in after lots of teasing."

"Come now, don't lay it all on yourself; you
know I proposed the cupboard," broke in Snodgrass, who was enjoying the joke amazingly.

"Never you mind what she says. I'm the wretch
that did it, sir," said the new member, with a
Welleresque nod to Mr. Pickwick. "But on my
honour, I never will do so again, and henceforth
dewote myself to the interest of this immortal
club."

"Hear! hear!" cried Jo, clashing the lid of
the warming-pan like a cymbal.

"Go on! go on!" added Winkle and Tupman,
while the President bowed benignly.

"I merely wish to say, that, as a slight token
of my gratitude for the honour done me, and as
a means of promoting friendly relations between
adjoining nations, I have set up a post-office in the
hedge in the lower corner of the garden; a fine,
spacious building, with padlocks on the doors,
and every convenience for the mails,—also the
females, if I may be allowed the expression. It's
the old martin-house; but I've stopped up the door,
and made the roof open, so it will hold all sorts of
things, and save our valuable time. Letters,
manuscripts, books and bundles can be passed in
there; and, as each nation has a key, it will be
uncommonly nice, I fancy. Allow me to present
the club key; and, with many thanks for your
favour, take my seat."

Great applause as Mr. Weller deposited a little
key on the table, and subsided; the warming-pan

clashed and waved wildly, and it was some time
before order could be restored. A long discussion
followed, and every one came out surprising, for
every one did her best ; so it was an unusually
lively meeting, and did not adjourn till a late hour,
when it broke up with three shrill cheers for the
new member.

No one ever regretted the admittance of Sam
Weller, for a more devoted, well-behaved, and jovial
member no club could have. He certainly did
add "spirit" to the meetings, and "a tone" to
the paper ; for his orations convulsed his hearers,
and his contributions were excellent, being patriotic,
classical, comical, or dramatic, but never sentimental. Jo regarded them as worthy of Bacon,
Milton, or Shakespeare ; and remodelled her own
works with good effect, she thought.

The P. O. was a capital little institution, and
flourished wonderfully, for nearly as many queer
things passed through it as through the real office.
Tragedies and cravats, poetry and pickles, garden
seeds and long letters, music and gingerbread,
rubbers, invitations, scoldings and puppies. The
old gentleman liked the fun, and amused himself
by sending odd bundles, mysterious messages, and
funny telegrams ; and his gardener, who was
smitten with Hannah's charms, actually sent a
love-letter to Jo's care. How they laughed when
the secret came out, never dreaming how many
love-letters that little post-office would hold in
the years to come !

CHAPTER XI.

EXPERIMENTS.

"The first of June; the Kings are off to the sea-shore to-morrow, and I'm free! Three months' vacation! how I shall enjoy it!" exclaimed Meg, coming home one warm day to find Jo laid upon the sofa in an unusual state of exhaustion, while Beth took off her dusty boots, and Amy made lemonade for the refreshment of the whole party.

"Aunt March went to-day, for which, oh, be joyful!" said Jo. "I was mortally afraid she'd ask me to go with her; if she had, I should have felt as if I ought to do it; but Plumfield is about as festive as a church-yard, you know, and I'd rather be excused. We had a flurry getting the old lady off, and I had a scare every time she spoke to me, for I was in such a hurry to be through that I was uncommonly helpful and sweet, and feared she'd find it impossible to part from me. I quaked till she was fairly in the carriage, and had a final fright, for, as it drove off, she popped out her head, saying, 'Josy-phine, won't you——?' I didn't hear any more, for I basely turned and fled; I did actually run, and whisked round the corner, where I felt safe."

"Poor old Jo! she came in looking as if bears

were after her," said Beth, as she cuddled her sister's feet with a motherly air.

"Aunt March is a regular samphire, is she not?" observed Amy, tasting her mixture critically.

"She means *vampire*, not sea-weed; but it don't matter; it's too warm to be particular about one's parts of speech," murmured Jo.

"What shall you do all your vacation?" asked Amy, changing the subject, with tact.

"I shall lie a-bed late, and do nothing," replied Meg, from the depths of the rocking-chair. "I've been routed up early all winter, and had to spend my days working for other people; so now I'm going to rest and revel to my heart's content."

"Hum!" said Jo; "that dozy way wouldn't suit me. I've laid in a heap of books, and I'm going to improve my shining hours reading on my perch in the old apple-tree, when I'm not having——"

"Don't say 'larks'!" implored Amy, as a return snub for the "samphire" correction.

"I'll say 'nightingales,' then, with Laurie; that's proper and appropriate, since he's a warbler."

"Don't let us do any lessons, Beth, for a while, but play all the time, and rest, as the girls mean to," proposed Amy.

"Well, I will, if mother don't mind. I want to learn some new songs, and my children need fixing up for the summer; they are dreadfully out of order, and really suffering for clothes."

"May we, mother?" asked Meg, turning to Mrs. March, who sat sewing, in what they called "Marmee's corner."

"You may try your experiment for a week, and see how you like it. I think by Saturday night you will find that all play and no work is as bad as all work and no play."

"Oh, dear, no! it will be delicious, I'm sure," said Meg, complacently.

"I now propose a toast, as my 'friend and pardner, Sairey Gamp,' says. Fun for ever and no grubbage," cried Jo, rising, glass in hand, as the lemonade went round.

They all drank it merrily, and began the experiment by lounging for the rest of the day. Next morning, Meg did not appear till ten o'clock; her solitary breakfast did not taste good, and the room seemed lonely and untidy, for Jo had not filled the vases, Beth had not dusted, and Amy's books lay scattered about. Nothing was neat and pleasant but "Marmee's corner," which looked as usual; and there she sat, to "rest and read," which meant yawn, and imagine what pretty summer dresses she would get with her salary. Jo spent the morning on the river with Laurie, and the afternoon reading and crying over "The Wide, Wide World," up in the apple-tree. Beth began by rummaging everything out of the big closet, where her family resided; but, getting tired before it was half done, she left her establishment topsy-turvy, and went to her music, rejoicing that she had no dishes to wash. Amy arranged her bower, put on her best white frock, smoothed her curls, and sat down to draw, under the honey-suckles, hoping some one would see and inquire who the young artist was. As no one appeared but an inquisitive daddy-long-legs, who examined her work with interest, she went for a walk, got caught in a shower, and came home dripping.

At tea-time they compared notes, and all agreed that it had been a delightful, though unusually long day. Meg, who went shopping in the after-noon, and got a " sweet blue muslin," had dis-covered, after she had cut the breadths off, that it wouldn't wash, which mishap made her slightly cross. Jo had burnt the skin off her nose boating, and got a raging headache by reading too long. Beth was worried by the confusion of her closet, and the difficulty of learning three or four songs at once ; and Amy deeply regretted the damage done her frock, for Katy Brown's party was to be the next day ; and now, like Flora McFlimsy, she had " nothing to wear." But these were mere trifles ; and they assured their mother that the experiment was working finely. She smiled, said nothing, and, with Hannah's help, did their neglected work, keeping home pleasant, and the domestic machinery running smoothly. It was astonishing what a peculiar and uncomfortable state of things was produced by the " resting and revelling " process. The days kept getting longer and longer ; the weather was unusually variable, and so were tem-pers ; an unsettled feeling possessed every one, and Satan found plenty of mischief for the idle hands to do. As the height of luxury, Meg put out some of her sewing, and then found time hang so heavily that she fell to snipping and spoiling her clothes, in her attempts to furbish them up, à la Moffat. Jo read till her eyes gave out, and she was sick of books ; got so fidgety that even good-natured Laurie had a quarrel with her, and so reduced in spirits that she desperately wished she had gone with Aunt March. Beth got on pretty well, for she was constantly forgetting that it was to be *all play and no work*, and fell back into her old ways, now and then ; but something in the air affected her, and, more than once, her tranquillity was much disturbed ; so much so, that, on one occasion, she actually shook poor dear Joanna, and told her she was " a fright." Amy fared worst of all, for her resources were small ; and, when her sisters left her to amuse and care for herself, she soon found that accomplished and important little self a great burden. She didn't like dolls ; fairy tales were childish, and one couldn't draw all the time. Tea-parties didn't amount to much, neither did pic-nics, unless very well conducted.

" If one could have a fine house, full of nice girls, or go travelling, the summer would be delightful ; but to stay at home with three selfish sisters, and a grown-up boy, was enough to try the patience of a Boaz," complained Miss Malaprop, after several days devoted to pleasure, fretting, and *ennui*.

No one would own that they were tired of the experiment ; but, by Friday night, each acknowledged to herself that they were glad the week was nearly done. Hoping to impress the lesson more deeply, Mrs. March, who had a good deal of humour, resolved to finish off the trial in an appropriate manner ; so she gave Hannah a holiday, and let the girls enjoy the full benefit of the play system.

When they got up on Saturday morning, there was no fire in the kitchen, no breakfast in the dining-room, and no mother anywhere to be seen.

" Mercy on us ! what *has* happened ? " cried Jo, staring about her in dismay.

Meg ran upstairs, and soon came back again,

looking relieved, but rather bewildered, and a little ashamed.

" Mother isn't sick, only very tired, and she says she is going to stay quietly in her room all day, and let us do the best we can. It's a very queer thing for her to do, she don't act a bit like herself ; but she says it *has* been a hard week for her, so we mustn't grumble, but take care of ourselves."

" That's easy enough, and I like the idea ; I'm aching for something to do—that is, some new amusement, you know," added Jo, quickly.

In fact it *was* an immense relief to them all to have a little work, and they took hold with a will, but soon realized the truth of Hannah's saying, " Housekeeping ain't no joke." There was plenty of food in the larder, and while Beth and Amy set the table, Meg and Jo got breakfast ; wondering, as they did so, why servants ever talked about hard work.

" I shall take some up to mother, though she said we were not to think of her, for she'd take care of herself," said Meg, who presided, and felt quite matronly behind the teapot.

So a tray was fitted out before any one began and taken up, with the cook's compliments. The boiled tea was very bitter, the omelette scorched, and the biscuits speckled with saleratus ; but Mrs. March received her repast with thanks, and laughed heartily over it after Jo was gone.

" Poor little souls, they will have a hard time, I'm afraid ; but they won't suffer, and it will do them good," she said, producing the more palatable viands with which she had provided herself, and disposing of the bad breakfast, so that their feelings might not be hurt ;—a motherly little deception, for which they were grateful.

Many were the complaints below, and great the chagrin of the head cook at her failures. "Never mind, I'll get the dinner, and be servant ; you be missis, keep your hands nice, see company, and give orders," said Jo, who knew still less than Meg about culinary affairs.

This obliging offer was gladly accepted ; and Margaret retired to the parlour, which she hastily put in order by whisking the litter under the sofa, and shutting the blinds, to save the trouble of dusting. Jo, with perfect faith in her own powers, and a friendly desire to make up the quarrel, immediately put a note in the office, inviting Laurie to dinner.

"You'd better see what you have got before you think of having company," said Meg, when informed of the hospitable but rash act.

"Oh, there's corned beef, and plenty of potatoes ; and I shall get some asparagus, and a lobster, ' for a relish,' as Hannah says. We'll have lettuce, and make a salad ; I don't know how, but the book tells. I'll have blanc-mange and strawberries for dessert ; and coffee, too, if you want to be elegant."

"Don't try too many messes, Jo, for you can't make anything but gingerbread and molasses candy fit to eat. I wash my hands of the dinner-party ; and, since you have asked Laurie on your own responsibility, you may just take care of him."

"I don't want you to do anything but be clever to him, and help to the pudding. You'll give me your advice if I get stuck, won't you ? " asked Jo, rather hurt.

" Yes ; but I don't know much, except about bread, and a few trifles. You had better ask mother's leave, before you order anything," returned Meg, prudently.

" Of course I shall ; I ain't a fool," and Jo went off in a huff at the doubts expressed of her powers.

" Get what you like, and don't disturb me ; I'm going out to dinner, and can't worry about things at home," said Mrs. March, when Jo spoke to her. " I never enjoyed housekeeping, and I'm going to take a holiday to-day, and read, write, go visiting and amuse myself."

The unusual spectacle of her busy mother rocking comfortably, and reading early in the morning, made Jo feel as if some natural phenomenon had occurred ; for an eclipse, an earthquake, or a volcanic eruption would hardly have seemed stranger.

" Everything is out of sorts, somehow," she said to herself, going down stairs. " There's Beth crying ; that's a sure sign that something is wrong with this family. If Amy is bothering, I'll shake her."

Feeling very much out of sorts herself, Jo hurried into the parlour to find Beth sobbing over Pip, the canary, who lay dead in the cage, with his little claws pathetically extended, as if imploring the food, for want of which he had died.

" It's all my fault—I forgot him—there isn't a seed or drop left—oh, Pip ! oh, Pip ! how could I be so cruel to you ? " cried Beth, taking the poor thing in her hands, and trying to restore him, while her tears fell thick and fast.

Jo peeped into his half-opened eye, felt his little

heart, and finding him stiff and cold, shook her head, and offered her domino-box for a coffin.

"Put him in the oven, and maybe he will get warm, and revive," said Amy, hopefully.

"He's been starved, and he shan't be baked, now he's dead. I'll make him a shroud, and he shall be buried in the grave; and I'll never have another bird, never, my Pip! for I am too bad to own one," murmured Beth, sitting on the floor with her pet folded in her hands.

"The funeral shall be this afternoon, and we will all go. Now, don't cry, Bethy; it's a pity, but nothing goes right this week, and Pip has had the worst of the experiment. Make the shroud, and lay him in my box; and, after the dinner-party, we'll have a nice little funeral," said Jo, beginning to feel as if she had undertaken a good deal.

Leaving the others to console Beth, she departed to the kitchen, which was in a most discouraging state of confusion. Putting on a big apron, she fell to work, and got the dishes piled up ready for washing, when she discovered that the fire was out.

"Here's a sweet prospect!" muttered Jo, slamming the stove door open, and poking vigorously among the cinders.

Having rekindled it, she thought she would go to market while the water heated. The walk revived her spirits; and, flattering herself that she had made good bargains, she trudged home again, after buying a very young lobster, some very old asparagus, and two boxs of acid strawberries. By the time she got cleared up, the dinner arrived, and the stove was red-hot. Hannah had left a pan of bread to rise, Meg had worked it up early, and set it on the hearth for a second rising, and forgotten it. Meg was entertaining Sallie Gardiner, in the parlour, when the door flew open, and a floury, crocky, flushed and dishevelled figure appeared, demanding, tartly—

" I say, isn't bread ' riz ' enough when it runs over the pans ? "

Sallie began to laugh ; but Meg nodded, and lifted her eyebrows as high as they would go, which caused the apparition to vanish, and put the sour bread into the oven without further delay. Mrs. March went out, after peeping here and there to see how matters went, also saying a word of comfort to Beth, who sat making a winding sheet, while the dear departed lay in state in the domino-box. A strange sense of helplessness fell upon the girls as the grey bonnet vanished round the corner, and despair seized them, when, a few minutes later, Miss Crocker appeared, and said she'd come to dinner. Now this lady was a thin, yellow spinster, with a sharp nose, and inquisitive eyes, who saw everything, and gossipped about all she saw. They disliked her, but had been taught to be kind to her, simply because she was old and poor, and had few friends. So Meg gave her the easy chair, and tried to entertain her, while she asked questions, criticised everything, and told stories of the people whom she knew.

Language cannot describe the anxieties, experiences, and exertions which Jo underwent that morning ; and the dinner she served up became a standing joke. Fearing to ask any more advice, she did her best alone, and discovered that something more than energy and good-will is necessary to make a cook. She boiled the asparagus hard for an hour, and was grieved to find the heads cooked off, and the stalks harder than ever. The bread burnt black; for the salad dressing so aggravated her, that she let everything else go, till she had convinced herself that she could not make it fit to eat. The lobster was a scarlet mystery to her, but she hammered and poked, till it was unshelled, and its meagre proportions concealed in a grove of lettuce leaves. The potatoes had to be hurried, not to keep the asparagus waiting, and were not done at last. The blanc-mange was lumpy, and the strawberries not as ripe as they looked, having been skilfully " deaconed."

" Well, they can eat beef, and bread and butter if they are hungry; only it's mortifying to have to spend your whole morning for nothing," thought Jo, as she rang the bell half an hour later than usual, and stood hot, tired and dispirited, surveying the feast spread for Laurie, accustomed to all sorts of elegance, and Miss Crocker, whose curious eyes would mark all failures, and whose tattling tongue would report them far and wide.

Poor Jo would gladly have gone under the table, as one thing after another was tasted and left ; while Amy giggled, Meg looked distressed, Miss Crocker pursed up her lips, and Laurie talked and laughed with all his might, to give a cheerful tone to the festive scene. Jo's one strong point was the fruit, for she had sugared it well, and had a pitcher of rich cream to eat with it. Her hot cheeks cooled a little, and she drew a long breath, as the

pretty glass plates went round, and every one
looked graciously at the little rosy islands floating
in a sea of cream. Miss Crocker tasted first, made
a wry face, and drank some water hastily. Jo,
who had refused, thinking there might not be
enough, for they dwindled sadly after the picking
over, glanced at Laurie, but he was eating away
manfully, though there was a slight pucker about
his mouth, and he kept his eye fixed on his plate.
Amy, who was fond of delicate fare, took a heaping
spoonful, choked, hid her face in her napkin, and
left the table precipitately.

"Oh, what is it?" exclaimed Jo, trembling.

"Salt instead of sugar, and the cream is sour,"
replied Meg.

Jo uttered a groan, and fell back in her chair;
remembering that she had given a last hasty
powdering to the berries out of one of the two
boxes on the kitchen table, and had neglected to
put the milk in the refrigerator. She turned scarlet,
and was on the verge of crying, when she met
Laurie's eyes, which *would* look merry in spite of his
heroic efforts; the comical side of the affair suddenly struck her, and she laughed till the tears
ran down her cheeks. So did every one else, even
"Croaker," as the girls called the old lady; and
the unfortunate dinner ended gaily, with bread
and butter, olives and fun.

"I haven't strength of mind enough to clear up
now, so we will sober ourselves with a funeral,"
said Jo, as they rose; and Miss Crocker made ready
to go, being eager to tell the new story at another
friend's dinner table.

They did sober themselves, for Beth's sake;

Laurie dug a grave under the ferns in the grove, little Pip was laid in, with many tears, by his tender-hearted mistress, and covered with moss, while a wreath of violets and chickweed was hung on the stone which bore his epitaph, composed by Jo, while she struggled with the dinner:—

> " Here lies Pip March,
> Who died the 7th of June,
> Loved and lamented sore,
> And not forgotten soon."

At the conclusion of the ceremonies, Beth retired to her room, overcome with emotion and lobster ; but there was no place of repose, for the beds were not made, and she found her grief much assuaged by beating up pillows and putting things in order. Meg helped Jo clear away the remains of the feast, which took half the afternoon, and left them so tired that they agreed to be contented with tea and toast for supper. Laurie took Amy to drive, which was a deed of charity, for the sour cream seemed to have a bad effect upon her temper. Mrs. March came home to find the three older girls hard at work in the middle of the afternoon ; and a glance at the closet gave her an idea of the success of one part of the experiment.

Before the housewives could rest, several people called, and there was a scramble to get ready to see them ; then tea must be got, errands done ; and one or two bits of sewing were necessary, but neglected till the last minute. As twilight fell, dewy and still, one by one they gathered in the porch where the June roses were budding beautifully, and each groaned or sighed as she sat down, as if tired or troubled.

"What a dreadful day this has been!" began Jo, usually the first to speak.

"It has seemed shorter than usual, but *so* uncomfortable," said Meg.

"Not a bit like home," added Amy.

"It can't seem so without Marmee and little Pip," sighed Beth, glancing, with full eyes, at the empty cage above her head.

"Here's mother, dear, and you shall have another bird to-morrow, if you want it."

As she spoke, Mrs. March came and took her place among them, looking as if her holiday had not been much pleasanter than theirs.

"Are you satisfied with your experiment, girls, or do you want another week of it?" she asked, as Beth nestled up to her, and the rest turned toward her with brightening faces, as flowers turn toward the sun.

"I don't!" cried Jo, decidedly.

"Nor I," echoed the others.

"You think, then, that it is better to have a few duties, and live a little for others, do you?"

"Lounging and larking don't pay," observed Jo, shaking her head. "I'm tired of it, and mean to go to work at something right off."

"Suppose you learn plain cooking; that's a useful accomplishment, which no woman should be without," said Mrs. March, laughing audibly at the recollection of Jo's dinner-party; for she had met Miss Crocker, and heard her account of it.

"Mother! did you go away and let everything be, just to see how we'd get on?" cried Meg, who had had suspicions all day.

"Yes; I wanted you to see how the comfort of all depends on each doing her share faithfully. While Hannah and I did your work, you got on pretty well, though I don't think you were very happy or amiable; so I thought, as a little lesson, I would show you what happens when every one thinks only of herself. Don't you feel that it is pleasanter to help one another, to have daily duties which make leisure sweet when it comes, and to bear or forbear, that home may be comfortable and lovely to us all?"

"We do, mother, we do!" cried the girls.

"Then let me advise you to take up your little burdens again : for though they seem heavy sometimes, they are good for us, and lighten as we learn to carry them. Work is wholesome, and there is plenty for every one; it keeps us from *ennui* and mischief; is good for health and spirits, and gives us a sense of power and independence better than money or fashion."

"We'll work like bees, and love it too; see if we don't!" said Jo. "I'll learn plain cooking for my holiday task; and the next dinner-party I have shall be a success."

"I'll make the set of shirts for father, instead of letting you do it, Marmee. I can and I will, though I'm not fond of sewing; that will be better than fussing over my own things, which are plenty nice enough as they are," said Meg.

"I'll do my lessons every day, and not spend so much time with my music and dolls. I am a stupid thing, and ought to be studying, not playing," was Beth's resolution; while Amy followed their example by heroically declaring, "I shall learn to make button-holes, and attend to my parts of speech."

"Very good ! then I am quite satisfied with the experiment, and fancy that we shall not have to repeat it ; only don't go to the other extreme, and delve like slaves. Have regular hours for work and play ; make each day both useful and pleasant, and prove that you understand the worth of time by employing it well. Then youth will be delightful, old age will bring few regrets, and life become a beautiful success, in spite of poverty."

"We'll remember, mother ! " and they did.

CHAPTER XII.

CAMP LAURENCE.

Beth was post-mistress, for, being most at home, she could attend to it regularly, and dearly liked the daily task of unlocking the little door and distributing the mail. One July day she came in with her hands full, and went about the house, leaving letters and parcels, like the penny post.

"Here's your posy, mother ! Laurie never forgets that," she said, putting the fresh nosegay in the vase that stood in " Marmee's corner," and was kept supplied by the affectionate boy.

"Miss Meg March, one letter, and a glove," continued Beth, delivering the articles to her sister, who sat near her mother, stitching wristbands.

" Why, I left a pair over there, and here is only one," said Meg, looking at the grey cotton glove.

"Didn't you drop the other in the garden ? "

"No, I'm sure I didn't ; for there was only one in the office."

"I hate to have odd gloves! Never mind, the other may be found. My letter is only a translation of the German song I wanted ; I guess Mr. Brooke did it, for this isn't Laurie's writing."

Mrs. March glanced at Meg, who was very pretty in her gingham morning gown, with the little curls blowing about her forehead, and very womanly, as she sat sewing at her little work-table, full of tidy white rolls ; so, unconscious of the thought in her mother's mind, she sewed and sung while her fingers flew, and her mind was busied with girlish fancies as innocent and fresh as the pansies in her belt, that Mrs. March smiled, and was satisfied.

"Two letters for Doctor Jo, a book, and a funny old hat, which covered the whole post-office, stuck outside," said Beth, laughing, as she went into the study, where Jo sat writing.

"What a sly fellow Laurie is! I said I wished bigger hats were the fashion, because I burn my face every hot day. He said, 'Why mind the fashions, wear a big hat, and be comfortable!' I said I would if I had one, and he has sent me this, to try me ; I'll wear it for fun, and show him I *don't* care for the fashion," and, hanging the antique broad-brim on a bust of Plato, Jo read her letters.

One from her mother made her cheeks glow, and her eyes fill, for it said to her—

"MY DEAR :

"I write a little word to tell you with how much satisfaction I watch your efforts to control your temper. You say nothing about your trials, failures, or successes, and think, perhaps, that no one sees them but the Friend whose help you daily ask, if I may trust the well-worn cover of your guide-book. *I*, too, have seen them all, and heartily believe in the sincerity of your resolution, since it begins to bear fruit. Go on, dear, patiently and bravely, and always believe that no one sympathises more tenderly with you than your loving

" MOTHER."

" That does me good ! that's worth millions of money, and pecks of praise. Oh, Marmee, I do try ! I will keep on trying, and not get tired, since I have you to help me."

Laying her head on her arms, Jo wet her little romance with a few happy tears, for she *had* thought that no one saw and appreciated her efforts to be good, and this assurance was doubly precious, doubly encouraging, because unexpected, and from the person whose commendation she most valued. Feeling stronger than ever to meet and subdue her Apollyon, she pinned the note inside her frock, as a shield and a reminder, lest she be taken unaware, and proceeded to open her other letter, quite ready for either good or bad news. In a big, dashing hand, Laurie wrote—

" DEAR JO,

What ho !

Some English girls and boys are coming to see me to-morrow, and I want to have a jolly time. If it's fine, I'm going to pitch my tent in Longmeadow, and row up the whole crew to lunch and croquet—

have a fire, make messes, gipsy fashion, and all
sorts of larks. They are nice people, and like
such things. Brooke will go, to keep us boys
steady, and Kate Vaughan will play propriety
for the girls. I want you all to come ; can't let
Beth off, at any price, and nobody shall worry her.
Don't bother about rations—I'll see to that, and
everything else—only do come, there's a good
fellow !

> " In a tearing hurry,
>   " Yours ever, LAURIE."

" Here's richness ! " cried Jo, flying to tell the
news to Meg. " Of course we can go, mother ! it will
be such a help to Laurie, for I can row, and Meg see
to the lunch, and the children be useful some
way."

" I hope the Vaughans are not fine, grown-up
people. Do you know anything about them,
Jo ? " asked Meg.

" Only that there are four of them.   Kate is older
than you, Fred and Frank (twins) about my age,
and a little girl (Grace), who is nine or ten.   Laurie
knew them abroad, and liked the boys ; I fancied,
from the way he primed up his mouth in speaking
of her, that he didn't admire Kate much."

" I'm so glad my French print is clean, it's just
the thing, and so becoming ! " observed Meg,
complacently.   " Have you anything decent, Jo ? "

" Scarlet and grey boating suit, good enough for
me ; I shall row and tramp about, so I don't want
any starch to think of. You'll come, Betty ? "

" If you won't let any of the boys talk to me."

" Not a boy ! "

" I like to please Laurie ; and I'm not afraid of Mr. Brooke, he is so kind ; but I don't want to play, or sing, or say anything. I'll work hard, and not trouble any one ; and you'll take care of me, Jo, so I'll go."

" That's my good girl ; you do try to fight off your shyness, and I love you for it ; fighting faults isn't easy, as I know, and a cheery word kind of gives a lift. Thank you, mother," and Jo gave the thin cheek a grateful kiss, more precious to Mrs. March than if it had given her back the rosy round-ness of her youth.

" I had a box of chocolate drops, and the picture I wanted to copy," said Amy, showing her mail.

" And I got a note from Mr. Laurence, asking me to come over and play to him to-night, before the lamps are lighted, and I shall go," added Beth, whose friendship with the old gentleman prospered finely.

" Now let's fly round, and do double duty to-day, so that we can play to-morrow with free minds," said Jo, preparing to replace her pen with a broom.

When the sun peeped into the girls' room early next morning, to promise them a fine day, he saw a comical sight. Each had made such preparation for the fête as seemed necessary and proper. Meg had an extra row of little curl papers across her forehead, Jo had copiously anointed her afflicted face with cold cream, Beth had taken Joanna to bed with her to atone for the approaching separa-tion, and Amy had capped the climax by putting a clothes-pin on her nose, to uplift the offending feature. It was one of the kind artists use to hold the paper on their drawing-boards; therefore, quite appropriate and effective for the purpose to which it was now put. This funny spectacle appeared to amuse the sun, for he burst out with such radiance that Jo woke up, and roused all her sisters by a hearty laugh at Amy's ornament.

Sunshine and laughter were good omens for a pleasure party, and soon a lively bustle began in both houses.

Beth, who was ready first, kept reporting what went on next door, and enlivened her sisters' toilets by frequent telegrams from the window.

" There goes the man with the tent! I see Mrs. Barker doing up the lunch in a hamper and a great basket. Now Mr. Laurence is looking up at the sky, and the weathercock; I wish he would go, too! There's Laurie looking like a sailor—nice boy! Oh, mercy me! here's a carriage full of people— a tall lady, a little girl, and two dreadful boys. One is lame, poor thing, he's got a crutch! Laurie didn't tell us that. Be quick, girls! it's getting late. Why, there is Ned Moffat, I do declare. Look, Meg! isn't that the man who bowed to you one day, don't you remember, when we were shopping ? "

" So it is; how queer that he should come! I thought he was in the Mountains. There is Sallie; I'm glad she got back in time. Am I all right, Jo ? " cried Meg, in a flutter.

" A regular daisy; hold up your dress, and put your hat straight; it looks sentimental tipped that way, and will fly off at the first puff. Now, then, come on ! "

" Oh, oh, Jo ! you ain't going to wear that awful

hat? It's too absurd! You shall *not* make a guy of yourself," remonstrated Meg, as Jo tied down, with a red ribbon, the broad-brimmed, old-fashioned Leghorn Laurie had sent for a joke.

" I just will, though! it's capital; so shady, light, and big. It will make fun; and I don't mind being a guy, if I'm comfortable." With that Jo marched straight away, and the rest followed; a bright little band of sisters, all looking their best, in summer suits, with happy faces under the jaunty hat-brims.

Laurie ran to meet, and present them to his friends, in the most cordial manner. The lawn was the reception-room, and for several minutes a lively scene was enacted there. Meg was grateful to see that Miss Kate, though twenty, was dressed with a simplicity which American girls would do well to imitate, and she was much flattered by Mr. Ned's assurances that he came especially to see her. Jo understood why Laurie " primed his mouth " while speaking of Kate, for that young lady had a stand-off-don't-touch-me air, which contrasted strongly with the free and easy demeanour of the other girls. Beth took an observation of the new boys, and decided that the lame one was not " dreadful," but gentle and feeble, and she would be kind to him on that account. Amy found Grace a well-mannered, merry little person; and, after staring dumbly at one another for a few minutes, they suddenly became very good friends.

Tents, lunch, and croquet utensils having been sent on beforehand, the party was soon embarked, and the two boats pushed off together, leaving Mr. Laurence waving his hat on the shore. Laurie and

Jo rowed one boat ; Mr. Brooke and Ned the other ; while Fred Vaughan, the riotous twin, did his best to upset both, by paddling about in a wherry, like a disturbed waterbug. Jo's funny hat deserved a vote of thanks, for it was of general utility ; it broke the ice in the beginning, by producing a laugh ; it created quite a refreshing breeze, flapping to and fro, as she rowed, and would make an excellent umbrella for the whole party, if a shower came up, she said. Kate looked rather amazed at Jo's proceedings, especially as she exclaimed " Christopher Columbus ! " when she lost her oar ; and Laurie said, " My dear fellow, did I hurt you ? " when he tripped over her feet in taking his place. But after putting up her glass to examine the queer girl several times, Miss Kate decided that she was " odd, but rather clever," and smiled upon her from afar.

Meg, in the other boat, was delightfully situated, face to face with the rowers, who both admired the prospect, and feathered their oars with " uncommon skill and dexterity." Mr. Brooke was a grave, silent young man, with handsome brown eyes, and a pleasant voice. Meg liked his quiet manners, and considered him a walking encyclopædia of useful knowledge. He never talked to her much ; but he looked at her a good deal, and she felt sure that he did not regard her with aversion. Ned being in college, of course put on all the airs which freshmen think it their bounden duty to assume ; he was not very wise, but very good-natured and merry, and, altogether, an excellent person to carry on a picnic. Sallie Gardiner was absorbed in keeping her white piqué dress clean,

and chatting with the ubiquitous Fred, who kept
Beth in constant terror by his pranks.

It was not far to Longmeadow ; but the tent
was pitched, and the wickets down, by the time
they arrived. A pleasant green field, with three
wide-spreading oaks in the middle, and a smooth
strip of turf for croquet.

"Welcome to Camp Laurence ! " said the young
host as they landed, with exclamations of delight.
"Brooke is commander-in-chief ; I am commissary-general ; the other fellows are staff officers ;
and you, ladies, are company. The tent is for
your especial benefit, and that oak is your drawing-
room ; this is the mess room, and the third is the
camp kitchen. Now let's have a game before it
gets hot, and then we'll see about dinner."

Frank, Beth, Amy, and Grace sat down to watch
the game played by the other eight. Mr. Brooke
chose Meg, Kate, and Fred, Laurie took Sallie, Jo,
and Ned. The Englishers played well ; but the
Americans played better, and contested every
inch of the ground as strongly as if the spirit of '76
inspired them. Jo and Fred had several skirmishes,
and once narrowly escaped high words. Jo was
through the last wicket, and had missed the stroke,
which failure ruffled her a good deal. Fred was close
behind her, and his turn came before hers ; he gave
a stroke, his ball hit the wicket, and stopped an inch
on the wrong side. No one was very near ; and
running up to examine, he gave it a sly nudge with
his toe, which put it just an inch on the right side.

"I'm through ! now, Miss Jo, I'll settle you
and get in first," cried the young gentleman, swinging his mallet for another blow.

" You pushed it ; I saw you ; it's my turn now,"
said Jo, sharply.

" Upon my word I didn't move it ! it rolled a
bit, perhaps, but that is allowed ; so stand off,
please, and let me have a go at the stake."

" We don't cheat in America ; but *you* can, if
you choose," said Jo, angrily.

" Yankees are a deal the most tricky, everybody knows. There you go," returned Fred,
croquetting her ball far away.

Jo opened her lips to say something rude ; but
checked herself in time, coloured up to her forehead, and stood for a minute, hammering down
a wicket with all her might, while Fred hit the
stake, and declared himself out, with much ex-
altation. She went off to get her ball, and was
a long time finding it, among the bushes ; but
she came back, looking cool and quiet, and
waited her turn patiently. It took several
strokes to regain the place she had lost ; and,
when she got there, the other side had nearly
won, for Kate's ball was the last but one, and lay
near the stake.

" By George, it's all up with us ! Good-by,
Kate ; Miss Jo owes me one, so you are finished,"
cried Fred, excitedly, as they all drew near to see
the finish.

" Yankees have a trick of being generous to their
enemies," said Jo, with a look that made the lad
redden, " especially when they beat them," she
added, as, leaving Kate's ball untouched, she won
the game by a clever stroke.

Laurie threw up his hat ; then remembered that it
wouldn't do to exult over the defeat of his guests,

and stopped in the middle of a cheer to whisper to his friend—

"Good for you, Jo! he did cheat, I saw him; we can't tell him so, but he won't do it again, take my word for it."

Meg drew her aside, under pretence of pinning up a loose braid, and said, approvingly—

"It was dreadfully provoking; but you kept your temper, and I'm so glad, Jo."

"Don't praise me, Meg, for I could box his ears this minute. I should certainly have boiled over, if I hadn't stayed among the nettles till I got my rage under enough to hold my tongue. It's simmering now, so I hope he'll keep out of my way," returned Jo, biting her lips, as she glowered at Fred from under her big hat.

"Time for lunch," said Mr. Brooke, looking at his watch. "Commissary-general, will you make the fire, and get water, while Miss March, Miss Sallie, and I spread the table? Who can make good coffee?"

"Jo can," said Meg, glad to recommend her sister. So Jo, feeling that her late lessons in cookery were to do her honour, went to preside over the coffee-pot, while the children collected dry sticks, and the boys made a fire, and got water from a spring near by. Miss Kate sketched, and Frank talked to Beth, who was making little mats of braided rushes, to serve as plates.

The commander-in-chief and his aids soon spread the table-cloth with an inviting array of eatables and drinkables, prettily decorated with green leaves. Jo announced that the coffee was ready, and everybody settled themselves to a hearty meal; for youth is seldom dyspeptic, and exercise develops wholesome appetites. A very merry lunch it was; for everything seemed fresh and funny, and frequent peals of laughter started a venerable horse, who fed near by. There was a pleasing inequality in the table, which produced many mishaps to cups and plates; acorns dropped into the milk, little black ants partook of the refreshments without being invited, and fuzzy caterpillars swung down from the tree, to see what was going on. Three white-headed children peeped over the fence, and an objectionable dog barked at them from the other side of the river with all his might and main.

"There's salt here, if you prefer it," said Laurie, as he handed Jo a saucer of berries.

"Thank you; I prefer spiders," she replied, fishing up two unwary little ones, who had gone to a creamy death. "How dare you remind me of that horrid dinner-party, when yours is so nice in every way?" added Jo, as they both laughed, and ate off one plate, the china having run short.

"I had an uncommonly good time that day, and haven't got over it yet. This is no credit to me, you know; I don't do anything; it's you, and Meg, and Brooke who make it go, and I'm no end obliged to you. What shall we do when we can't eat any more?" asked Laurie, feeling that his trump card had been played when lunch was over.

"Have games till it's cooler. I brought 'Authors,' and I daresay Miss Kate knows something new and nice. Go and ask her; she's company, and you ought to stay with her more."

"Aren't you company, too? I thought she'd suit Brooke; but he keeps talking to Meg, and Kate just stares at them through that ridiculous glass of hers. I'm going, so you needn't try to preach propriety, for you can't do it, Jo."

Miss Kate did know several new games ; and as the girls would not, and the girls could not, eat any more, they all adjourned to the drawing-room to play " Rigmarole."

" One person begins a story, any nonsense you like, and tells as long as they please, only taking care to stop short at some exciting point, when the next takes it up, and does the same. It's very funny when well done, and makes a perfect jumble of tragical comic stuff to laugh over. Please start it, Mr. Brooke," said Kate, with a commanding gesture, which surprised Meg, who treated the tutor with as much respect as any other gentleman.

Lying on the grass, at the feet of the two young ladies, Mr. Brooke obediently began his story, with the handsome brown eyes steadily fixed upon the sunshiny river.

" Once on a time, a knight went out into the world to seek his fortune, for he had nothing but his sword and his shield. He travelled a long while, nearly eight-and-twenty years, and had a hard time of it, till he came to the palace of a good king, who had offered a reward to anyone who could tame and train a fine, unbroken colt, of which he was very fond. The knight agreed to try, and got on slowly but surely ; for the colt was a gallant fellow, and soon learned to love his new master, though he was freakish and wild. Every day, when he gave his lessons to this pet of the king's, the knight rode him through the city ; and, as he rode, he looked every where for a certain beautiful face which he had seen many times in his dreams, but never found. One day, as he went prancing down a quiet street, he saw at the window of a ruinous castle a lovely face. He was delighted, inquired who lived in this old castle, and was told that several captive princesses were kept there by a spell, and spun all day to lay up money to buy their liberty. The knight wished intensely that he could free them ; but he was poor, and could only go by each day, watching for the sweet face, and longing to see it out in the sunshine. At last he resolved to get into the castle, and ask how he could help them. He went and knocked ; the great door flew open, and he beheld——"

"A ravishingly lovely lady, who exclaimed, with a cry of rapture, 'At last ! at last ! ' " continued Kate, who had read French novels, and admired the style. " ' 'Tis she ! ' cried Count Gustave, and fell at her feet in an ecstasy of joy. 'Oh, rise ! ' she said, extending a hand of marble fairness. 'Never ! till you tell me how I may rescue you,' swore the knight, still kneeling. 'Alas, my cruel fate condemns me to remain here till my tyrant is destroyed.' 'Where is the villain ?' 'In the mauve salon ; go, brave heart, and save me from despair.' 'I obey, and return victorious or dead ! ' With these thrilling words he rushed away, and, flinging open the door of the mauve salon, was about to enter, when he received——"

"A stunning blow from the big Greek lexicon, which an old fellow in a black gown fired at him," said Ned. "Instantly Sir What's-his-name recovered himself, pitched the tyrant out of the window, and turned to join the lady, victorious, but with a bump on his brow ; found the door locked, tore up the curtains, made a rope ladder, got half-way down when the ladder broke, and he went head first into the moat, sixty feet below. Could swim like a duck, paddled round the castle till he came to a little door guarded by two stout fellows ; knocked their heads together till they cracked like a couple of nuts, then, by a trifling exertion of his prodigious strength, he smashed in the door, went up a pair of stone steps covered with dust a foot thick, toads as big as your fist, and spiders that would frighten you into hysterics, Miss March. At the top of these steps he came plump upon a sight that took away his breath and chilled his blood——"

" A tall figure, all in white, with a veil over its face, and a lamp in its wasted hand," went on Meg. " It beckoned, gliding noiselessly before him down a corridor as dark and cold as any tomb. Shadowy effigies in armour stood on either side, a dead silence reigned, the lamp burned blue, and the ghostly figure ever and anon turned its face towards him, showing the glitter of awful eyes through its white veil. They reached a curtained door, behind which sounded lovely music ; he sprang forward to enter, but the spectre plucked him back, and waved, threateningly, before him, a——"

" Snuff-box," said Jo, in a sepulchral tone, which convulsed the audience. " ' Thankee,' said the knight, politely, as he took a pinch, and sneezed seven times so violently that his head fell off. ' Ha ! ha ! ' laughed the ghost ; and, having peeped through the keyhole at the princesses spinning away for dear life, the evil spirit picked up her victim and put him in a large tin box, where there were eleven other knights packed together without their heads, like sardines, who all rose and began to——"

"Dance a hornpipe," cut in Fred, as Jo paused for breath; "and as they danced, the rubbishy old castle turned to a man-of-war in full sail. 'Up with the jib, reef the tops'l halliards, helm hard a lee, and man the guns,' roared the captain, as a Portuguese pirate hove in sight, with a flag black as ink flying from her foremast. 'Go in and win my hearties,' says the captain; and a tremendous fight began. Of course the British beat—they always do; and, having taken the pirate captain prisoner, sailed slap over the schooner, whose decks were piled with dead, and whose lee-scuppers ran blood, for the order had been 'Cutlasses, and die hard.' 'Bosen's mate, take a bight of the flying jib sheet, and start this villain if he don't confess his sins double quick,' said the British captain. The Portuguese held his tongue like a brick, and walked the plank, while the jolly tars cheered like mad. But the sly dog dived, came up under the man-of-war, scuttled her, and down she went, with all sails set, 'To the bottom of the sea, where——"

"Oh, gracious! what *shall* I say?" cried Sallie, as Fred ended his rigmarole, in which he had jumbled together, pell-mell, nautical phrases and facts, out of one of his favourite books. "Well, they went to the bottom, and a nice mermaid welcomed them, but was much grieved on finding the box of headless knights, and kindly pickled them in brine, hoping to discover the mystery about them; for, being a woman, she was curious. By and by a diver came pown, and the mermaid said, 'I'll give you this

box of pearls if you can take it up ; ' for she wanted
to restore the poor things to life, and couldn't
raise the heavy load herself. So the diver hoisted
it up, and was much disappointed, on opening it,
to find no pearls. He left it in a great lonely field,
where it was found by a——"

"Little goose-girl, who kept a hundred fat geese
in the field," said Amy, when Sallie's invention gave
out. "The little girl was sorry for them, and asked
an old woman what she should do to help them.
'Your geese will tell you, they know everything,'
said the old woman. So she asked what she should
use for new heads, since the old ones were lost,
and all the geese opened their hundred mouths,
and screamed——"

"'Cabbages!'" continued Laurie, promptly.
"'Just the thing,' said the girl, and ran to get twelve
fine ones from her garden. She put them on, the
knights revived at once, thanked her, and went on
their way rejoicing, never knowing the difference,
for there was so many heads like them in the world,
that no one thought anything of it. The knight in
whom I'm interested went back to find the pretty
face, and learned that the princesses had spun themselves free, and all gone to be married, but one.
He was in a great state of mind at that ; and mount-
ing the colt, who stood by him through thick and
thin, rushed to the castle to see which was left.
Peering over the hedge, he saw the queen of his
affections picking flowers in her garden. 'Will you
give me a rose ? ' said he. 'You must come and
get it ; I can't come to you ; it isn't proper,' said
she, as sweet as honey. He tried to climb over the
hedge, but it seemed to grow higher and higher ;

then he tried to push through, but it grew thicker and thicker, and he was in despair. So he patiently broke twig after twig, till he had made a little hole, through which he peeped, saying imploringly, ' Let me in ! let me in ! ' But the pretty princess did not seem to understand, for she picked her roses, quietly, and left him to fight his way in. Whether he did or not, Frank will tell you."

" I can't ; I'm not playing, I never do," said Frank, dismayed at the sentimental predicament out of which he was to rescue the absurd couple. Beth had disappeared behind Jo, and Grace was asleep.

" So the poor knight is to be left sticking in the hedge, is he ? " asked Mr. Brooke, still watching the river, and playing with the wild rose in his button-hole.

" I guess the princess gave him a posy, and opened the gate, after awhile," said Laurie, smiling to himself, as he threw acorns at his tutor.

" What a piece of nonsense we have made ! With practice we might do something quite clever. Do you know ' Truth ? ' " asked Sallie, after they had laughed over their story.

" I hope so," said Meg, soberly.

" The game, I mean ? "

" What is it ? "

" Why you pile up your hands, choose a number, and draw out in turn, and the person who draws at the number has to answer truly any question put by the rest. It's great fun."

" Let's try it," said Jo, who liked new experiments.

Miss Kate and Mr. Brooke, Meg and Ned,

declined; but Fred, Sallie, Jo and Laurie piled and drew; and the lot fell to Laurie.

"Who are your heroes?" asked Jo.

"Grandfather and Napoleon."

"What lady do you think prettiest?" said Sallie.

"Margaret."

"Which do you like best?" from Fred.

"Jo, of course."

"What silly questions you ask!" and Jo gave a disdainful shrug as the rest laughed at Laurie's matter-of-fact tone.

"Try again; Truth isn't a bad game," said Fred.

"It's a very good one for you," retorted Jo, in a low voice.

Her turn came next.

"What is your greatest fault?" asked Fred, by way of testing in her the virtue he lacked himself.

"A quick temper."

"What do you most wish for?" said Laurie.

"A pair of boot-lacings," returned Jo, guessing and defeating his purpose.

"Not a true answer; you must say what you really do want most."

"Genius; don't you wish you could give it to me, Laurie?" and she slyly smiled in his disappointed face.

"What virtues do you most admire in a man?" asked Sallie.

"Courage and honesty."

"Now my turn," said Fred, as his hand came last.

" Let's give it to him," whispered Laurie to Jo, who nodded, and asked at once—

" Didn't you cheat at croquet ? "

" Well, yes, a little bit."

" Good ! Didn't you take your story out of ' The Sea Lion ? ' " said Laurie.

" Rather."

" Didn't you think the English nation perfect in every respect ? " asked Sallie.

" I should be ashamed of myself if I didn't."

" He's a true John Bull. Now, Miss Sallie, you shall have a chance without waiting to draw. I'll harrow up your feelings first by asking you if you don't think you are something of a flirt," said Laurie, as Jo nodded to Fred, as a sign that peace was declared.

" You impertinent boy ! of course I'm not," exclaimed Sallie, with an air that proved the contrary.

" What do you hate most ? " asked Fred.

" Spiders and rice pudding."

" What do you like best ? " asked Jo.

" Dancing and French gloves."

" Well, *I* think Truth is a very silly play ; let's have a sensible game of Authors, to refresh our minds," proposed Jo.

Ned, Frank, and the little girls joined in this, and, while it went on, the three elders sat apart, talking. Miss Kate took out her sketch again, and Margaret watched her, while Mr. Brooke lay on the grass, with a book, which he did not read.

" How beautifully you do it ; I wish I could draw," said Meg, with mingled admiration and regret in her voice.

" Why don't you learn ?   I should think you had taste and talent for it," replied Miss Kate, graciously.

" I haven't time."

" Your mamma prefers other accomplishments, I fancy. So did mine ; but I proved to her that I had talent, by taking a few lessons privately, and then she was quite willing I should go on. Can't you do the same with your governess ? "

" I have none."

" I forgot ; young ladies in America go to school more than with us. Very fine schools they are, too, papa says. You go to a private one, I suppose ? "

" I don't go at all ; I'm a governess myself."

" Oh, indeed ! " said Miss Kate ; but she might as well have said, " Dear me, how dreadful ! " for her tone implied it, and something in her face made Meg colour, and wish she had not been so frank.

Mr. Brooke looked up, and said, quickly, " Young ladies in America love independence as much as their ancestors did, and are admired and respected for supporting themselves.

" Oh, yes ; of course ! it's very nice and proper in them to do so. We have many most respectable and worthy young women, who do the same ; and are employed by the nobility, because being the daughters of gentlemen, they are both well-bred and accomplished, you know," said Miss Kate, in a tone that hurt Meg's pride, and made her work seem not only more distasteful, but degrading.

" Did the German song suit, Miss March ? " inquired Mr. Brooke, breaking an awkward pause.

" Oh, yes ! it was very sweet, and I'm much

obliged to whoever translated it for me ; " and Meg's downcast face brightened.

" Don't you read German ? " asked Miss Kate, with surprise.

" Not very well. My father, who taught me, is away, and I don't get on very fast alone, for I've no one to correct my pronunciation."

" Try a little now ; here is Schiller's ' Mary Stuart,' and a tutor who loves to teach," and Mr. Brooke laid his book on her lap, with an inviting smile.

" It's so hard, I'm afraid to try," said Meg, gratefully, but bashful in the presence of the accomplished young lady beside her.

" I'll read a bit to encourage you ; " and Miss Kate read one of the most beautiful passages, in a perfectly correct, but perfectly expressionless manner.

Mr. Brooke made no comment, as she returned the book to Meg, who said, innocently—

" I thought it was poetry."

" Some of it is ; try this passage."

There was a queer smile about Mr. Brooke's mouth, as he opened at poor Mary's lament.

Meg, obediently, following the long grass-blade which her new tutor used to point with, read, slowly and timidly, unconsciously making poetry of the hard words, by the soft intonation of her musical voice. Down the page went the green guide, and presently, forgetting her listener in the beauty of the sad scene, Meg read as if alone, giving a little touch of tragedy to the words of the unhappy queen. If she had seen the brown eyes then, she would have stopped ; but she never looked up, and the lesson was not spoilt for her.

"Very well, indeed!" said Mr. Brooke, quite ignoring her many mistakes, and looking as if he did, indeed, "love to teach."

"You've a nice accent, and, in time, will be a clever reader. I advise you to learn, for German is a valuable accomplishment to teachers. I must look after Grace, she is romping;" and Miss Kate strolled away, adding to herself, with a shrug, "I didn't come to chaperone a governess. What odd people these Yankees are! I'm afraid Laurie will be quite spoilt among them."

"I forgot that English people rather turn up their noses at governesses, and don't treat them as we do," said Meg, looking after the retreating figure with an annoyed expression.

"Tutors, also, have rather a hard time of it there, as I know to my sorrow. There's no place like America for us workers, Miss Margaret," and Mr. Brooke looked so contented and cheerful, that Meg was ashamed to lament her hard lot.

"I'm glad I live in it, then. I don't like my work, but I get a good deal of satisfaction out of it, after all, so I won't complain; I only wish I liked teaching as you do."

"I think you would, if you had Laurie for a pupil. I shall be very sorry to lose him next year," said Mr. Brooke, busily punching holes in the turf.

"Going to college, I suppose?" Meg's lips asked that question, but her eyes added, "And what becomes of you?"

"Yes; it's high time he went, for he is nearly ready, and as soon as he is off I shall turn soldier."

"I'm glad of that!" exclaimed Meg; "I should

think every young man would want to go ; though it is hard for the mothers and sisters, who stay at home," she added, sorrowfully.

"I have neither, and very few friends, to care whether I live or die," said Mr. Brooke, rather bitterly, as he absently put the dead rose in the hole he had made, and covered it up, like a little grave.

"Laurie and his grandfather would care a great deal, and we should all be very sorry to have any harm happen to you," said Meg, heartily.

"Thank you ; that sounds pleasant," began Mr. Brooke, looking cheerful again ; but, before he could finish his speech, Ned, mounted on an old horse, came lumbering up, to display his equestrian skill before the young ladies, and there was no more quiet that day.

"Don't you love to ride ? " asked Grace of Amy, as they stood resting, after a race round the field with the others, led by Ned.

"I dote upon it ; my sister Meg used to ride, when papa was rich, but we don't keep any horses now—except Ellen Tree," added Amy, laughing.

"Tell me about Ellen Tree ; is it a donkey ? " asked Grace.

"Why, you see, Jo is crazy about horses, and so am I, but we've only got an old side-saddle and no horse. Out in our garden is an apple tree, that has a nice low branch ; so I put the saddle on it, fixed some reins on the part that turns up, and we bounce away on Ellen Tree whenever we like."

"How funny ! " laughed Grace. " I have a pony at home, and ride nearly every day in the park, with Fred and Kate."

Frank, sitting just behind the little girls, heard

what they were saying, and pushed his crutch away from him with an impatient gesture, as he watched the active lads going through all sorts of comical gymnastics. Beth, who was collecting the scattered Author cards, looked up, and said, in her shy yet friendly way--

" I'm afraid you are tired ; can I do anything for you ? "

"Talk to me, please ; it's dull, sitting by myself," answered Frank, who had evidently been used to being made much of at home.

If he had asked her to deliver a Latin oration, it would not have seemed a more impossible task to bashful Beth ; but there was no place to run to, no Jo to hide behind now, and the poor boy looked so wistfully to her, that she bravely resolved to try.

" What do you like to talk about ? " she asked fumbling over the cards, and dropping half as she tried to tie them up.

" Well, I like to hear about cricket, and boating, and hunting," said Frank, who had not yet learned to suit his amusements to his strength.

" My heart ! whatever shall I do ! I don't know anything about them," thought Beth ; and, forgetting the boy's misfortune in her flurry, she said, hoping to make him talk, " I never saw any hunting, but I suppose you know all about it."

" I did once ; but I'll never hunt again, for I got hurt leaping a confounded five-barred gate ; so there's no more horses and hounds for me," said Frank with a sigh that made Beth hate herself for her innocent blunder.

" Your deer are much prettier than our ugly buffaloes," she said, turning to the prairies for help, and feeling glad that she had read one of the boys' books in which Jo delighted.

Buffaloes proved soothing and satisfactory ; and, in her eagerness to amuse another, Beth forgot herself, and was quite unconscious of her sister's surprise and delight at the unusual spectacle of Beth talking away to one of the dreadful boys, against whom she had begged protection.

"Bless her heart ! She pities him, so she is good to him," said Jo, beaming at her from the croquet ground.

"I haven't heard Frank laugh so much for ever so long," said Grace to Amy, as they sat discussing dolls, and making tea-sets out of the acorn-cups.

" My sister Beth is a very fastidious girl, when she likes to be," said Amy, well pleased at Beth's success. She meant " fascinating," but, as Grace didn't know the exact meaning of either word, " fastidious " sounded well, and made a good impression.

An impromptu circus, fox and geese, and an amicable game of croquet, finished the afternoon. At sunset the tent was struck, hampers packed, wickets pulled up, boats loaded, and the whole party floated down the river, singing at the tops of their voices. Ned, getting sentimental, warbled a serenade with the pensive refrain :—

> "Alone, alone, ah ! woe, alone."

and at the lines—

> "We each are young, we each have a heart,
> Oh, why should we stand thus coldly apart ? "

he looked at Meg with such a lackadaisical expression; that she laughed outright, and spoilt his song.

" How can you be so cruel to me ? " he whispered, under cover of a lively chorus ; " you've kept close to that starched-up Englishwoman all day, and now you snub me."

" I didn't mean to ; but you looked so funny I really couldn't help it," replied Meg, passing over the first part of his reproach ; for it was quite true that she *had* shunned him, remembering the Moffat party and the talk after it.

Ned was offended, and turned to Sallie for consolation, saying to her, rather pettishly, " There isn't a bit of flirt in that girl, is there ? "

" Not a particle ; but she's a dear," returned Sallie, defending her friend, even while confessing her shortcomings.

" She's not a stricken deer, anyway," said Ned, crying to be witty, and succeeding as well as very young gentlemen usually do.

On the lawn, where it had gathered, the little party separated with cordial good-nights and good-byes, for the Vaughans were going to Canada. As the four sisters went home through the garden, Miss Kate looked after them, saying, without the patronising tone in her voice, " In spite of their demonstrative manners, American girls are very nice when one knows them."

" I quite agree with you," said Mr. Brooke.

CHAPTER XIII.

CASTLES IN THE AIR.

LAURIE lay luxuriously swinging to and fro in his hammock, one warm September afternoon, wondering what his neighbours were about, but too lazy to go and find out. He was in one of his moods; for the day had been both unprofitable and unsatisfactory, and he was wishing he could live it over again. The hot weather made him indolent; and he had shirked his studies, tried Mr. Brooke's patience to the utmost, displeased his grandfather by practising half the afternoon, frightened the maid servants half out of their wits, by mischievously hinting that one of his dogs was going mad, and, after high words with the stableman about some fancied neglect of his horse, he had flung himself into his hammock, to fume over the stupidity of the world in general, till the peace of the lovely day quieted him in spite of himself. Staring up into the green gloom of the horse-chestnut trees above him, he dreamed dreams of all sorts, and was just imagining himself tossing on the ocean, in a voyage round the world, when the sound of voices brought him ashore in a flash. Peeping through the meshes of the hammock, he saw the Marches coming out, as if bound on some expedition.

" What in the world are those girls about now ? " thought Laurie, opening his sleepy eyes to take a good look, for there was something rather peculiar in the appearance of his neighbours. Each wore a large, flapping hat, a brown linen pouch slung over one shoulder, and carried a long staff ; Meg had a cushion, Jo a book, Beth a dipper, and Amy a portfolio. All walked quietly through the garden, out at the little back gate, and began to climb the hill that lay between the house and the river.

" Well, that's cool ! " said Laurie to himself, " to have a picnic and never ask me. They can't be going in the boat, for they haven't got the key. Perhaps they forgot it ; I'll take it to them and see what's going on."

Though possessed of half a dozen hats, it took him some time to find one ; then there was a hunt for the key, which was at last discovered in his pocket, so that the girls were quite out of sight when he leaped the fence and ran after them. Taking the shortest way to the boat-house, he waited for them to appear ; but no one came, and he went up the hill to take an observation. A grove of pines covered one part of it, and from the heart of this green spot came a clearer sound than the soft sigh of the pines, or the drowsy chirp of the crickets.

" Here's a landscape ! " thought Laurie, peeping through the bushes, and looking wide awake and good-natured already.

It *was* rather a pretty little picture ; for the sisters sat together in the shady nook, with sun and shadow flickering over them, the aromatic wind lifting their hair and cooling their hot cheeks, and all the little wood-people going on with their affairs as if these were no strangers, but old friends. Meg sat upon her cushion, sewing daintily with her white hands, and looking as fresh and sweet as a rose, in her pink dress, among the green. Beth was sorting the cones that lay thick under the hemlock near by, for she made pretty things of them. Amy was sketching a group of ferns, and Jo was knitting as she read aloud. A shadow passed over the boy's face as he watched them, feeling that he ought to go, because uninvited; yet lingering, because home seemed very lonely, and this quiet party in the woods most attractive to his restless spirit. He stood so still, that a squirrel, busy with its harvesting, ran down a pine close beside him, saw him suddenly, and skipped back, scolding so shrilly that Beth looked up, espied the wistful face behind the birches, and beckoned with a reassuring smile.

"May I come in, please? or shall I be a bother?" he asked.

Meg lifted her eyebrows, but Jo scowled at her defiantly, and said, at once, "Of course you may. We should have asked you before, only we thought you wouldn't care for such a girl's game as this."

"I always like your games; but if Meg don't want me, I'll go away."

"I've no objection, if you do something; it's against the rule to be idle here," replied Meg, gravely, but graciously.

"Much obliged; I'll do anything if you'll let me stop a bit, for it's as dull as the desert of Sahara down there. Shall I sew, read, cone, draw, or do all at once? Bring on your bears; I'm ready."

" Finish this story while I set my heel," said Jo, handing him the book.

" Yes'm," was the meek answer, as he began, doing his best to prove his gratitude for the favour of an admission into the " Busy Bee Society."

The story was not a long one, and, when it was finished, he ventured to ask a few questions as a reward of merit.

" Please, mum, could I inquire if this highly instructive and charming institution is a new one ? "

" Well, you see we used to play ' Pilgrim's Progress,' and we have been going on with it in earnest, all winter and summer."

" Yes, I know," said Laurie, nodding wisely.

" Who told you ? " demanded Jo.

" Spirits."

" No, it was me ; I wanted to amuse him one night when you were all away, and he was rather dismal. He did like it, so don't scold Jo said Beth, meekly.

" You can't keep a secret. Never mind ; it saves trouble now."

" Go on, please," said Laurie, as Jo became absorbed in her work, looking a trifle displeased.

" Oh, didn't she tell you about this new plan of ours ? Well, we have tried not to waste our holidays, but each one has had a task, and worked at it with a will. The vacation is nearly over, the stints are all done, and we are so glad that we didn't dawdle."

" Yes, I should think so " ; and Laurie thought regretfully of his own idle days.

" Mother likes to have us out of doors as much

as possible ; so we bring our work here, and have nice times. For the fun of it we bring our things in these bags, wear the old hats, use poles to climb the hill, and play pilgrims, as we used to do years ago. We call this hill the 'Delectable Mountain,' for we can look far away and see the country where we hope to live some time."

Jo pointed, and Laurie sat up to examine ; for through an opening in the wood one could look across the wide, blue river,—the meadows on the other side,—far over the outskirts of the great city, to the green hills that rose to meet the sky. The sun was low, and the heavens glowed with the splendour of an autumn sunset. Gold and purple clouds lay on the hill-tops ; and rising high into the ruddy light were silvery white peaks, that shone like the airy spires of some Celestial City.

" How beautiful that is ! " said Laurie, softly, for he was quick to see and feel beauty of any kind.

" It's often so and we like to watch it, for it is never the same, but always splendid," replied Amy, wishing she could paint it.

" I wish the beautiful country up there was real, and we could ever go to it," said Beth, musingly.

" There is a lovelier country even than that, where we *shall* go, by and by, when we are good enough," answered Meg.

" It seems so long to wait, so hard to do ; I want to fly away at once, as those swallows fly, and go in at that splendid gate."

" You'll get there, Beth, sooner or later ; no fear of that," said Jo ; " I'm the one that will have to fight and work, and climb and wait, and maybe never get in after all."

"You'll have me for company, if that's any comfort. I shall have to do a deal of travelling before I come in sight of your Celestial City. If I arrive late, you'll say a good word for me, won't you, Beth?"

Something in the boy's face troubled his little friend; but she said cheerfully, with her quiet eyes on the changing clouds, "If people really want to go, and really try all their lives, I think they will get in; for I don't believe there are any locks on that door, or any guards at the gate. I always imagine it is as it is in the picture, where the shining ones stretch out their hands to welcome poor Christian as he comes up from the river."

"Wouldn't it be fun if all the castles in the air which we make could come true, and we could live in them?" said Jo, after a little pause.

"I've made such quantities it would be hard to choose which I'd have," said Laurie, lying flat, and throwing cones at the squirrel who had betrayed him.

"You'd have to take your favourite one. What is it?" asked Meg.

"If I tell mine, will you tell yours?"

"Yes, if the girls will too."

"We will. Now, Laurie!"

"After I'd seen as much of the world as I want to, I'd like to settle in Germany, and have just as much music as I choose. I'm to be a famous musician myself, and all creation is to rush to hear me; and I'm never to be bothered about money or business, but just enjoy myself, and live for what

I like. That's my favourite castle. What's yours, Meg ? "

Margaret seemed to find it a little hard to tell hers, and moved a brake before her face, as if to disperse imaginary gnats, while she said, slowly, " I should like a lovely house, full of all sorts of luxurious things ; nice food, pretty clothes, handsome furniture, pleasant people, and heaps of money. I am to be mistress of it, and manage as I like, with plenty of servants, so I never need work a bit. How I should enjoy it ! for I wouldn't be idle, but do good, and make every one love me dearly."

" Wouldn't you have a master for your castle in the air ? " asked Laurie, slyly.

" I said ' pleasant people,' you know "; and Meg carefully tied up her shoe as she spoke, so that no one saw her face.

" Why don't you say you'd have a splendid, wise, good husband, and some angelic little children ? You know your castle wouldn't be perfect without," said blunt Jo, who had no tender fancies yet, and rather scorned romance, except in books.

" You'd have nothing but horses, inkstands, and novels in yours," answered Meg, petulantly.

" Wouldn't I, though ? I'd have a stable full of Arabian steeds, rooms piled with books, and I'd write out of a magic inkstand, so that my works should be as famous as Laurie's music. I want to do something splendid before I go into my castle—something heroic, or wonderful—that won't be forgotten after I'm dead, I don't know what, but I'm on the watch for it, and mean to astonish you all, some day. I think I shall write books, and get rich and famous; that would suit me, so that is *my* favourite dream."

"Mine is to stay at home safe with father and mother, and help take care of the family," said Beth, contentedly.

"Don't you wish for anything else?" asked Laurie.

"Since I had my little piano I am perfectly satisfied. I only wish we may all keep well, and be together; nothing else."

"I have lots of wishes; but the pet one is to be an artist, and go to Rome, and do fine pictures, and be the best artist in the whole world," was Amy's modest desire.

"We're an ambitious set, aren't we? Every one of us, but Beth, wants to be rich and famous, and gorgeous in every respect. I do wonder if any of us will ever get our wishes," said Laurie, chewing grass like a meditative calf.

"I've got the key to my castle in the air; but whether I can unlock the door remains to be seen," observed Jo, mysteriously.

"I've got the key to mine, but I'm not allowed to try it. Hang college!" muttered Laurie, with an impatient sigh.

"Here's mine!" and Amy waved her pencil.

"I haven't got any," said Meg, forlornly.

"Yes, you have," said Laurie, at once.

"Where?"

"In your face."

"Nonsense! that's of no use."

"Wait and see if it doesn't bring you something worth having," replied the boy, laughing at the thought of a charming little secret which he fancied he knew.

"If we are all alive ten years hence, let's meet and see how many of us have got our wishes, or how much nearer we are then than now," said Jo, always ready with a plan.

"I hope I shall have done something to be proud of by that time; but I'm such a lazy dog, I'm afraid I shall ' dawdle,' Jo."

"You need a motive, mother says; and when you get it, she is sure you'll work splendidly.

"Is she? By Jupiter I will, if I only get the chance!" cried Laurie, sitting up with sudden energy. "I ought to be satisfied to please grand-father, and I do try, but it's working against the grain, you see, and comes hard. He wants me to be an India merchant, as he was, and I'd rather be shot; I hate tea, and silks, and spices, and every sort of rubbish his old ships bring, and I don't care how soon they go to the bottom when I own them. Going to college ought to satisfy him, for if I give him four years he ought to let me off from the business; but he's set, and I've got to do just as he did, unless I break away and please myself, as my father did. If there was any one left to stay with the old gentleman, I'd do it to-morrow."

Laurie spoke excitedly, and looked ready to carry his threat into execution on the slightest provocation; for he was growing up very fast, and, in spite of his indolent ways, had a young man's hatred of subjection and restless longing to try the world for himself.

"I advise you to sail away in one of your ships;

and never come home again till you have tried your own way," said Jo, whose imagination was fired by the thought of such a daring exploit, and whose sympathy was considerably excited by what she called "Teddy's wrongs."

"That's not right, Jo; and you mustn't talk in that way, and Laurie mustn't take your bad advice. You should do just what your grandfather wishes, my dear boy," said Meg, in her most maternal tone. "Do your best at college, and when he sees that you try to please him, I'm sure he won't be hard or unjust to you. As you say, there is no one else to stay with and love him, and you'd never forgive yourself if you left him without his permission. Don't be dismal, or fret, but do your duty; and you'll get your reward, as good Mr. Brooke has, by being respected and loved."

"What do you know about him?" asked Laurie, grateful for the good advice, but objecting to the lecture.

"Only what your grandpa told mother about him; how he took good care of his own mother till she died, and wouldn't go abroad as tutor to some nice person, because he wouldn't leave her; and how he provides now for an old woman who nursed his mother; and never tells any one, but is just as generous, and patient, and good as he can be."

"So he is, dear old fellow!" said Laurie, heartily, as Meg paused, looking flushed and earnest, with her story. "It's like grandpa to find out all about him, without letting him know, and to tell all his goodness to others, so that they might like him. Brooke couldn't understand why your mother was so kind to him, asking him over with me, and treating him in her beautiful friendly way. He thought she was just perfect, and talked about it for days and days, and went on about you all, in flaming style. If ever I do get my wish, you see what I'll do for Brooke."

"Begin to do something now, by not plaguing his life out," said Meg, sharply.

"How do you know I do, miss ? "

"I can always tell by his face, when he goes away. If you have been good, he looks satisfied, and walks briskly ; if you have plagued him, he's sober, and walks slowly, as if he wanted to go back and do his work better."

"Well, I like that ! So you keep an account of my good and bad marks in Brooke's face, do you ? I see him bow and smile as he passes your window, but I didn't know you'd got up a telegraph."

"We haven't ; don't be angry, and oh, don't tell him I said anything ! It was only to show that I cared how you get on, and what is said here is said in confidence, you know," cried Meg, much alarmed at the thought of what might follow from her careless speech.

"*I* don't tell tales," replied Laurie, with his "high and mighty" air, as Jo called a certain expression which he occasionally wore. "Only if Brooke is going to be a thermometer, I must mind and have fair weather for him to report."

"Please don't be offended ; I didn't mean to preach or tell tales, or be silly ; I only thought Jo was encouraging you in a feeling which you'd be sorry for by and by. You are so kind to us, we feel as if you were our brother, and say just what we think ; forgive me, I meant it kindly ! " and Meg offered her hand with a gesture both affectionate and timid.

Ashamed of his momentary pique, Laurie squeezed the kind little hand, and said, frankly, " I'm the one to be forgiven ; I'm cross, and have been out of sorts all day. I like to have you tell me my faults, and be sisterly ; so don't mind if I am grumpy sometimes ; I thank you all the same."

Bent on showing that he was not offended, he made himself as agreeable as possible ; wound cotton for Meg, recited poetry to please Jo, shook down cones for Beth, and helped Amy with her ferns,—proving himself a fit person to belong to the " Busy Bee Society." In the midst of an animated discussion on the domestic habits of turtles (one of which amiable creatures having strolled up from the river), the faint sound of a bell warned them that Hannah had put the tea " to draw," and they would have just time to get home to supper.

" May I come again ? " asked Laurie.

" Yes, if you are good, and love your book, as the boys in the primer are told to do," said Meg, smiling.

That night, when Beth played to Mr. Laurence in the twilight, Laurie, standing in the shadow of the curtain, listened to the little David, whose simple music always quieted his moody spirit, and watched the old man, who sat with his grey head on his hand, thinking tender thoughts of the dead child he had loved so much. Remembering the conversation of the afternoon, the boy said to himself, with the resolve to make the sacrifice cheerfully, " I'll let my castle go, and stay with the dear old gentleman while he needs me, for I am all he has."

CHAPTER XIV.

SECRETS.

Jo was very busy up in the garret, for the October days began to grow chilly, and the afternoons were short. For two or three hours the sun lay warmly in at the high window, showing Jo seated on the old sofa writing busily, with her papers spread out upon a trunk before her, while Scrabble, the pet rat, promenaded the beams overhead, accompanied by his oldest son, a fine young fellow, who was evidently very proud of his whiskers. Quite absorbed in her work, Jo scribbled away till the last page was filled, when she signed her name with a flourish, and threw down her pen, exclaiming—

" There, I've done my best ! If this don't suit I shall have to wait till I can do better."

Lying back on the sofa, she read the manuscript carefully through, making dashes here and there, and putting in many exclamation points, which looked like little balloons ; then she tied it up with a smart red ribbon, and sat a minute looking at it with a sober, wistful expression, which plainly showed how earnest her work had been. Jo's desk up here was an old tin kitchen, which hung against the wall. In it she kept her papers, and a few books, safely shut away from Scrabble, who, being likewise of a literary turn, was fond of making a circulating library of such books as were left in his way, by eating the leaves. From this tin receptacle Jo produced another manuscript ; and putting both in her pocket, crept quietly down stairs, leaving her friends to nibble her pens and taste her ink.

She put on her hat and jacket as noiselessly as possible, and, going to the back entry window, got out upon the roof of a low porch, swung herself down to the grassy bank, and took a roundabout way to the road. Once there she composed herself, hailed a passing omnibus, and rolled away to town, looking very merry and mysterious.

If any one had been watching her, he would have thought her movements decidedly peculiar ; for, on alighting, she went off at a great pace till she reached a certain number in a certain busy street ; having found the place with some difficulty, she went into the doorway, looked up the dirty stairs, and, after standing stock still a minute, suddenly dived into the street, and walked away as rapidly as she came. This manœuvre she repeated several times, to the great amusement of a black-eyed young gentleman lounging in the window of a building opposite. On returning for the third time, Jo gave herself a shake, pulled her hat over her eyes, and walked up the stairs, looking as if she was going to have all her teeth out.

There was a dentist's sign, among others, which adorned the entrance, and, after staring a moment at the pair of artificial jaws which slowly opened and shut to draw attention to a fine set of teeth, the young gentleman put on his coat, took his hat, and went down to post himself in the opposite door-way, saying, with a smile and a shiver—

" It's like her to come alone, but if she has a bad time, she'll need some one to help her home."

In ten minutes Jo came running down stairs with a very red face, and the general appearance of a person who had just passed through a trying ordeal of some sort. When she saw the young gentleman she looked anything but pleased, and passed him with a nod ; but he followed, asking with an air of sympathy—

" Did you have a bad time ? "

" Not very."

" You got through quick."

" Yes, thank goodness ! "

" Why did you go alone ? "

" Didn't want any one to know."

" You're the oddest fellow I ever saw. How many did you have out ? "

Jo looked at her friend as if she did not understand him ; then began to laugh, as if mightily amused at something.

" There are two which I want to have come out, but I must wait a week."

" What are you laughing at ? You are up to some mischief, Jo," said Laurie, looking mystified.

" So are you. What were you doing, sir, up in that billiard saloon ? "

" Begging your pardon, ma'am, it wasn't a billiard saloon, but a gymnasium, and I was taking a lesson in fencing."

" I am glad you were not in the saloon, because I hope you never go to such places. Do you ? "

" Not often."

" I wish you wouldn't."

" It's no harm, Jo, I have billiards at home, but it's no fun unless you have good players ; so, as I'm fond of it, I come sometimes and have a game with Ned Moffat or some of the other fellows."

" Oh dear, I'm so sorry, for you'll get to liking it better and better, and will waste time and money, and grow like those dreadful boys. I did hope you'd stay respectable, and be a satisfaction to your friends," said Jo, shaking her head.

" Can't a fellow take a little innocent amusement now and then without losing his respectability ? " asked Laurie, looking nettled.

" That depends upon how and where he takes it. I don't like Ned and his set, and wish you'd keep out of it. Mother won't let us have him at our house, though he wants to come, and if you grow like him she won't be willing to have us frolic together."

" Won't she ? " asked Laurie, anxiously.

Laurie walked in silence a few minutes, and Jo watched him, wishing she had held her tongue, for his eyes looked angry, though his lips still smiled as if at her warnings.

" Are you going to deliver lectures all the way home ? " he asked presently.

" Of course not ; why ? "

" Because if you are, I'll take a 'bus ; if you are not, I'd like to walk with you, and tell you something very interesting."

" I won't preach any more, and I'd like to hear the news immensely."

" Very well, then ; come on. It's a secret, and if I tell you, you must tell me yours."

" I haven't got any," began Jo, but stopped suddenly, remembering that she had.

" You know you have ; you can't hide anything, so up and 'fess, or I won't tell," cried Laurie.

" Is your secret a nice one ? "

" Oh, isn't it ! all about people you know, and such fun ! You ought to hear it, and I've been aching to tell this a long time. Come ! you begin."

" You'll not say anything about it at home, will you ? "

" Not a word."

" And you won't tease me in private ? "

" I never tease."

" Yes, you do ; you get everything you want out of people. I don't know how you do it, but you are a born wheedler."

" Thank you ! fire away ! "

" Well, I've left two stories with a newspaper man, and he's to give his answer next week," whispered Jo, in her confidant's ear.

" Hurrah for Miss March, the celebrated American authoress ! " cried Laurie, throwing up his hat and catching it again, to the great delight of two ducks, four cats, five hens, and half a dozen Irish children ; for they were out of the city now.

" Hush ! it won't come to anything, I dare say ; but I couldn't rest till I had tried, and I said nothing about it, because I didn't want any one else to be disappointed."

" It won't fail ! Why, Jo, your stories are works of Shakespeare compared to half the rubbish that's published every day. Won't it be fun to see them in print; and shan't we feel proud of our authoress?"

Jo's eyes sparkled, for it's always pleasant to be believed in; and a friend's praise is always sweeter than newspaper puffs.

"Where's *your* secret? Play fair, Teddy, or I'll never believe you again," she said, trying to extinguish the brilliant hopes that blazed up at a word of encouragement.

"I may get into a scrape for telling; but I didn't promise not to, so I will, for I never feel easy in my mind till I've told you any plummy bit of news I get. I know where Meg's glove is."

"Is that all?" said Jo, looking disappointed, as Laurie nodded and twinkled, with a face full of mysterious intelligence.

"It's quite enough for the present, as you'll agree when I tell you where it is."

"Tell, then."

Laurie bent and whispered three words in Jo's ear, which produced a comical change. She stood and glared at him for a minute, looking both surprised and displeased, then walked on, saying sharply, "How do you know?"

"Saw it."

"Where?"

"Pocket."

"All this time?"

"Yes; isn't that romantic?"

"No, it's horrid."

"Don't you like it?"

"Of course I don't; it's ridiculous; it won't be allowed. My patience! what would Meg say?"

"You are not to tell any one ; mind that."

" I didn't promise."

" That was understood, and I trusted you."

" Well, I won't for the present, anyway ; but I'm disgusted, and wish you hadn't told me."

" I thought you'd be pleased."

" At the idea of anybody coming to take Meg away ? No, thank you."

" You'll feel better about it when somebody comes to take you away."

" I'd like to see any one try it," cried Jo, fiercely.

" So should I ! " and Laurie chuckled at the idea.

" I don't think secrets agree with me ; I feel rumpled up in my mind since you told me that," said Jo, rather ungratefully.

" Race down this hill with me, and you'll be all right," suggested Laurie.

No one was in sight ; the smooth road sloped invitingly before her, and, finding the temptation irresistible, Jo darted away, soon leaving hat and comb behind her, and scattering hair-pins as she ran. Laurie reached the goal first, and was quite satisfied with the success of his treatment.

" I wish I was a horse ; then I could run for miles in this splendid air, and not lose my breath. It was capital ; but see what a guy it's made me. Go, pick up my things, like a cherub as you are," said Jo, dropping down under a maple tree, which was carpeting the bank with crimson leaves.

Laurie leisurely departed to recover the lost property, and Jo bundled up her braids, hoping no one would pass by till she was tidy again. But some one did pass, and who should it be but Meg, looking particularly lady-like in her state and festival suit, for she had been making calls.

"What in the world are you doing here?" she asked.

"Getting leaves," meekly answered Jo, sorting the rosy handful she had just swept up.

"And hair-pins," added Laurie, throwing half-a-dozen into Jo's lap. "They grow on this road, Meg; so do combs and brown straw hats."

"You have been running, Jo; how could you? When *will* you stop such romping ways?" said Meg, reprovingly, as she settled her cuffs and smoothed her hair, with which the wind had taken liberties.

"Never till I'm stiff and old, and have to use a crutch. Don't try to make me grow up before my time, Meg; it's hard enough to have you change all of a sudden; let me be a girl as long as I can."

As she spoke, Jo bent over her work to hide the trembling of her lips; for lately she had felt that Margaret was fast getting to be a woman, and Laurie's secret made her dread the separation which must surely come some time, and now seemed very near. He saw the trouble in her face, and drew Meg's attention from it by asking, quickly, "Where have you been calling, all so fine?"

"At the Gardiners'; and Sallie has been telling me all about Belle Moffat's wedding. It was very splendid, and they have gone to spend the winter in Paris; think how delightful that must be!"

"Do you envy her, Meg?" said Laurie.

"I'm afraid I do."

"I'm glad of it!" muttered Jo, tying on her hat with a jerk.

"Why?" asked Meg, looking surprised.

"Because, if you care much about riches, you will never go and marry a poor man," said Jo, frowning at Laurie, who was mutely warning her to mind what she said.

"I shall never ' go and marry ' any one," observed Meg, walking on with great dignity, while the others followed, laughing, whispering, skipping stones, and "behaving like children," as Meg said to herself, though she might have been tempted to join them if she had not had her best dress on.

For a week or two Jo behaved so queerly that her sisters got quite bewildered. She rushed to the door when the postman rang; was rude to Mr. Brooke whenever they met; would sit looking at Meg with a woe-begone face, occasionally jumping up to shake, and then to kiss her, in a very mysterious manner; Laurie and she were always making signs to one another, and talking about "Spread Eagles," till the girls declared they had both lost their wits. On the second Saturday after Jo got out of the window, Meg, as she sat sewing at her window, was scandalized by the sight of Laurie chasing Jo all over the garden, and finally capturing her in Amy's bower. What went on there, Meg could not see, but shrieks of laughter were heard, followed by the murmur of voices, and a great flapping of newspapers.

"What shall we do with that girl? She never *will* behave like a young lady," sighed Meg, as she watched the race with a disapproving face.

"I hope she won't; she is so funny and dear as she is," said Beth, who had never betrayed that she was a little hurt at Jo's having secrets with any one but her.

"It's very trying, but we never can make her *comme la fo*," added Amy, who sat making some new frills for herself, with her curls tied up in a very becoming way,—two agreeable things, which made her feel unusually elegant and ladylike.

In a few minutes Jo bounced in, laid herself on the sofa, and affected to read.

"Have you anything interesting there?" asked Meg, with condescension.

"Nothing but a story; don't amount to much, I guess," returned Jo, carefully keeping the name of the paper out of sight.

"You'd better read it aloud; that will amuse us, and keep you out of mischief," said Amy in her most grown-up tone.

"What's the name?" asked Beth, wondering why Jo kept her face behind the sheet.

"The Rival Painters."

"That sounds well; read it," said Meg.

With a loud "hem!" and a long breath, Jo began to read very fast. The girls listened with interest, for the tale was romantic, and somewhat pathetic, as most of the characters died in the end.

"I like that about the splendid picture," was Amy's approving remark as Jo paused.

"I prefer the lovering part. Viola and Angelo are two of our favourite names; isn't that queer?" said Meg, wiping her eyes, for the "lovering part" was tragical.

"Who wrote it?" asked Beth, who had caught a glimpse of Jo's face.

The reader suddenly sat up, cast away the paper, displaying a flushed countenance, and, with a funny mixture of solemnity and excitement, replied in a loud voice, " Your sister !"

" You ? " cried Meg, dropping her work.

" It's very good," said Amy, critically.

" I knew it ! I knew it ! oh, my Jo, I *am* so proud ! " and Beth ran to hug her sister and exult over this splendid success.

Dear me, how delighted they all were, to be sure ; how Meg wouldn't believe it till she saw the words " Miss Josephine March " actually printed in the paper ; how graciously Amy criticised the artistic parts of the story, and offered hints for a sequel, which unfortunately couldn't be carried out, as the hero and heroine were dead ; how Beth got excited, and skipped and sung with joy ; how Hannah came in to exclaim, " Sakes alive, well I never ! " in great astonishment at " that Jo's doin's " ; how proud Mrs. March was when she knew it ; how Jo laughed with tears in her eyes, as she declared she might as well be a peacock and done with it ; and how the " Spread Eagle " might be said to flap his wings triumphantly over the house of March, as the paper passed from hand to hand.

" Tell us about it." " When did it come ? " " How much did you get for it ? " " What *will* father say ? " " Won't Laurie laugh ? " cried the family, all in one breath, as they clustered above Jo ; for these foolish, affectionate people made a jubilee of every little household joy.

" Stop jabbering, girls, and I'll tell you everything," said Jo, wondering if Miss Burney felt any grander over her "Evelina" than she did over her "Rival Painters." Having told how she disposed of her tales, Jo added—"And when I went to get my answer the man said he liked them both, but didn't pay beginners, only let them print in his paper, and noticed the stories. It was good practice, he said; and, when the beginners improved, any one would pay. So I let him have the two stories, and to-day this was sent to me, and Laurie caught me with it, and insisted on seeing it; so I let him; and he said it was good, and I shall write more, and he's going to get the next paid for, and oh—I *am* so happy, for in time I may be able to support myself and help the girls."

Jo's breath gave out here; and, wrapping her head in the paper, she bedewed her little story with a few natural tears; for to be independent, and earn the praise of those she loved, were the dearest wishes of her heart, and this seemed to be the first step toward that happy end.

CHAPTER XV.

A TELEGRAM.

"November is the most disagreeable month in the whole year," said Margaret, standing at the window one dull afternoon, looking out at the frost-bitten garden.

"That's the reason why I was born in it," observed Jo, pensively, quite unconscious of the blot on her nose.

" If something very pleasant should happen now, we should think it a delightful month," said Beth, who took a hopeful view of everything, even November.

" I dare say ; but nothing pleasant ever *does* happen in this family," said Meg, who was out of sorts. " We go grubbing along day after day, without a bit of change, and very little fun. We might as well be in a tread-mill."

Beth, who sat at the other window, said, smiling, " Two pleasant things are going to happen right away ; Marmee is coming down the street, and Laurie is tramping through the garden as if he had something nice to tell."

In they both came, Mrs. March with her usual question, " Any letter from father, girls ? " and Laurie to say, in his persuasive way, " Won't some of you come for a drive ? I've been pegging away at mathematics till my head is in a muddle, and I'm going to freshen my wits by a brisk turn. It's a dull day, but the air isn't bad, and I'm going to take Brooke home, so it will be gay inside, if it isn't out. Come, Jo, you and Beth will go, won't you ? "

" Of course we will."

" Can I do anything for you, Madam Mother ? " asked Laurie, with the affectionate look and tone he always gave her.

" No, thank you, except call at the office, if you'll be so kind, dear. It's our day for a letter, and the penny postman hasn't been. Father is as regular as the sun, but there's some delay on the way, perhaps."

A sharp ring interrupted her, and a minute after Hannah came in with a letter.

" It's one of them horrid telegraph things, mum," she said, handing it as if she was afraid it would explode.

At the word " telegraph," Mrs. March snatched it, read the two lines it contained, and dropped back into her chair as white as if the little paper had sent a bullet to her heart. Laurie dashed down stairs for water, Meg and Hannah supported her, and Jo read—

" MRS. MARCH :

" Your husband is very ill. Come at once.

" S. HALE,

" Blank Hospital, Washington."

How still the room was as they listened breathlessly! how strangely the day darkened outside! and how suddenly the whole world seemed to change, as the girls gathered about their mother, feeling as if all the happiness and support of their lives was about to be taken from them. Mrs. March was herself again directly ; read the message over, and stretched out her arms to her daughters, saying, in a tone they never forgot, " I shall go at once, but it may be too late ; oh, children, children! help me to bear it ! "

For several minutes there was nothing but the sound of sobbing in the room, mingled with broken words of comfort, tender assurances of help, and hopeful whispers, that died away in tears. Poor Hannah was the first to recover, and with unconscious wisdom, she set all the rest a good example ; for, with her, work was the panacea for most afflictions.

"The Lord keep the dear man! I won't waste no time a cryin', but git your things ready right away, mum," she said, heartily, as she wiped her face on her apron, gave her mistress a warm shake of the hand with her own hard one, and went away to work, like three women in one.

"She's right; there's no time for tears now. Be calm, girls, and let me think."

They tried to be calm, poor things, as their mother sat up, looking pale, but steady, and put away her grief to think and plan for them.

"Where's Laurie?" she asked presently, when she had collected her thoughts, and decided on the first duties to be done.

"Here, ma'am; oh, let me do something!" cried the boy, hurrying from the next room, whither he had withdrawn, feeling that their first sorrow was too sacred for even his friendly eyes to see.

"Send a telegram saying I will come at once. The next train goes early in the morning; I'll take that."

"What else? The horses are ready; I can go anywhere—do anything," he said, ready to fly to the ends of the earth.

"Leave a note at Aunt March's. Jo, give me pen and paper."

Tearing off the blank side of one of her newly-copied pages, Jo drew the table before her mother, well knowing that money for the long, sad journey, must be borrowed, and feeling as if she could do anything to add a little to the sum for her father.

"Now go, dear; but don't kill yourself driving at a desperate pace; there is no need of that."

Mrs. March's warning was evidently thrown away ; for five minutes later Laurie tore by the window, on his own fleet horse, riding as if for his life.

" Jo, run to the rooms, and tell Mrs. King that I can't come. On the way get these things. I'll put them down ; they'll be needed, and I must go prepared for nursing. Hospital stores are not always good. Beth, go and ask Mr. Laurence for a couple of bottles of old wine ; I'm not too proud to beg for father ; he shall have the best of everything. Amy, tell Hannah to get down the black trunk ; and Meg, come and help me find my things, for I'm half bewildered."

Writing, thinking, and directing all at once, might well bewilder the poor lady, and Meg begged her to sit quietly in her room for a little while, and let them work. Every one scattered, like leaves before a gust of wind ; and the quiet, happy household was broken up as suddenly as if the paper had been an evil spell.

Mr. Laurence came hurrying back with Beth, bringing every comfort the kind old gentleman could think of for the invalid, and friendliest promises of protection for the girls, during the mother's absence, which comforted her very much. There was nothing he didn't offer, from his own dressing-gown to himself as escort. But that last was impossible. Mrs. March would not hear of the old gentleman's undertaking the long journey ; yet an expression of relief was visible when he spoke of it, for anxiety ill fits one for travelling. He saw the look, knit his heavy eyebrows, rubbed his hands, and marched abruptly away, saying he'd be back directly. No one had time to think of him again till, as Meg ran through the entry, with a pair of rubbers in one hand and a cup of tea in the other, she came suddenly upon Mr. Brooke.

"I'm very sorry to hear this, Miss March," he said, in the kind, quiet tone which sounded very pleasantly to her perturbed spirit. "I came to offer myself as escort to your mother. Mr. Laurence has commissions for me in Washington, and it will give me real satisfaction to be of service to her there."

Down dropped the rubbers, and the tea was very near following, as Meg put out her hand, with a face so full of gratitude, that Mr. Brooke would have felt repaid for a much greater sacrifice than the trifling one of time and comfort which he was about to make.

"How kind you all are! Mother will accept, I'm sure; and it will be such a relief to know that she has some one to take care of her. Thank you very, very much!"

Everything was arranged by the time Laurie returned with a note from Aunt March, enclosing the desired sum, and a few lines repeating what she had often said before, that she had always told them it was absurd for March to go into the army, always predicted that no good would come of it, and she hoped they would take her advice next time. Mrs. March put the note in the fire, the money in her purse, and went on with her preparations, with her lips folded tightly, which Jo would have understood if she had been there.

The short afternoon wore away; all the other errands were done, and Meg and her mother busy at some necessary needlework, while Beth and Amy got tea, and Hannah finished her ironing with what she called "a slap and a bang," but still Jo did not come. They began to get anxious; and Laurie went off to find her, for no one ever knew what freak Jo might take into her head. He missed her, however, and she came walking in with a very queer expression of countenance, for there was a mixture of fun and fear, satisfaction and regret in it, which puzzled the family as much as did the roll of bills she laid before her mother, saying, with a little choke in her voice, "That's my contribution towards making father comfortable, and bringing him home!"

"My dear, where did you get it! Twenty-five dollars! Jo, I hope you haven't done anything rash?"

"No, it's mine honestly; I didn't beg, borrow, nor steal it. I earned it; and I don't think you'll blame me, for I only sold what was my own."

As she spoke, Jo took off her bonnet, and a general outcry arose, for all her abundant hair was cut short.

"Your hair! Your beautiful hair." "Oh, Jo, how could you? Your one beauty." "My dear girl, there was no need of this." "She don't look my Jo any more, but I love her dearly for it!"

As every one exclaimed, and Beth hugged the cropped head tenderly, Jo assumed an indifferent air, which did not deceive any one a particle, and said, rumpling up the brown bush, and trying to look as if she liked it, "It doesn't affect the fate of the nation, so don't wail, Beth. It will be good for my vanity; I was getting too proud of my wig. It will do my brains good to have that mop taken off; my head feels deliciously light and cool, and the barber said I could soon have a curly crop, which will be boyish, becoming, and easy to keep in order. I'm satisfied; so please take the money and let's have supper."

"Tell me all about it, Jo; *I* am not quite satisfied, but I can't blame you, for I know how willingly you sacrificed your vanity, as you call it, to your love. But, my dear, it was not necessary; I'm afraid you will regret it, one of these days," said Mrs. March.

"No, I won't!" returned Jo, stoutly, feeling much relieved that her prank was not entirely condemned.

"What made you do it?" asked Amy, who would as soon have thought of cutting off her head as her pretty hair.

"Well, I was wild to do something for father," replied Jo, as they gathered about the table, for healthy young people can eat even in the midst of trouble. "I hate to borrow as much as mother does, and I knew Aunt March would croak; she always does, if you ask for a ninepence. Meg gave all her quarterly salary toward the rent, and I only got some clothes with mine, so I felt wicked, and was bound to have some money, if I sold the nose off my face to get it."

"You needn't feel wicked, my child, you had no winter things, and got the simplest, with your own hard earnings," said Mrs. March, with a look that warmed Jo's heart.

"I hadn't the least idea of selling my hair at first, but as I went along I kept thinking *what* I could do, and feeling as if I'd like to dive into some of the rich stores and help myself. In a barber's window I saw tails of hair with the prices marked ; and one black tail, longer, but not so thick as mine, was forty dollars. It came over me all of a sudden that I had one thing to make money out of, and, without stopping to think, I walked in, asked if they bought hair, and what they would give for mine."

"I don't know how you dared to do it," said Beth.

"Oh, he was a little man who looked as if he merely lived to oil his hair. He rather stared, at first, as if he wasn't used to having girls bounce into his shop and ask him to buy their hair. He said he didn't care about mine, it wasn't the fashionable colour, and he never paid much for it in the first place ; the work put into it made it dear, and so on. It was getting late, and I was afraid, if it wasn't done right away, that I shouldn't have it done at all, and you know, when I start to do a thing, I hate to give it up ; so I begged him to take it, and told him why I was in such a hurry. It was silly, I dare say, but it changed his mind, for I got rather excited, and told the story in my topsy-turvy way, and his wife heard, and said so kindly—

" ' Take it, Thomas, and oblige the young lady ; I'd do as much for our Jimmy, any day, if I had a spire of hair worth selling.' "

"Who was Jimmy ? " asked Amy.

"Her son," she said, "who is in the army. How friendly such things make strangers feel, don't they ? She talked away all the time the man clipped, and diverted my mind nicely."

" Didn't you feel dreadfully, when the first cut came ? " asked Meg, with a shiver.

"I took a last look at my hair while the man got his things, and that was the end of it. I never snivel over trifles like that ; I will confess, though, I felt queer when I saw the dear old hair laid out on the table, and felt only the short, rough ends on my head. It almost seemed as if I'd an arm or a leg off. The woman saw me look at it, and picked out a long lock for me to keep. I'll give it to you, Marmee, just to remember past glories by ; for a crop is so comfortable I don't think I shall ever have a mane again."

Mrs. March folded the wavy, chestnut lock, and laid it away with a short grey one in her desk. She only said, " Thank you, deary," but something in her face made the girls change the subject, and talk as cheerfully as they could about Mr. Brooke's kindness, the prospect of a fine day to-morrow, and the happy times they would have when father came home to be nursed.

No one wanted to go to bed, when, at ten o'clock, Mrs. March put by the last finished job, and said, " Come, girls." Beth went to the piano and played the father's favourite hymn ; all began bravely, but broke down one by one till Beth was left alone, singing with all her heart, for to her music was always a sweet consoler.

"Go to bed, and don't talk, for we must be up early, and shall need all the sleep we can get. Good-night, my darlings," said Mrs. March, as the hymn ended, for no one cared to try another.

They kissed her quietly, and went to bed as silently as if the dear invalid lay in the next room.

Beth and Amy soon fell asleep in spite of the great trouble, but Meg lay awake thinking the most serious thoughts she had ever known in her short life. Jo lay motionless, and her sister fancied that she was asleep, till a stifled sob made her exclaim, as she touched a wet cheek—

" Jo, dear, what is it ? "

" My—my hair," burst out poor Jo, trying vainly to smother her emotion in the pillow.

It did not sound at all comical to Meg, who kissed and caressed the afflicted heroine in the tenderest manner.

" I'm not sorry," protested Jo, with a choke. " I'd do it again to-morrow, if I could. It's only the vain, selfish part of me that goes and cries in this silly way. Don't tell any one, it's all over now. I thought you were asleep, so I just made a little private moan for my one beauty. How came you to be awake ? "

" I can't sleep, I'm so anxious," said Meg.

" Think about something pleasant, and you'll soon drop off."

" I tried it, but felt wider awake than ever."

" What did you think of ? "

" Handsome faces ; eyes particularly," answered Meg smilingly, to herself, in the dark.

" What colour do you like best ? "

" Brown—that is sometimes—blue are lovely."

Jo laughed, and Meg sharply ordered her not to talk, then amiably promised to make her hair curl, and fell asleep to dream of living in her castle in the air.

The clocks were striking midnight, and the rooms were very still as a figure glided quietly from bed to bed, smoothing a coverlid here, setting a pillow there, and pausing to look long and tenderly at each unconscious face, to kiss each with lips that mutely blessed, and to pray the fervent prayers which only mothers utter. As she lifted the curtain to look out into the dreary night, the moon broke suddenly from behind the clouds, and shone upon her like a bright benignant face, which seemed to whisper in the silence, " Be comforted, there is always light behind the clouds."

CHAPTER XVI.

LETTERS.

In the cold grey dawn the sisters lit their lamp, and read their chapter with an earnestness never felt before, for now the shadow of a real trouble had come, showing them how rich in sunshine their lives had been. The little books were full of help and comfort ; and, as they dressed, they agreed to say good-bye cheerfully, hopefully, and to send their mother on her anxious journey unsaddened by tears or complaints from them. Everything seemed very strange when they went down ; so dim and still outside, so full of light and bustle within. Breakfast at that early hour seemed odd, and even Hannah's familiar face seemed unnatural as she flew about her kitchen with her night-cap on. The big trunk stood ready in the hall, mother's cloak and bonnet lay on the sofa, and mother herself sat trying to eat, but looking so pale and worn with sleeplessness and anxiety, that the girls found it very hard to keep their resolution.

Nobody talked much, but, as the time drew very near, and they sat waiting for the carriage, Mrs. March said to the girls—

"Children, I leave you to Hannah's care, and Mr. Laurence's protection ; Hannah is faithfulness itself, and our good neighbour will guard you as if you were his own. I have no fears for you, yet I am anxious that you should take this trouble rightly. Don't grieve and fret when I'm gone, or think that you can comfort yourselves by being idle, and trying to forget. Go on with your work as usual, for work is a blessed solace. Hope, and keep busy ; and, whatever happens, remember that you never can be fatherless."

The rattle of an approaching carriage made them all start and listen. That was the hard minute, but the girls stood it well ; no one cried, no one ran away, or uttered a lamentation, though their hearts were very heavy as they sent loving messages to father, remembering, as they spoke, that it might be too late to deliver them. They kissed their mother quietly, clung about her tenderly, and tried to wave their hands cheerfully, when she drove away.

Laurie and his grandfather came over to see her off, and Mr. Brooke looked so strong, and sensible, and kind, that the girls christened him " Mr. Greatheart," on the spot.

"Good-bye, my darlings ! God bless and keep us all," whispered Mrs. March, as she kissed one dear little face after the other, and hurried into the carriage.

As she rolled away, the sun came out, and, looking back, she saw it shining on the group at the gate, like a good omen. They saw it also, and smiled and waved their hands; and the last thing she beheld, as she turned the corner, was the four bright faces, and behind them, like a body-guard, old Mr. Laurence, faithful Hannah, and devoted Laurie.

"I feel as if there had been an earthquake," said Jo, as their neighbours went home to breakfast, leaving them to rest and refresh themselves.

"It seems as if half the house was gone," added Meg, forlornly.

Beth opened her lips to say something, but could only point to the pile of nicely-mended hose which lay on mother's table, showing that even in her last hurried moments she had thought and worked for them. It was a little thing, but it went straight to their hearts; and, in spite of their brave resolutions, they all broke down, and cried bitterly.

Hannah wisely allowed them to relieve their feelings; and, when the shower showed signs of clearing up, she came to the rescue, armed with a coffee-pot.

"Now, my dear young ladies, remember what your ma said, and don't fret; come and have a cup of coffee all round, and then let's fall to work, and be a credit to the family."

Coffee was a treat, and Hannah showed great tact in making it that morning.

"'Hope and keep busy;' that's the motto for us, so let's see who will remember it best. I shall go to Aunt March as usual; oh, won't she lecture, though!" said Jo, with returning spirit.

"I shall go to my Kings, though I'd much rather

stay at home and attend to things here," said Meg,
wishing she hadn't made her eyes so red.

"No need of that ; Beth and I can keep house
perfectly well. I think anxiety is very interesting,"
put in Amy, eating sugar.

The girls couldn't help laughing, and felt the
better for it, though Meg shook her head at the
young lady who could find consolation in a sugar-
bowl.

The sight of the turnovers made Jo sober again ;
and, when the two went out to their daily tasks,
they looked sorrowfully back at the window where
they were accustomed to see their mother's face.
It was gone ; but Beth had remembered the little
household ceremony, and there she was, nodding
away at them like a rosy-faced mandarin.

"That's so like my Beth ! " said Jo, waving her
hat, with a grateful face. "Good-bye, Meggy ;
I hope the Kings won't train to-day. Don't fret
about father, dear," she added, as they parted.

"And I hope Aunt March won't croak. Your
hair *is* becoming, and it looks very boyish and nice,"
returned Meg, trying not to smile at the curly head,
which looked comically small on her tall sister's
shoulders.

"That's my only comfort," and touching her hat
à la Laurie, away went Jo, feeling like a shorn sheep
on a wintry day.

News from their father comforted the girls very
much ; for, though dangerously ill, the presence
of the best and tenderest of nurses had already done
him good. Mr. Brooke sent a bulletin every day,
and, as the head of the family, Meg insisted on reading the despatches, which grew more and more

cheering as the week passed. At first, every one was eager to write, and plump envelopes were carefully poked into the letter-box, by one or other of the sisters, who felt rather important with their Washington correspondence. As one of these packets contained characteristic notes from the party, we will rob an imaginary mail, and read them :—

" MY DEAREST MOTHER—

" It is impossible to tell you how happy your last letter made us, for the news was so good we couldn't help laughing and crying over it. How very kind Mr. Brooke is, and how fortunate that Mr. Laurence's business detains him near you so long, since he is so useful to you and father. The girls are all as good as gold. Jo helps me with the sewing, and insists on doing all sorts of hard jobs. I should be afraid she might overdo, if I didn't know that her ' moral fit' wouldn't last long. Beth is as regular about her tasks as a clock, and never forgets what you told her. She grieves about father, and looks sober, except when she is at her little piano. Amy minds me nicely, and I take great care of her. She does her own hair, and I am teaching her to make button-holes and mend her own stockings. She tries very hard, and I know you will be pleased with her improvement when you come. Mr. Laurence watches over us like a motherly old hen, as Jo says ; and Laurie is very kind and neighbourly. He and Jo keep us merry, for we get pretty blue sometimes, and feel like orphans, with you so far away. Hannah is a perfect saint ; she does not scold at all, and always calls me ' Miss Margaret,' which is quite proper, you know, and treats me with respect.

We are all well and busy, but we long, day and night, to have you back. Give my dearest love to father, and believe me, ever your own

" MEG."

This note, prettily written on scented paper, was a great contrast to the next, which was scribbled on a big sheet of thin, foreign paper, ornamented with blots, and all manner of flourishes and curly-tailed letters :—

" MY PRECIOUS MARMEE—

"Three cheers for dear old father! Brooke was a trump to telegraph right off, and let us know the minute he was better. I rushed up garret the moment the letter came, and tried to thank God for being so good to us ; but I could only cry and say, ' I'm glad ! I'm glad ! ' Didn't that do as well as a regular prayer ? for I felt a great many in my heart. We have such funny times ; and now I can enjoy 'em, for everyone is so desperately good, it's like living in a nest of turtle-doves. You'd laugh to see Meg head the table, and try to be motherish. She gets prettier every day, and I'm in love with her sometimes. The children are regular archangels, and I—well, I'm Jo, and never shall be anything else. Oh, I must tell you that I came near having a quarrel with Laurie. I freed my mind about a silly little thing, and he was offended. I was right, but didn't speak as I ought, and he marched home, saying that he wouldn't come again until I begged pardon. I declared I wouldn't, and got mad. It lasted all day ; I felt bad, and wanted you very much. Laurie and I are both so proud, it's hard to beg pardon ; but I thought he'd come to it, for I *was* in the right.   He didn't come ; and just at night I remembered what you said when Amy fell into the river.   I read my little book, felt better, resolved not to let the sun set on *my* anger, and ran over to tell Laurie I was sorry. I met him at the gate, coming for the same thing. We both laughed, begged each other's pardon, and felt all good and comfortable again.

" I made a ' pome ' yesterday, when I was helping Hannah wash ; and, as father likes my silly little things, I put it in to amuse him. Give him the lovingest hug that ever was, and kiss yourself a dozen times, for your

" TOPSY-TURVY JO."

" A SONG FROM THE SUDS."

" Queen of my tub, I merrily sing,
    While the white foam rises high ;
And sturdily wash, and rinse, and wring,
    And fasten the clothes to dry ;
Then out in the free fresh air they swing,
    Under the sunny sky.

" I wish we could wash from our hearts and souls
    The stains of the week away,
And let water and air by their magic make
    Ourselves as pure as they ;
Then on the earth there would be indeed
    A glorious washing-day !

" Along the path of a useful life,
    Will heart's-ease ever bloom ;
The busy mind has no time to think
    Of sorrow, or care, or gloom ;
And anxious thoughts may be swept away,
    As we busily wield a broom.

> " I am glad a task to me is given,
>   To labour at day by day ;
> For it brings me health, and strength, and hope,
>   And I cheerfully learn to say,—
> ' Head you may think, Heart you may feel,
>   But Hand you shall work alway ! ' "

" DEAR MOTHER—

" There is only room for me to send my love,
and some pressed pansies from the root I have been
keeping safe in the house for father to see. I read
every morning, try to be good all day, and sing
myself to sleep with father's tune. I can't sing
' Land of the Leal ' now ; it makes me cry. Every one
is very kind, and we are as happy as we can be without you. Amy wants the rest of the page, so I must
stop. I didn't forget to cover the holders, and I
wind the clock and air the rooms every day.

" Kiss dear father on the cheek he calls mine. Oh,
do come soon to your loving

" LITTLE BETH."

" MA CHERE MAMMA—

" We are all well I do my lessons always and never
corroborate the girls. Meg is a great comfort to me
and lets me have jelly every night at tea its so good
for me Jo says because it keeps me sweet tempered.
Laurie is not as respeckful as he ought to be now I'm
almost in my teens, he calls me Chick and hurts
my feelings by talking French to me very fast
when I say Merci or Bon jour as Hattie King does.
The sleeves of my blue dress were all worn out
and Meg put in new ones but the full front came
wrong and they are more blue than the dress. I
felt bad but did not fret I bear my troubles well

but I do wish Hannah would put more starch in
my aprons and have buck wheats every day. Can't
she ? Didn't I make that interrigation point nice.
Meg says my punchtuation and spelling are disgrace-
ful and I am mortyfied but dear me I have so many
things to do I can't stop. Adieu, I send heaps of
love to Papa.

" Your affectionate daughter,
" AMY CURTIS MARCH."

" DEAR MISS MARCH—

" I jes drop a line to say we git on fust rate.
The girls is clever and fly round right smart. Miss
Meg is goin to make a proper good housekeeper ; she
has the liking for it, and gits the hang of things
surprisin quick. Jo does beat all for goin ahead,
but she don't stop to cal'k'late fust, and you never
know where she'd like to bring up. She done
out a tub of clothes on Monday, but she starched
'em afore they was wrenched, and blued a pink
dress till I thought I should a died a laughin. Beth
is the best of little creeters, and a sight of help to me,
bein so forehanded and dependable. She tries
to learn everything, and really goes to market beyond
her years ; likewise keeps accounts, with my help,
quite wonderful. We have got on very economical
so fur ; I don't let the girls hev coffee only once a
week, accordin to your wish, and keep em on plain
wholesome vittles. Amy does well about frettin,
wearin her best clothes and eatin sweet stuff.
Mr. Laurie is as full of didoes as usual, and turns the
house upside down frequent ; but he heartens up
the girls, and so I let em hev full swing. The old
man sends heaps of things, and is rather wearin, but

means wal, and it aint my place to say nothin. My bread is riz, so no more at this time. I send my duty to Mr. March, and hope he's seen the last of his Pewmonia.

> " Yours respectful,
> " HANNAH MULLET."

" HEAD NURSE OF WARD II.—

" All serene on the Rappahannock, troops in fine condition, commissary department well conducted, the Home Guard under Colonel Teddy always on duty, Commander-in-Chief General Laurence reviews the Army daily, Quartermaster Mullet keeps order in camp, and Major Lion does picket duty at night. A salute of twenty-four guns was fired on receipt of good news from Washington, and a dress parade took place at headquarters. Commander-in-Chief sends best wishes, in which he is heartily joined by

> " COLONEL TEDDY."

" DEAR MADAM—

" The little girls are all well ; Beth and my boy report daily ; Hannah is a model servant, guards pretty Meg like a dragon. Glad the fine weather holds ; pray make Brooke useful, and draw on me for funds if expenses exceed your estimate. Don't let your husband want anything. Thank God he is mending.

> " Your sincere friend and servant,
> " JAMES LAURENCE."

CHAPTER XVII.

LITTLE FAITHFUL.

FOR a week the amount of virtue in the old house would have supplied the neighbourhood. It was really amazing, for every one seemed in a heavenly frame of mind, and self-denial was all the fashion. Relieved of their first anxiety about their father, the girls insensibly relaxed their praiseworthy efforts a little, and began to fall back into the old ways. They did not forget their motto, but hoping and keeping busy seemed to grow easier; and, after such tremendous exertions, they felt that Endeavour deserved a holiday, and gave it a good many.

Jo caught a bad cold through neglecting to cover the shorn head enough, and was ordered to stay at home till she was better, for Aunt March didn't like to hear people read with colds in their heads. Jo liked this, and after an energetic rummage from garret to cellar, subsided on to the sofa to nurse her cold with arsenicum and books. Amy found that house-work and art did not go well together, and returned to her mud pies. Meg went daily to her kingdom, and sewed, or thought she did, at home, but much time was spent in writing long letters to her mother, or reading the Washing-

ton despatches over and over. Beth kept on with
only slight relapses into idleness or grieving. All
the little duties were faithfully done each day,
and many of her sisters also, for they were forgetful
and the house seemed like a clock, whose pen-
dulum was gone a-visiting. When her heart got
heavy with longings for mother, or fears for father,
she went away into a certain closet, hid her face
in the folds of a certain dear old gown, and made
her little moan, and prayed her little prayer quietly
by herself. Nobody knew what cheered her up
after a sober fit, but every one felt how sweet
and helpful Beth was, and fell into a way of
going to her for comfort or advice in their small
affairs.

All were unconscious that this experience was
a test of character; and, when the first excitement was over felt that they had done well, and
deserved praise. So they did ; but their mistake
was in ceasing to do well, and they learned this
lesson through anxiety and regret.

"Meg, I wish you'd go and see the Hummels ;
you know mother told us not to forget them," said
Beth, ten days after Mrs. March's departure.

"I'm too tired to go this afternoon," replied
Meg, rocking comfortably, as she sewed.

"I *have* been every day, but the baby is sick,
and I don't know what to do for it. Mrs. Hummel
goes away to work, and Lottchen takes care of it ;
but it gets sicker and sicker, and I think you or
Hannah ought to go."

Beth spoke earnestly, and Meg promised to go
to-morrow.

"Ask Hannah for some nice little mess, and take

it round, Beth; the air will do you good," said Jo, adding apologetically, " I'd go, but I want to finish my story."

"My head aches, and I'm tired, so I thought maybe some of you would go," said Beth.

"Amy will be in presently, and she will run down for us," suggested Meg.

So Beth lay down on the sofa, the others returned to their work, and the Hummels were forgotten. An hour passed, Amy did not come; Meg went to her room to try on a new dress; Jo was absorbed in her story, and Hannah was sound asleep before the kitchen fire, when Beth quietly put on her hood, filled her basket with odds and ends for the poor children, and went out into the chilly air with a heavy head and a grieved look in her patient eyes. It was late when she came back, and no one saw her creep upstairs and shut herself into her mother's room. Half an hour after Jo went to " mother's closet " for something, and there found Beth sitting on the medicine chest, looking very grave, with red eyes, and a camphor bottle in her hand.

"Christopher Columbus! what's the matter? " cried Jo, as Beth put out her hand as if to warn her off, and asked quickly—

"You've had scarlet fever, haven't you? "

"Years ago, when Meg did. Why? "

"Then I'll tell you—oh, Jo, the baby's dead! "

"What baby? "

"Mrs. Hummel's; it died in my lap before she got home," cried Beth, with a sob.

"My poor dear, how dreadful for you! I ought to have gone," said Jo, taking her sister in her lap as she sat down in her mother's big chair, with a remorseful face.

"It wasn't dreadful, Jo, only so sad! I saw in a minute that it was sicker, but Lottchen said her mother had gone for a doctor, so I took baby and let Lotty rest. It seemed asleep, but all of a sudden it gave a little cry, and trembled, and then lay very still. I tried to warm its feet, and Lotty gave it some milk, but it didn't stir, and I knew it was dead."

"Don't cry, dear! what did you do?"

"I just sat and held it softly till Mrs. Hummel came with the doctor. He said it was dead, and looked at Heinrich and Minna, who have got sore throats. 'Scarlet fever, ma'am; ought to have called me before,' he said, crossly. Mrs. Hummel told him she was poor, and had tried to cure baby herself, but now it was too late, and she could only ask him to help the others, and trust to charity for his pay. He smiled then, and was kinder, but it was very sad, and I cried with them till he turned all of a sudden, and told me to go home and take belladonna, or I'd have the fever."

"No, you won't!" cried Jo, hugging her close, with a frightened look. "Oh, Beth, if you should be sick I never could forget myself! What *shall* we do?"

"Don't be frightened, I guess I shan't have it badly; I looked in mother's book, and saw that it begins with headache, sore throat, and queer feelings like mine, so I did take some belladonna, and I feel better," said Beth, laying her cold hands on her hot forehead.

"If mother was only at home!" exclaimed Jo,

seizing the book, and feeling that Washington was an immense way off. She read a page, looked at Beth, felt her head, peeped into her throat, and then said, gravely, " You've been over the baby every day for more than a week, and among the others who are going to have it, so I'm afraid you're going to have it, Beth. I'll call Hannah; she knows all about sickness."

" Don't let Amy come ; she never had it, and I should hate to give it to her. Can't you and Meg have it over again ? " asked Beth, anxiously.

" I guess not ; don't care if I do ; serve me right, selfish pig, to let you go, and stay writing rubbish myself ! " muttered Jo, as she went to consult Hannah.

The good soul was wide awake in a minute, and took the lead at once, assuring Jo that there was no need to worry ; every one had scarlet fever, and, if rightly treated, nobody died ; all of which Jo believed, and felt much relieved as they went up to call Meg.

" Now I'll tell you what we'll do," said Hannah, when she had examined and questioned Beth ; " we will have Dr. Bangs, just to take a look at you, dear, and see that we start right ; then we'll send Amy off to Aunt March's, for a spell, to keep her out of harm's way, and one of you girls can stay at home and amuse Beth for a day or two."

" I shall stay, of course, I'm oldest," began Meg, looking anxious and self-reproachful.

" *I* shall, because it's my fault she is sick ; I told mother I'd do the errands, and I haven't," said Jo, decidedly.

"Which will you have, Beth? there ain't no need of but one," said Hannah.

"Jo, please"; and Beth leaned her head against her sister, with a contented look, which effectually settled that point.

"I'll go and tell Amy," said Meg, feeling a little hurt, yet rather relieved, on the whole, for she did not like nursing, and Jo did.

Amy rebelled outright, and passionately declared that she had rather have the fever than go to Aunt March. Meg reasoned, pleaded, and commanded, all in vain. Amy protested that she would *not* go; and Meg left her in despair, to ask Hannah what should be done. Before she came back, Laurie walked into the parlour to find Amy sobbing, with her head in the sofa cushions. She told her story, expecting to be consoled; but Laurie only put his hands in his pockets and walked about the room, whistling softly, as he knit his brows in deep thought. Presently he sat down beside her, and said, in his most wheedlesome tone, "Now be a sensible little woman, and do as they say. No, don't cry, but hear what a jolly plan I've got. You go to Aunt March's, and I'll come and take you out every day, driving or walking, and we'll have capital times. Won't that be better than moping here?"

"But it's dull at Aunt March's, and she is so cross," said Amy.

"It won't be dull with me popping in every day to tell you how Beth is, and take you out gallivanting. The old lady likes me, and I'll be as clever as possible to her, so she won't peck at us, whatever we do."

"Will you take me out in the trotting wagon with Puck ? "

"On my honour as a gentleman."

"And come every single day ? "

"See if I don't."

"And bring me back the minute Beth is well ? "

"The identical minute."

"Well—I guess—I will," said Amy, slowly.

"Good girl ! Sing out for Meg, and tell her you'll give in," said Laurie, with an approving pat, which annoyed Amy more than the "giving in."

Meg and Jo came running down to behold the miracle which had been wrought ; and Amy, feeling very precious and self-sacrificing, promised to go if the doctor said Beth was going to be ill.

"How is the little dear ? " asked Laurie ; for Beth was his pet, and he felt more anxious about her than he liked to show.

"She is lying down on mother's bed, and feels better. The baby's death troubled her, but I dare say she has only got cold. Hannah *says* she thinks so ; but she *looks* worried, and that makes me fidgety," answered Meg.

"What a trying world it is ! " said Jo, rumpling up her hair in a fretful sort of way. " No sooner do we get out of one trouble than down comes another. There don't seem to be anything to hold on to when mother's gone ; so I'm all at sea."

"Well, don't make a porcupine of yourself, it isn't becoming. Settle your wig, Jo, and tell me if I shall telegraph to your mother, or do anything ? " asked Laurie, who never had been reconciled to the loss of his friend's one beauty.

"That is what troubles me," said Meg. " I

think we ought to tell her if Beth is really ill, but Hannah says we mustn't, for mother can't leave father, and it will only make them anxious. Beth won't be sick long, and Hannah knows just what to do, and mother said we were to mind her, so I suppose we must, but it don't seem quite right to me."

"Hum, well, I can't say; suppose you ask grandfather, after the doctor has been."

"We will; Jo, go and get Dr. Bangs at once," commanded Meg; "we can't decide anything till he has been."

"Stay where you are, Jo; I'm errand boy to this establishment," said Laurie, taking up his cap.

"I'm afraid you are busy," began Meg.

"No, I've done my lessons for the day."

"Do you study in vacation time?" asked Jo.

"I follow the good example my neighbours set me," was Laurie's answer, as he swung himself out of the room.

"I have great hopes of my boy," observed Jo, watching him fly over the fence, with an approving smile.

"He does very well—for a boy," was Meg's somewhat ungracious answer, for the subject did not interest her.

Dr. Bangs came, said Beth had symptoms of the fever, but thought she would have it lightly, though he looked sober over the Hummel story. Amy was ordered off at once, and provided with something to ward off danger; she departed in great state, with Jo and Laurie as escort.

Aunt March received them with her usual condescension.

"What do you want now?" she asked, looking sharply over her spectacles.

Laurie retired to the window, and Jo told her story.

"No more than I expected, if you are allowed to go poking about among poor folks. Amy can stay and make herself useful if she isn't sick, which I've no doubt she will be,—looks like it now. Don't cry, child; it worries me to hear people sniff."

Amy *was* on the point of crying, but Laurie slyly pulled the parrot's tale, which caused Polly to utter an astonished croak in such a funny way, that she laughed instead.

"What do you hear from your mother?" asked the old lady, gruffly.

"Father is much better," replied Jo, trying to keep sober.

"Oh, is he? Well, that won't last long, I fancy, March never had any stamina," was the cheerful reply.

"Ha, ha! never say die, take a pinch of snuff, good-by, good-by!" squalled Polly, dancing on her perch, and clawing at the old lady's cap as Laurie tweaked him in the rear.

"Hold your tongue, you disrespectful old bird! and, Jo, you'd better go at once; it isn't proper to be gadding about so late with a rattle-pated boy like——"

"Hold your tongue, you disrespectful old bird!" cried Polly, tumbling off the chair with a bounce, and running to peck the "rattle-pated" boy, who was shaking with laughter.

"I don't think I *can* bear it, but I'll try,"

thought Amy, as she was left alone with Aunt March.

"Get along, you're a fright," screamed Polly, and at that rude speech Amy could not restrain a sniff.

CHAPTER XVIII.

DARK DAYS.

BETH did have the fever, and was much sicker than anyone, but Hannah and the doctor suspected. The girls knew nothing about illness and Mr. Laurence was not allowed to see her, so Hannah had everything all her own way, and busy Dr. Bangs did his best, but left a good deal to the excellent nurse. Meg stayed at home, lest she should infect the Kings, and kept house, feeling very anxious and a little guilty, when she wrote letters in which no mention was made of Beth's illness. She could not think it right to deceive her mother, but she had been bidden to mind Hannah, and Hannah wouldn't hear of " Mrs. March bein' told, and worried just for sech a trifle." Jo devoted herself to Beth day and night, not a hard task, for Beth was very patient, and bore her pain uncomplainingly as long as she could control herself. But there came a time when, during the fever fits, she began to talk in a hoarse, broken voice, and play on the coverlet, as if on her beloved little piano ; a time when she did not know the familiar faces round her, but addressed them by wrong names, and called imploringly for her mother. Then Jo grew frightened,

Meg begged to be allowed to write the truth, and even Hannah said she would " think of it, though there was no danger *yet*." A letter from Washington added to their trouble, for Mr. March had had a relapse.

How dark the days seemed now, how sad and lonely the house, and how heavy were the hearts of the sisters as they worked and waited, while the shadow of death hovered over the once happy home ! Then it was that Margaret, sitting alone with tears dropping often on her work, felt how rich she had been in things more precious than any luxuries money could buy ; in love, protection, peace, and health, the real blessings of life. Then it was that Jo, living in the darkened room, with that suffering little sister always before her eyes, and that pathetic voice always in her ears, learned to see the beauty and the sweetness of Beth's nature, to feel how deep and tender a place she filled in all hearts, and to acknowledge the worth of Beth's unselfish ambition, to live for others, and make home happy by the exercise of those simple virtues which all may possess, and which all should love and value more than talent, wealth, or beauty. And Amy, in her exile, longed eagerly to be at home, that she might work for Beth, feeling now that no service would be hard or irksome, and remembering, with regretful grief, how many neglected tasks those willing hands had done for her. Laurie haunted the house like a restless ghost, and Mr. Laurence locked the grand piano, because he could not bear to be reminded of the young neighbour who used to make the twilight pleasant for him. Everyone missed Beth, and even those who knew her best were surprised to find how many friends shy little Beth had made.

Meanwhile she lay on her bed with old Johanna at her side, for even in her wanderings she did not forget her forlorn *protégé*. She longed for her cats, but would not have them brought, lest they should get sick; and, in her quiet hours, she was full of anxiety about Jo. She sent loving messages to Amy, bade them tell her mother that she would write soon; and often begged for pencil and paper to try to say a word, that father might not think she had neglected him. But soon these intervals of consciousness ended, and she lay hour after hour tossing to and fro with incoherent words on her lips, or sank into a heavy sleep which brought her no refreshment. Dr. Bangs came twice a day, Hannah sat up at night, Meg kept a telegram in her desk all ready to send off at any minute, and Jo never stirred from Beth's side.

The first of December was a wintry day indeed to them, for a bitter wind blew, snow fell fast, and the year seemed getting ready for its death. When Dr. Bangs came that morning, he looked long at Beth, held the hot hand in both his own a minute, and laid it gently down, saying, in a low tone, to Hannah—

"If Mrs. March *can* leave her husband, she'd better be sent for."

Hannah nodded without speaking, for her lips twitched nervously; Meg dropped down into a chair as the strength seemed to go out of her limbs at the sound of those words, and Jo, after standing with a pale face for a minute, ran to the parlour, snatched up the telegram, and, throwing on her things, rushed out into the storm. She was soon back, and, while noiselessly taking off her cloak, Laurie came in with a letter, saying Mr. March was mending again. Jo read it thankfully, but the heavy weight did not seem lifted off her heart, and her face was so full of misery that Laurie asked—

"What is it ? is Beth worse ? "

"I've sent for mother," said Jo, tugging at her rubber boots.

"Good for you, Jo ! Did you do it on your own responsibility ? "

"No, the doctor told us to."

"Oh, Jo, it's not so bad as that ? " cried Laurie.

"Yes, it is ; she don't know us, she don't even talk about the flocks of green doves, as she calls the vine leaves on the wall ; she don't look like my Beth, and there's nobody to help us bear it ; mother and father both gone, and God seems so far away."

As the tears streamed fast down poor Jo's cheeks, she stretched out her hand in a helpless sort of way, as if groping in the dark, and Laurie took it in his, whispering—

"I'm here, hold on to me, Jo dear ! "

She could not speak, but she did "hold on," and the warm grasp of the friendly human hand comforted her sore heart, and seemed to lead her nearer to the Divine arm which alone could uphold her in her trouble. Laurie longed to say something tender and comfortable, but no fitting words came to him, so he stood silent, gently stroking her bent head as her mother used to do. Soon she dried the tears which had relieved her, and looked up.

"Thank you, Teddy, I'm better now ; I

don't feel so forlorn, and will try to bear it if it comes."

"Keep hoping for the best ; that will help you lots, Jo. Soon your mother will be here, and then everything will be right."

"I'm so glad father is better ; now she won't feel so bad about leaving him. Oh, me ! it does seem as if all the troubles came in a heap, and I got the heaviest part on my shoulders," sighed Jo, spreading her wet handkerchief, over her knees, to dry.

"Doesn't Meg pull fair ? " asked Laurie, looking indignant.

"Oh, yes, she tries to, but she don't love Bethy as I do ; and she won't miss her as I shall. Beth is my conscience, and I *can't* give her up ; I can't ! I can't ! "

Down went Jo's face into the wet handkerchief, and she cried despairingly, for she had kept up bravely till now, and never shed a tear. Laurie drew his hand across his eyes, but could not speak till he had subdued the choky feeling in his throat, and steadied his lips. Presently, as Jo's sobs quieted, he said, hopefully, " I don't think she will die ; she's so good, and we all love her so much."

" The good and dear people always do die," groaned Jo, but she stopped crying, for her friend's words cheered her up.

" Poor girl ! you're worn out. It isn't like you to be forlorn. Stop a bit ; I'll hearten you up in a jiffy."

Laurie went off two stairs at a time, and Jo laid her wearied head down on Beth's little brown hood, which no one had thought of removing from the table where she left it. It must have possessed some magic, for the submissive spirit of its gentle owner seemed to enter into Jo; and, when Laurie came running down with a glass of wine, she took it with a smile, and said, bravely, " I drink—Health to my Beth ! You are a good doctor, Teddy, and *such* a comfortable friend ; how can I ever repay you ? " she added.

" I'll send in my bill by and by ; and to-night I'll give you something that will warm the cockles of your heart better than quarts of wine," said Laurie, beaming at her with a face of suppressed satisfaction at something.

"What is it ? " cried Jo, forgetting her woes for a minute, in her wonder.

" I telegraphed to your mother yesterday, and Brooke answered she'd come at once, and she'll be here to-night, and everything will be all right. Aren't you glad I did it ? "

Laurie spoke very fast, and turned red and excited all in a minute, for he had kept his plot secret, for fear of disappointing the girls or harming Beth. Jo grew quite white, flew out of her chair, and the moment he stopped speaking she electrified him by throwing her arms round his neck, and crying out, with a joyful cry, " Oh, Laurie ! oh, mother ! I *am* so glad ! " She did not weep again, but laughed hysterically, and trembled and clung to her friend as if she was a little bewildered by the sudden news. Laurie, though decidedly amazed, behaved with great presence of mind ; he patted her back soothingly, and, finding that she was recovering, followed it up by a bashful kiss or two, which brought Jo round at once. Holding on to the banisters, she put him gently away, saying breathlessly, "Oh, don't! I didn't mean to; it was dreadful of me; but you were such a dear to go and do it in spite of Hannah, that I couldn't help flying at you. Tell me all about it, and don't give me wine again, it makes me act so."

"I don't mind," laughed Laurie, as he settled his tie. "Why, you see I got fidgety, and so did grandpa. We thought Hannah was overdoing the authority business, and your mother ought to know. She'd never forgive us if Beth—well, if anything happened, you know. So I got grandpa to say it was high time we did something, and off I pelted to the office yesterday, for the doctor looked sober, and Hannah most took my head off when I proposed a telegram. I never *can* bear to be ' marmed over ; ' so that settled my mind, and I did it. Your mother will come, I know, and the late train is in at two a.m. I shall go for her ; and you've only got to bottle up your rapture, and keep Beth quiet, till that blessed lady gets here."

"Laurie, you're an angel! How shall I ever thank you ? "

"Fly at me again ; I rather like it," said Laurie, looking mischievous—a thing he had not done for a fortnight.

"No, thank you. I'll do it by proxy, when your grandpa comes. Don't tease, but go home and rest, for you'll be up half the night. Bless you, Teddy ; bless you ! "

Jo had backed into a corner ; and, as she finished her speech, she vanished precipitately into the kitchen, where she sat down upon a dresser, and told the assembled cats that she was " happy, oh, *so* happy ! " while Laurie departed, feeling that he had made rather a neat thing of it.

"That's the interferingest chap I ever see ; but I forgive him, and do hope Mrs. March is coming on right away," said Hannah, with an air of relief, when Jo told the good news.

Meg had a quiet rapture, and then brooded over the letter, while Jo set the sick room in order, and Hannah " knocked up a couple of pies in case of company unexpected." A breath of fresh air seemed to blow through the house, and something better than sunshine brightened the quiet rooms ; everything appeared to feel the hopeful change ; and every time the girls met, their pale faces broke into smiles as they hugged one another, whispering, encouragingly, " Mother's coming, dear ! mother's coming ! " Every one rejoiced but Beth ; she lay in that heavy stupor, alike unconscious of hope and joy, doubt and danger. It was a piteous sight— the once rosy face so changed and vacant—the once busy hand so weak and wasted—the once smiling lips quite dumb—and the once pretty, well-kept hair scattered rough and tangled on the pillow. All day she lay so, only rousing now and then to mutter, " Water ! " with lips so parched they could hardly shape the word ; all day Jo and Meg hovered over her, watching, waiting, hoping, and trusting in God and mother ; and all night the snow fell, the bitter wind raged, and the hours dragged slowly by. But night came at last ; and every time the clock struck the sisters, still sitting on either side the bed, looked at each other with brightening eyes, for each hour brought help nearer. The doctor had been in to say that some change for better or worse would probably take place about midnight, at which time he would return.

Hannah, quite worn out, lay down on the sofa at the bed's foot, and fell asleep ; Mr. Laurence marched to and fro in the parlour, feeling that he would rather face a rebel battery than Mrs. March's anxious countenance as she entered ; Laurie lay on the rug, pretending to rest, but staring into the fire with the thoughtful look which made his black eyes beautifully soft and clear.

The girls never forgot that night, for no sleep came to them as they kept their watch, with that dreadful sense of powerlessness which comes to us in hours like those.

" If God spares Beth I never will complain again," whispered Meg, earnestly.

" If God spares Beth I'll try to love and serve Him all my life," answered Jo, with equal fervour.

" I wish I had no heart, it aches so," sighed Meg.

" If life is often as hard as this, I don't see how we ever shall get through it," added her sister, despondently.

Here the clock struck twelve, and both forgot themselves in watching Beth, for they fancied a change passed over her wan face. The house was still as death, and nothing but the wailing of the wind broke the deep hush. Weary Hannah slept on, and no one but the sisters saw the pale shadow which seemed to fall upon the little bed. An hour went by, and nothing happened except Laurie's quiet departure for the station. Another hour —still no one came ; and anxious fears of delay in the storm, accidents by the way, or worst of all, a great grief at Washington, haunted the poor girls.

It was past two, when Jo, who stood at the window thinking how dreary the world looked in its winding-sheet of snow, heard a movement by the bed, and, turning quickly, saw Meg kneeling before their mother's easy chair, with her face hidden. A dreadful fear passed coldly over Jo as she thought, " Beth is dead, and Meg is afraid to tell me."

She was back at her post in an instant, and to her excited eyes a great change seems to have taken place. The fever flush, and the look of pain, were gone, and the beloved little face looked so pale and peaceful in its utter repose, that Jo felt no desire to weep or to lament. Leaning low over this dearest of her sisters, she kissed the damp forehead with her heart on her lips, and softly whispered, " Good-by, my Beth ; good-by ! "

As if waked by the stir, Hannah started out of her sleep, hurried to the bed, looked at Beth, felt her hands, listened at her lips, and then, throwing her apron over her head, sat down to rock to and fro, exclaiming, under her breath, " The fever's turned ; she's sleepin' nat'ral ; her skin's damp, and she breathes easy. Praise be given ! Oh, my goodness me ! "

Before the girls could believe the happy truth, the doctor came to confirm it. He was a homely man, but they thought his face quite heavenly when he smiled, and said, with a fatherly look at them, " Yes, my dears ; I think the little girl will pull through this time. Keep the house quiet ; let her sleep, and when she wakes, give her——"

What they were to give, neither heard ; for both crept into the dark hall, and, sitting on the stairs, held each other close, rejoicing with hearts too full for words. When they went back to be kissed and cuddled by faithful Hannah, they found Beth lying, as she used to do, with her cheek pillowed on her hand, the dreadful pallor gone, and breathing quietly, as if just fallen asleep.

"If mother would only come now," said Jo, as the winter night began to wane.

"See," said Meg, coming up with a white, half-opened rose, " I thought this would hardly be ready to lay in Beth's hand to-morrow if she—went away from us. But it has blossomed in the night, and now I mean to put in it my vase here, so that when the darling wakes, the first thing she sees will be the rose, and mother's face."

Never had the sun risen so beautifully, and, never had the world seemed so lovely, as it did to the heavy eyes of Meg and Jo, as they looked out in the early morning, when their long, sad vigil was done.

"It looks like a fairy world," said Meg, smiling to herself, as she stood behind the curtain watching the dazzling sight.

"Hark!" cried Jo, starting to her feet.

Yes, there was a sound of bells at the door below, a cry from Hannah, and then Laurie's voice, saying, in a joyful whisper, "Girls! she's come! she's come!"

CHAPTER XIX.

AMY'S WILL.

WHILE these things were happening at home, Amy was having hard times at Aunt March's. She felt her exile deeply, and, for the first time in her life, realized how much she was beloved and petted at home. Aunt March never petted any one; she did not approve of it; but she meant to be kind, for the well-behaved little girl pleased her very much, and Aunt March had a soft place in her old heart for her nephew's children, though she didn't think proper to confess it. She really did her best to make Amy happy, but dear, me, what mistakes she made! Some old people keep young at heart in spite of wrinkles and grey hairs, can sympathise with little children's cares and joys, make them feel at home, and can hide wise lessons under pleasant plays, giving and receiving friendship in the sweetest way. But Aunt March had not this gift, and she worried Amy almost to death with her rules and orders, her prim ways, and long, prosy talks. Finding the child more docile and amiable than her sister, the old lady felt it her duty to try and counteract, as far as possible, the bad effects of home freedom and indulgence. So she took Amy in hand, and taught her as she herself had been taught sixty years ago; a process which carried dismay to Amy's soul, and made her feel like a fly in the web of a very strict spider.

She had to wash the cups every morning, and polish up the old-fashioned spoons, the fat silver teapot, and the glasses, till they shone. Then she must dust the room, and what a trying job that was! Not a speck escaped Aunt March's eye, and all the furniture had claw legs, and much carving, which was never dusted to suit. Then Polly must be fed, the lap-dog combed, and a dozen trips up-stairs and down, to get things or deliver orders, for the old lady was very lame, and seldom left her big chair. After these tiresome labours she must do her lessons, which was a daily trial of every virtue she possessed. Then she was allowed one hour for exercise or play, and didn't she enjoy it? Laurie came every day, and wheedled Aunt March till Amy was allowed to go out with him, when they walked and rode, and had capital times. After dinner she had to read aloud, and sit still while the old lady slept, which she usually did for an hour, as she dropped off over the first page. Then patch-work or towels appeared, and Amy sewed with outward meekness and inward rebellion till dusk, when she was allowed to amuse herself as she liked, till tea-time. The evenings were the worst of all, for Aunt March fell to telling long stories about her youth, which were so unutterably dull, that Amy was always ready to go to bed, intending to cry over her hard fate, but usually going to sleep before she had squeezed out more than a tear or two.

If it had not been for Laurie and old Esther, the maid, she felt that she never could have got through that dreadful time. The parrot alone was enough to drive her distracted, for he soon felt that she did not admire him, and revenged himself by being as mischievous as possible. He pulled her hair whenever she came near him, upset his bread and milk to plague her when she had newly cleaned his cage, made Mop bark by pecking at him while Madame dozed; called her names before company, and behaved in all respects like a reprehensible old bird. Then she could not endure the dog, a fat, cross beast, who snarled and yelped at her when she made his toilet, and who laid on his back with all his legs in the air, and a most idiotic expression of countenance, when he wanted something to eat, which was about a dozen times a day. The cook was bad-tempered, the old coachman deaf, and Esther the only one who ever took any notice of the young lady.

Esther was a Frenchwoman, who had lived with "Madame," as she called her mistress, for many years, and who rather tyrannized over the old lady, who could not get along without her. Her real name was Estelle; but Aunt March ordered her to change it, and she obeyed, on condition that she was never asked to change her religion. She took a fancy to Mademoiselle, and amused her very much, with odd stories of her life in France, when Amy sat with her while she got up Madame's laces. She also allowed her to roam about the great house, and examine the curious and pretty things stored away in the big wardrobes and the ancient chests; for Aunt March hoarded like a magpie. Amy's chief delight was an Indian cabinet full of queer drawers, like pigeon-holes, and secret places in which were kept all sorts of ornaments, some precious, some merely curious, all more or less antique. To examine and arrange these things gave Amy great satisfaction, especially the jewel-cases; in which, on velvet cushions, reposed the ornaments which had adorned a belle forty years ago. There was the garnet set which Aunt March wore when she came out, the pearls her father gave her on her wedding day, her lover's diamonds, the jet mourning rings and pins, the queer lockets with portraits of dead friends, and weeping willows made of hair inside, the baby bracelets her one little daughter had worn, Uncle March's big watch, with a red seal so many childish hands had played with, and in a box, all by itself, lay Aunt March's wedding ring, too small now for her fat finger, but put carefully away, like the most precious jewel of them all.

"Which would Mademoiselle choose, if she had her will?" asked Esther, who always sat near to watch over and lock up the valuables.

"I like the diamonds best, but there is no neck-lace among them, and I'm fond of necklaces, they are so becoming. I should choose this if I might," replied Amy, looking with great admiration at a string of gold and ebony beads, from which hung a heavy cross of the same.

"I, too, covet that, but not as a necklace! ah, no! to me it is a rosary, and as such I should use it like a good Catholic," said Esther, eyeing the handsome thing wistfully.

"Is it meant to use as you use the string of

good-smelling wooden beads hanging over your glass ? " asked Amy.

" Truly, yes, to pray with. It would be pleasing to the saints if one used so fine a rosary as this, instead of wearing it as a vain bijou."

" You seem to take a deal of comfort in your prayers, Esther, and always come down looking quiet and satisfied. I wish I could."

" If Mademoiselle was a Catholic, she would find true comfort ; but, as that is not to be, it would be well if you went apart each day to meditate, and to pray, as did the good mistress whom I served before Madame. She had a little chapel, and in it found solacement for much trouble."

" Would it be right for me to do so too ? " asked Amy, who, in her loneliness, felt the need of help of some sort, and found that she was apt to forget her little book, now that Beth was not there to remind her of it.

" It would be excellent and charming ; and I shall gladly arrange the little dressing-room for you, if you like it. Say nothing to Madame, but when she sleeps go you and sit alone awhile to think good thoughts, and ask the dear God to preserve your sister."

Esther was truly pious, and quite sincere in her advice ; for she had an affectionate heart, and felt much for the sisters in their anxiety. Amy liked the idea, and gave her leave to arrange the light closet next her room, hoping it would do her good.

" I wish I knew where all these pretty things would go when Aunt March dies," she said, as she slowly replaced the shining rosary, and shut the jewel-cases one by one.

" To you and your sisters. I know it ; Madame confides in me ; I witnessed her will, and it is to be so," whispered Esther, smiling.

" How nice ! but I wish she'd let us have them now. Pro-cras-ti-nation is not agreeable," observed Amy, taking a last look at the diamonds.

" It is too soon yet for the young ladies to wear these things. The first one who is affianced will have the pearls—Madame has said it ; and I have a fancy that the little turquoise ring will be given to you when you go, for Madame approves your good behaviour and charming manners."

" Do you think so ? Oh, I'll be a lamb, if I can only have that lovely ring ! It's ever so much prettier than Kitty Bryant's. I do like Aunt March, after all " ; and Amy tried on the blue ring with a delighted face, and a firm resolve to earn it.

From that day she was a model of obedience, and the old lady complacently admired the success of her training. Esther fitted up the closet with a little table, placed a footstool before it, and over it a picture, taken from one of the shut-up rooms. She thought it was of no great value, but, being appropriate, she borrowed it. It was, however, a very valuable copy of one of the famous pictures of the world, and Amy's beauty-loving eyes were never tired of looking up at the sweet face of the divine mother, while tender thoughts of her own were busy at her heart. On the table she laid her little testament and hymn-book, kept a vase always full of the best flowers Laurie brought her, and came every day to "sit alone, thinking good thoughts, and praying the dear God to preserve her sister." Esther had given her a rosary of black beads, with a silver cross, but Amy hung it up, and did not use it, feeling doubtless as to its fitness for Protestant prayers.

The little girl was very sincere in all this, for, being left alone outside the safe home-nest, she felt the need of some kind hand to hold by so sorely, that she instinctively turned to the strong and tender Friend, whose fatherly love most closely surrounds His little children. She missed her mother's help to understand and rule herself, but having been taught where to look, she did her best to find the way, and walk it confidingly. But Amy was a young pilgrim, and just now her burden seemed very heavy. She tried to forget herself, to keep cheerful, and be satisfied with doing right, though no one saw or praised her for it. In her first effort at being very, very good, she decided to make her will, as Aunt March had done; so that if she *did* fall ill and die, her possessions might be justly and generously divided. It cost her a pang even to think of giving up the little treasures which in her eyes were as precious as the old lady's jewels.

During one of her play hours she wrote out the important document as well as she could, with some help from Esther as to certain legal terms; and, when the good-natured Frenchwoman had signed her name, Amy felt relieved, and laid it by to show Laurie, whom she wanted as a second witness. As it was a rainy day she went upstairs to amuse herself in one of the large chambers, and took Polly with her for company. In this room there was a wardrobe full of old-fashioned costumes, with which Esther allowed her to play, and it was her favourite amusement to array herself in the faded brocades, and parade up and down before the long mirror, making stately courtesies, and sweeping her train about, with a rustle which delighted her ears. So busy was she on this day, that she did not hear Laurie's ring, nor see his face peeping in at her, as she gravely promenaded to and fro, flirting her fan and tossing her head, on which she wore a great pink turban, contrasting oddly with her blue brocade dress and yellow quilted petticoat. She was obliged to walk carefully, for she had on high-heeled shoes, and, as Laurie told Jo afterwards, it was a comical sight to see her mince along in her gay suit, with Polly sidling and bridling just behind her, imitating her as well as he could, and occasionally stopping to laugh, or exclaim, "Ain't we fine ? Get along you fright ! Hold your tongue ! Kiss me, dear ; ha ! ha !"

Having with some difficulty restrained an explosion of merriment, lest it should offend her majesty, Laurie tapped, and was graciously received.

"Sit down and rest while I put these things away ; then I want to consult you about a very serious matter," said Amy, when she had shown her splendour and driven Polly into a corner. "That bird is the trial of my life," she continued, removing the pink mountain from her head, while Laurie seated himself astride of a chair.

" I'd wring your neck if you were mine, you old torment ! " cried Laurie, shaking his fist at the bird.

" Now I'm ready," said Amy, shutting the wardrobe and taking a paper out of her pocket. " I want you to read that, please, and tell me if it is legal and right. I felt that I ought to do it, for life is uncertain, and I don't want any ill-feeling over my tomb."

Laurie bit his lips, and turning a little from the pensive speaker, read the following document with praiseworthy gravity :—

" MY LAST WILL AND TESTMENT.

" I, Amy Curtis March, being in my sane mind, do give and bequeethe all my earthly property— viz. to wit :—namely

" To my father, my best pictures, sketches, maps, and works of art, including frames. Also my $100, to do what he likes with.

" To my mother, all my clothes, except the blue apron with pockets—also my likeness, and my medal, with much love.

" To my dear sister Margaret, I give my turkquoise ring (if I get it), also my green box with the doves on it, also my piece of real lace for her neck, and my sketch of her as a memorial of her ' little girl.'

" To Jo I leave my breast-pin, the one I mended with sealing wax, also my bronze inkstand—she lost the cover—and my most precious plaster rabbit, because I am sorry I burnt up her story.

"To Beth (if she lives after me) I give my dolls and the little bureau, my fan, my linen collars, and my new slippers if she can wear them, being thin, when she gets well. And I herewith also leave her my regret that I ever made fun of old Joanna.

"To my friend and neighbour Theodore Laurence I bequeethe my paper marshay portfolio, my clay model of a horse—though he did say it hadn't any neck. Also in return for his great kindness in the hour of affliction any one of my artistic works he likes, Noter Dame is the best.

"To our venerable benefactor Mr. Laurence I leave my purple box with a looking glass in the cover, which will be nice for his pens and remind him of the departed girl who thanks him for his favours to her family, specially Beth.

"I wish my favourite playmate Kitty Bryant to have the blue silk apron and my gold-bead ring with a kiss.

"To Hannah I give the band-box she wanted and all the patchwork I leave hoping she 'will remember me, when it you see.'

"And now having disposed of my most valuable property I hope all will be satisfied and not blame the dead. I forgive every one, and trust we may all meet when the trump shall sound. Amen.

"To this will and testiment I set my hand and seal on this 20th day of Nov. Anni Domino 1861.

"AMY CURTIS MARCH.

" *Witnesses* :—

    " ESTELLE VALNOR,
    " THEODORE LAURENCE."

The last name was written in pencil, and Amy explained that he was to re-write it in ink, and seal it up for her properly.

"What put it into your head? Did any one tell you about Beth's giving away her things?" asked Laurie, soberly, as Amy laid a bit of red tape, with sealing-wax, a taper, and a standish before him.

She explained; then asked, anxiously, "What about Beth?"

"I'm sorry I spoke; but as I did, I'll tell you. She felt so ill one day, that she told Jo she wanted to give her piano to Meg, her bird to you, and the poor old doll to Jo, who would love it for her sake. She was sorry she had so little to give, and left locks of hair to the rest of us, and her best love to grandpa. *She* never thought of a will."

Laurie was signing and sealing as he spoke, and did not look up till a great tear dropped on the paper. Amy's face was full of trouble; but she only said, "Don't people put sort of postscrips to their wills, sometimes?"

"Yes; 'codicils' they call them."

"Put one in mine then—that I wish *all* my curls cut off, and given round to my friends. I forgot it; but I want it done, though it will spoil my looks."

Laurie added it, smiling at Amy's last and greatest sacrifice. Then he amused her for an hour, and was much interested in all her trials. But when he came to go, Amy held him back to whisper, with trembling lips and tears in her eyes, "Is there really any danger about Beth?"

" I'm afraid there is ; but we must hope for the best, so don't cry, dear " ; and Laurie put his arm about her with a brotherly gesture which was very comforting.

When he had gone, she went to her little chapel, and, sitting in the twilight, prayed for Beth with streaming tears and an aching heart, feeling that a million turquoise rings would not console her for the loss of her gentle little sister.

CHAPTER XX.

CONFIDENTIAL.

I DON'T think I have any words in which to tell the meeting of the mother and daughters ; such hours are beautiful to live, but very hard to describe, so I will leave it to the imagination of my readers ; merely saying that the house was full of genuine happiness, and that Meg's tender hope was realized ; for when Beth woke from that long, healing sleep, the first objects on which her eyes fell *were* the little rose and mother's face. Too weak to wonder at anything, she only smiled, and nestled close into the loving arms about her, feeling that the hungry longing was satisfied at last. Then she slept again, and the girls waited upon their mother, for she would not unclasp the thin hand which clung to hers, even in sleep. Hannah had " dished up " an astonishing breakfast for the traveller, finding it impossible to vent her excitement in any other way ; and Meg and Jo fed their mother like dutiful young storks, while they listened to her whispered account of father's state, Mr. Brooke's promise to stay and nurse him, the delays which the storm occasioned on the homeward journey, and the unspeakable comfort Laurie's hopeful face had given her when she arrived, worn out with fatigue, anxiety and cold.

What a strange yet pleasant day it was; so brilliant and gay without, for all the world seemed abroad to welcome the first snow; so quiet and reposeful within, for every one slept, spent with watching, and a Sabbath stillness reigned through the house, while nodding Hannah mounted guard at the door. With a blissful sense of burdens lifted off, Meg and Jo closed their weary eyes, and lay at rest, like storm-beaten boats safe at anchor in a quiet harbour. Mrs. March would not leave Beth's side, but rested in the big chair, waking often to look at, touch, and brood over her child, like a miser over some recovered treasure.

Laurie, meanwhile, posted off to comfort Amy, and told his story so well that Aunt March actually "sniffed" herself, and never once said, "I told you so." Amy came out so strong on this occasion that I think the good thoughts in the little chapel really began to bear fruit. She dried her tears quickly, restrained her impatience to see her mother, and never even thought of the turquoise ring, when the old lady heartily agreed in Laurie's opinion, that she behaved "like a capital little woman." Even Polly seemed impressed, for he called her "good girl," blessed her buttons, and begged her to "come and take a walk, dear," in his most affable tone. She would very gladly have gone out to enjoy the bright wintry weather ; but, discovering that Laurie was dropping with sleep in spite of manful efforts to conceal the fact, she persuaded him to rest on the sofa, while she wrote a note to her mother. She was a long time about it ; and, when she returned, he was stretched out with both arms under his head, sound asleep, while Aunt March had pulled down the curtains, and sat doing nothing in an unusual fit of benignity.

After a while, they began to think he was not going to wake till night, and I'm not sure he would, had he not been effectually roused by Amy's cry of joy at sight of her mother. There probably were a good many happy little girls in and about the city that day, but it is my private opinion that Amy was the happiest of all, when she sat in her mother's lap and told her trials, receiving consolation and compensation in the shape of approving smiles and fond caresses. They were alone together in the chapel, to which her mother did not object, when its purpose was explained to her.

"On the contrary, I like it very much, dear," she said, looking from the dusty rosary to the well-worn little book, and the lovely picture with its garland of evergreen. "It is an excellent plan to have some place where we can go to be quiet, when things vex or grieve us. There are a good many hard times in this life of ours, but we can always bear them if we ask help in the right way. I think my little girl is learning this."

"Yes, mother ; and when I go home I mean to

have a corner in the big closet to put my books, and the copy of that picture which I've tried to make. The woman's face is not good, it's too beautiful for me to draw, but the baby's done better, and I love it very much. I like to think He was a little child once, for then I don't seem so far away, and that helps me."

As Amy pointed to the smiling Christ-child on his mother's knee, Mrs. March saw something on the lifted hand that made her smile. She said nothing, but Amy understood the look, and after a minute's pause, she added, gravely—

"I wanted to speak to you about this, but I forgot it. Aunt gave me the ring to-day; she called me to her and kissed me, and put it on my finger, and said I was a credit to her, and she'd like to keep me always. She gave me that funny guard to keep the turquoise on, as it's too big. I'd like to wear them, mother! Can I?"

"They are very pretty, but I think you're rather too young for such ornaments, Amy," said Mrs. March, looking at the plump little hand, with the band of sky-blue stones on the forefinger, and the quaint guard, formed of two tiny golden hands clasped together.

"I'll try not to be vain," said Amy; "I don't think I like it only because it's so pretty; but I want to wear it as the girl in the story wore her bracelet, to remind me of something."

"Do you mean Aunt March?" asked her mother, laughing.

"No, to remind me not to be selfish." Amy looked so earnest and sincere about it, that her

mother stopped laughing, and listened respectfully
to the little plan.

"I've thought a great deal lately about 'my
bundle of naughties,' and being selfish is the
largest one in it ; so I'm going to try hard to cure
it, if I can.   Beth isn't selfish, and that's the
reason every one loves her, and feels so bad at the
thoughts of losing her.   People wouldn't feel half
so bad about me if I were sick, and I don't deserve
to have them ; but I'd like to be loved and missed
by a great many friends, so I'm going to try and
be like Beth all I can.   I'm apt to forget my resolutions ; but, if I had something always about me
to remind me I should do better.   May I try this
way ? "

"Yes ; but I have more faith in the corner of
the big closet.   Wear your ring, dear, and do your
best ; I think you will prosper, for the sincere
wish to be good is half the battle.   Now, I must
go back to Beth.   Keep up your heart, little
daughter, and we will soon have you home again."

That evening, while Meg was writing to her
father, to report the traveller's safe arrival, Jo
slipped upstairs into Beth's room, and, finding her
mother in her usual place, stood a minute twisting
her fingers in her hair, with a worried gesture and
an undecided look.

"What is it, deary ? " asked Mrs. March, holding
out her hand, with a face which invited confidence.

"I want to tell you something, mother."

"About Meg ? "

"How quick you guessed !   Yes, it's about her,
and though it's a little thing, it fidgets me."

"Beth is asleep; speak low and tell me all about it. That Moffat hasn't been here, I hope?" asked Mrs. March, quickly.

"No; I should have shut the door in his face if he had," said Jo, settling herself on the floor at her mother's feet. "Last summer Meg left a pair of gloves over at the Laurences', and only one was returned. We forgot all about it, till Teddy told me that Mr. Brooke had it. He kept it in his waistcoat pocket, and once it fell out, and Teddy joked him about it, and Mr. Brooke owned that he liked Meg but didn't dare say so, she was so young and he so poor. Now isn't it a *dread*ful state of things?"

"Do you think Meg cares for him?" asked Mrs. March with an anxious look.

"Mercy me! I don't know anything about love, and such nonsense!" cried Jo, with a funny mixture of interest and contempt. "In novels, the girls show it by starting and blushing, fainting away, growing thin, and acting like fools. Now, Meg don't do anything of the sort; she eats and drinks and sleeps, like a sensible creature; she looks straight in my face when I talk about that man, and only blushes a little bit when Teddy talks about lovers."

"Then you fancy that Meg is *not* interested in John?"

"Who?" cried Jo, staring.

"Mr. Brooke; I call him 'John' now; we fell into the way of doing so at the hospital, and he likes it."

"Oh, dear! I know you'll take his part; he's

been good to father, and you won't send him away, but let Meg marry him, if she wants to. Mean thing! to go petting papa and truckling to you, just to wheedle you into liking him."

"My dear, don't get angry about it, and I will tell you how it happened. John went with me at Mr. Laurence's request, and was so devoted to poor father, that we couldn't help getting fond of him. He was perfectly open, honourable about Meg; for he told us he loved her, but would earn a comfortable home before he asked her to marry him. He only wanted our leave to love her and work for her, and the right to make her love him if he could. He is a truly excellent young man, and we could not refuse to listen to him; but I will not consent to Meg's engaging herself so young."

"Of course not; it would be idiotic! I knew there was mischief brewing; I felt it; and now it's worse than I imagined. I just wish I could marry Meg myself, and keep her safe in the family."

This odd arrangement made Mrs. March smile; but she said, gravely, "Jo, I confide in you, and don't wish you to say anything to Meg yet. When John comes back, and I see them together, I can judge better of her feelings towards him."

"She'll see his in those handsome eyes that she talks about, and then it will be all up with her. She's got such a soft heart, it will melt like butter in the sun if any one looks sentimentally at her. She read the short reports he sent more than your letters, and pinched me when I spoke of it, and likes brown eyes, and don't think John an ugly

name, and she'll go and fall in love, and there's an
end of peace and fun, and cosy times, together.
Brooke will scratch up a fortune somehow—carry
her off and make a hole in the family; and I shall
break my heart, and everything will be abominably
uncomfortable."

Jo leaned her chin on her knees in a disconsolate
attitude. Mrs. March sighed, and Jo looked up
with an air of relief.

"You don't like it, mother? I'm glad of it;
let's send him about his business, and not tell
Meg a word of it."

"I did wrong to sigh, Jo. It is natural and
right you should all go to homes of your own in
time; but I do want to keep my girls as long as I
can; and I am sorry that this happened so soon,
for Meg is only seventeen, and it will be some years
before John can make a home for her. Your
father and I have agreed that she shall not bind
herself in any way, nor be married, before twenty.
If she and John love one another, they can wait,
and test the love by doing so. She is conscientious,
and I have no fear of her treating him unkindly.
My pretty, tender-hearted girl! I hope things will
go happily with her."

"Hadn't you rather have her marry a rich
man?" asked Jo, as her mother's voice faltered
a little over the last words.

"Money is a good and useful thing, Jo; and I
hope my girls will never feel the need of it too
bitterly, nor be tempted by too much. I should
like to know that John was firmly established in
some good business, which gave him an income

large enough to keep free from debt, and make Meg comfortable. I'm not ambitious for a splendid fortune, a fashionable position, or a great name for my girls. If rank and money come with love and virtue also, I should accept them gratefully, and enjoy your good fortune; but I know by experience how much genuine happiness can be had in a plain little house, where the daily bread is earned, and some privations give sweetness to the few pleasures; I am content to see Meg begin humbly, for, if I am not mistaken, she will be rich in the possession of a good man's heart, and that is better than a fortune."

" I understand, mother, and quite agree; but I'm disappointed about Meg, for I'd planned to have her married to Teddy by and by, and sit in the lap of luxury all her days. Wouldn't it be nice ? "

" He is younger than she, you know," began Mrs. March ; but Jo broke in,—

" Oh, that don't matter; for he's old for his age, and tall; and can be quite grown-up in his manners, if he likes. Then he's rich, and generous, and good; and *I* say it's a pity my plan is spoilt."

" I'm afraid Laurie is hardly grown-up enough for Meg, and altogether too much of a weathercock, just now, for any one to depend on. Don't make plans, Jo ; but let time and their own hearts mate your friends. We can't meddle safely in such matters, and had better not get 'romantic rubbish,' as you call it, into our heads, lest it spoil our friendship."

" Well, I won't; but I hate to see things all going

criss-cross, and getting snarled up, when a pull here, and a snip there, would straighten it out. I wish wearing flat-irons on our heads would keep us from growing up. But buds will be roses, and kittens cats—more's the pity ! "

" What's that about flat-irons and cats ! " asked Meg, as she crept into the room, with the finished letter in her hand.

" Only one of my stupid speeches. I'm going to bed ; come on, Peggy," said Jo, unfolding herself like an animated puzzle.

" Quite right, and beautifully written. Please add that I send my love to John," said Mrs. March, after glancing over the letter.

" Do you call him ' John ' ? " asked Meg, smiling, with her innocent eyes looking down into her mother's.

" Yes ; he has been like a son to us, and we are very fond of him," replied Mrs. March, returning the look with a keen one.

" I'm glad of that ; he is so lonely. Good-night, mother, dear. It is so inexpressibly comfortable to have you here," Meg said.

The kiss her mother gave her was a very tender one ; and, as she went away, Mrs. March said, with a mixture of satisfaction and regret, " She does not love John yet, but wil' soon learn to."

CHAPTER XXI.

LAURIE MAKES MISCHIEF AND JO MAKES PEACE.

Jo's face was a study next day, for the secret rather weighed upon her, and she found it hard not to look mysterious and important. Meg observed it, but did not trouble herself to make inquiries, for she had learned that the best way to manage Jo was by the law of contraries, so she felt sure of being told everything if she did not ask. She was rather surprised, therefore, when the silence remained unbroken, and Jo assumed a patronising air, which decidedly aggravated Meg, who in her turn assumed an air of dignified reserve, and devoted herself to her mother. This left Jo to her own devices ; for Mrs. March had taken her place as nurse, and bid her rest, exercise, and amuse herself after her long confinement. Amy being gone, Laurie was her only refuge ; and, much as she enjoyed his society, she rather dreaded him just then, for he was an incorrigible tease, and she feared he would coax her secret from her.

She was quite right ; for the mischief-loving lad no sooner suspected a mystery, than he set himself to finding it out, and led Jo a trying life of it. He wheedled, bribed, ridiculed, threatened, and scolded ; affected indifference, that he might surprise the truth from her ; declared he knew, then that he didn't care ; and, at last, by dint of perseverance, he satisfied himself that it concerned Meg and Mr. Brooke. Feeling indignant that he was not taken into his tutor's confidence, he set his wits to work to devise some proper retaliation for the slight.

Meg meanwhile had apparently forgotten the matter, and was absorbed in preparations for her father's return ; but all of a sudden a change seemed to come over her, and, for a day or two, she was quite unlike herself. She started when spoken to, blushed when looked at, was very quiet, and sat over her sewing with a timid, troubled look on her face. To her mother's inquiries she answered that she was quite well, and Jo's she silenced by begging to be let alone.

" She feels it in the air—love, I mean—and she's going very fast. She's got most of the symptoms, is twittery and cross, don't eat, lies awake, and mopes in corners. I caught her singing that song about ' the silver-voiced brook,' and once she said ' John,' as you do, and then turned as red as a poppy. Whatever shall we do ? " said Jo, looking ready for any measures, however violent.

" Nothing but wait. Let her alone, be kind and patient, and father's coming will settle everything," replied her mother.

" Here's a note to you, Meg, all sealed up. How odd ! Teddy never seals mine," said Jo, next day, as she distributed the contents of the little post-office.

Mrs. March and Jo were deep in their own affairs,

when a sound from Meg made them look up to see her staring at her note, with a frightened face.

" My child, what is it ? " cried her mother, running to her, while Jo tried to take the paper which had done the mischief.

" It's all a mistake—he didn't send it—oh, Jo, how could you do it ? " and Meg hid her face in her hands, crying as if her heart was quite broken.

" Me ! I've done nothing ! What's she talking about ? " cried Jo, bewildered.

Meg's mild eyes kindled with anger, as she pulled a crumpled note from her pocket, and threw it at Jo, saying, reproachfully—

" You wrote it, and that bad boy helped you. How could you be so rude, so mean, and cruel to us both ? "

Jo hardly heard her, for she and her mother were reading the note, which was written in a peculiar hand.

" My Dearest Margaret—

" I can no longer restrain my passion, and must know my fate before I return. I dare not tell your parents yet, but I think they would consent if they knew that we adored one another. Mr. Laurence will help me to some good place, and then, my sweet girl, you will make me happy. I implore you to say nothing to your family yet, but to send one word of hope through Laurie to
" Your devoted
" John."

" Oh, the little villain ! that's the way he meant

to pay me for keeping my word to mother. I'll give him a hearty scolding, and bring him over to beg pardon," cried Jo, burning to execute justice. But her mother held her back, saying, with a severe look —

"Stop, Jo, you must clear yourself first. You have played so many pranks, that I'm afraid you have had a hand in this."

"On my word, mother, I haven't! I never saw that note before, and don't know anything about it, as true as I live!" said Jo, so earnestly that they believed her. "If I *had* taken a part in it I'd have done it better than this, and have written a sensible note. I should think you'd have known Mr. Brooke wouldn't write such stuff as that," she added, scornfully tossing down the paper.

"It's like his writing," faltered Meg, comparing it with the note in her hand.

"Oh, Meg, you didn't answer it?" cried Mrs. March, quickly.

"Yes, I did!" and Meg hid her face again, overcome with shame.

"Here's a scrape! *Do* let me bring that wicked boy over to explain, and be lectured. I can't rest till I get hold of him!" and Jo made for the door again.

"Hush! let me manage this, for it is worse than I thought. Margaret, tell me the whole story," commanded Mrs. March, sitting down by Meg, without looking up.

"I was worried at first, and meant to tell you; then I remembered how you liked Mr. Brooke, so I thought you wouldn't mind if I kept my little secret for a few days. I'm so silly that I liked to think no one knew ; and, while I was deciding what to say, I felt like the girls in books, who have such things to do. Forgive me, mother, I'm paid for my silliness now ; I never can look him in the face again."

"What did you say to him ? " asked Mrs. March.

"I only said I was too young to do anything about it yet ; that I didn't wish to have secrets from you, and he must speak to father. I was very grateful for his kindness, and would be his friend, but nothing more for a long while."

Mrs. March smiled, as if well pleased, and Jo clapped her hands, exclaiming, with a laugh—

"You are almost equal to Caroline Percy, who was a pattern of prudence ! Tell on, Meg. What did he say to that ? "

"He writes in a different way entirely ; telling me that he never sent any love-letter at all, and is very sorry that my roguish sister, Jo, should take such liberties with our names. It's very kind and respectful, but think how dreadful for me ! "

Meg leaned against her mother, looking the image of despair, and Jo tramped about the room, calling Laurie names. All of a sudden she stopped, caught up the two notes, and, after looking at them closely, said, decidedly, "I don't believe Brooke ever saw either of these letters. Teddy wrote both, and keeps yours to crow over me with because I wouldn't tell him my secret."

"Don't have any secrets, Jo ; tell it to mother,

and keep out of trouble, as I should have done,"
said Meg, warningly.

"Bless you, child! mother told me."

"That will do, Jo. I'll comfort Meg while you
go and get Laurie. I shall sift the matter to the
bottom, and put a stop to such pranks at once."

Away ran Jo, and Mrs. March gently told Meg
Mr. Brooke's real feelings. "Now, dear, what are
your own? Do you love him enough to wait till
he can make a home for you, or will you keep yourself quite free for the present?"

"I've been so scared and worried, I don't want
to have anything to do with lovers for a long while
—perhaps never," answered Meg, petulantly. "If
John *doesn't* know anything about this nonsense,
don't tell him, and make Jo and Laurie hold their
tongues. I won't be deceived and plagued, and
made a fool of—it's a shame!"

Seeing that Meg's usually gentle temper was roused
and her pride hurt by this mischievous joke, Mrs.
March soothed her by promises of entire silence and
great discretion for the future. The instant Laurie's
step was heard in the hall, Meg fled into the study,
and Mrs. March received the culprit alone. Jo had
not told him why he was wanted, fearing he wouldn't
come; but he knew the minute he saw Mrs. March's
face, and stood twirling his hat with a guilty air,
which convicted him at once. Jo was dismissed,
but chose to march up and down the hall like a
sentinel, having some fear that the prisoner might
bolt. The sound of voices in the parlour rose and
fell for half-an-hour; but what happened during
that interval the girls never knew.

When they were called in, Laurie was standing by their mother with such a penitent face, that Jo forgave him on the spot, but did not think it wise to betray the fact. Meg received his humble apology, and was much comforted by the assurance that Brooke knew nothing of the joke.

"I'll never tell him to my dying day—wild horses shan't drag it out of me; so you'll forgive me, Meg, and I'll do anything to show how out-and-out sorry I am," he added, looking very much ashamed of himself.

"I'll try; but it was a very ungentlemanly thing to do. I didn't think you could be so sly and malicious, Laurie," replied Meg, trying to hide her maidenly confusion under a gravely reproachful air.

"It was altogether abominable, and I don't deserve to be spoken to for a month; but you will, though, won't you?" and Laurie folded his hands together with such an imploring gesture, and rolled up his eyes in such a meekly repentant way, as he spoke, in his irresistibly persuasive tone, that it was impossible to frown upon him, in spite of his scandalous behaviour. Meg pardoned him, and Mrs. March's grave face relaxed, in spite of her efforts to keep sober, when she heard him declare that he would atone for his sins by all sorts of penances, and abase himself like a worm before the injured damsel.

Jo stood aloof, meanwhile, trying to harden her heart against him, and succeeded only in primming up her face into an expression of entire disapprobation. Laurie looked at her once or twice, but, as she showed no sign of relenting, he felt injured, and turned his back on her till the others were done with him, when he made her a low bow, and walked off without a word.

As soon as he had gone, she wished she had been more forgiving ; and, when Meg and her mother went upstairs, she felt lonely, and longed for Teddy. After resisting for some time, she yielded to the impulse, and, armed with a book to return, went over to the big house.

" Is Mr. Laurence in ? " asked Jo of a housemaid, who was coming downstairs.

" Yes, miss ; but I don't believe he's seeable just yet."

" Why not ; is he ill ? "

" La, no, miss ! but he's had a scene with Mr. Laurie, who is in one of his tantrums about something which vexes the old gentleman, so I dursn't go nigh him."

" Where is Laurie ? "

" Shut up in his room, and he won't answer, though I've been a-tapping. I don't know what's to become of the dinner, for it's ready, and there's no one to eat it."

" I'll go and see what the matter is. I'm not afraid of either of them."

Up went Jo, and knocked smartly at the door of Laurie's little study.

" Stop that, or I'll open the door and make you ! " called out the young gentleman, in a threatening tone.

Jo immediately pounded again ; the door flew open, and in she bounced, before Laurie could recover from his surprise. Seeing that he really *was* out of temper, Jo, who knew how to manage him, assumed a contrite expression, and, going artistically down upon her knees, said, meekly, " Please forgive me for being so cross. I came to make it up, and can't go away till I have."

" It's all right ; get up, and don't be a goose, Jo," was the cavalier reply to her petition.

" Thank you ; I will. Could I ask what's the matter ? You don't look exactly easy in your mind."

" I've been shaken, and I won't bear it ! " growled Laurie indignantly.

" Who did it ? " demanded Jo.

" Grandfather ; if it had been anyone else I'd have—" and the injured youth finished his sentence by an energetic gesture of the right arm.

" That's nothing ; I often shake you, and you don't mind," said Jo, soothingly.

" Pooh ! you're a girl, and it's fun ; but I'll allow no man to shake *me*."

" I don't think anyone would care to try it, if you looked as much like a thunder-cloud as you do now. Why were you treated so ? "

" Just because I wouldn't say what your mother wanted me for. I'd promised not to tell, and of course I wasn't going to break my word."

" Couldn't you satisfy your grandpa in any other way ? "

" No ; he *would* have the truth, the whole truth, and nothing but the truth. I'd have told my part of the scrape, if I could, without bringing Meg in. As I couldn't, I held my tongue, and bore the scolding till the old gentleman collared me. Then I got angry, and bolted, for fear I should forget myself."

" It wasn't nice, but he's sorry I know; so go down and make it up. I'll help you."

" Hanged if I do! I'm not going to be lectured and pummelled by everyone, just for a bit of a frolic. I *was* sorry about Meg, and begged pardon like a man; but I won't do it again, when I wasn't in the wrong."

" He didn't know that."

" He ought to trust me, and not act as if I was a baby. It's no use, Jo; he's got to learn that I'm able to take care of myself, and don't need any one's apron string to hold on by."

" What pepper-pots you are!" sighed Jo. " How do you mean to settle this affair?"

" Well, he ought to beg pardon, and believe me when I say I can't tell him what the row's about."

" Bless you! he won't do that."

" I won't go down till he does."

" Now, Teddy, be sensible; let it pass, and I'll explain what I can. You can't stay here, so what's the use of being melodramatic?"

" I don't intend to stay here long, anyway. I'll slip off and take a journey somewhere, and when grandpa misses me he'll come round fast enough."

" I dare say, but you ought not to go and worry him."

" Don't preach. I'll go to Washington and see Brooke; it's gay there, and I'll enjoy myself after the troubles."

"**What fun** you'd have! I wish I could run off too!" said Jo, forgetting her part of Mentor in lively visions of martial life at the capital.

"Come on then! Why not? You go and surprise your father, and I'll stir up old Brooke. It will be a glorious joke; let's do it, Jo! We'll leave a letter saying we are all right, and trot off at once. I've got money enough; it will do you good, and be no harm, as you go to your father."

For a moment Jo looked as if she would agree; for, wild as the plan was, it just suited her. She was tired of care and confinement, longed for change, and thoughts of her father blended temptingly with the novel charms of camp and hospitals, liberty and fun. Her eyes kindled as they turned wistfully towards the window, but they fell on the old house opposite, and she shook her head with sorrowful decision.

"If I was a boy, we'd run away together, and have a capital time; but as I'm a miserable girl, I must be proper, and stop at home. Don't tempt me, Teddy, it's a crazy plan."

"That's the fun of it!" began Laurie, who had got a wilful fit on him, and was possessed to break out of bounds in some way.

"Hold your tongue!" cried Jo, covering her ears. "'Prunes and prisms' are my doom, and I may as well make up my mind to it. I came here to moralize, not to hear about things that make me skip to think of."

"I knew Meg would wet-blanket such a proposal, but I thought you had more spirit," began Laurie, insinuatingly.

" Bad boy, be quiet.   Sit down and think of your own sins, don't go making me add to mine.   If I get your grandpa to apologise for the shaking, will you give up running away ? " asked Jo, seriously.

" Yes, but you won't do it," answered Laurie, who wished to " make up," but felt that his outraged dignity must be appeased first.

" If I can manage the young one I can the old one," muttered Jo, as she walked away, leaving Laurie bent over a railroad map, with his head propped up on both hands.

"Come in ! " and Mr. Laurence's gruff voice sounded gruffer than ever, as Jo tapped at his door.

" It's only me, sir, come to return a book," she said, blandly, as she entered.

" Want any more ? " asked the old gentleman, looking grim and vexed, but trying not to show it.

" Yes, please, I like old Sam so well, I think I'll try the second volume," returned Jo, hoping to propitiate him by accepting a second dose of " Boswell's Johnson," as he had recommended that lively work.

The shaggy eyebrows unbent a little, as he rolled the steps towards the shelf where the Johnsonian literature was placed. Jo skipped up, and sitting on the top step, affected to be searching for her book, but was really wondering how best to introduce the dangerous object of her visit. Mr. Laurence seemed to suspect that something was brewing in her mind ; for, after taking several brisk turns about the room, he faced round on her, speaking so abruptly, that "Rasselas" tumbled face downward on the floor.

"What has that boy been about? Don't try to shield him, now! I know he has been in mischief, by the way he acted when he came home. I can't get a word from him; and, when I threatened to shake the truth out of him, he bolted upstairs, and locked himself into his room."

"He did do wrong, but we forgave him, and all promised not to say a word to anyone," began Jo, reluctantly.

"That won't do; he shall not shelter himself behind a promise from you soft-hearted girls. If he's done anything amiss, he shall confess, beg pardon, and be punished. Out with it, Jo! I won't be kept in the dark."

Mr. Laurence looked so alarming, and spoke so sharply, that Jo would have gladly run away, if she could, but she was perched aloft on the steps, and he stood at the foot, a lion in the path, so she had to stay and brave it out.

"Indeed, sir, I cannot tell, mother forbid it. Laurie has confessed, asked pardon, and been punished quite enough. We don't keep silence to shield him, and it will make more trouble if you interfere. Please don't; it was partly my fault, but it's all right now, so let's forget it, and talk about the 'Rambler,' or something pleasant."

"Hang the 'Rambler!' come down and give me your word this harum-scarum boy of mine hasn't done anything ungrateful or impertinent. If he has, after all your kindness to him, I'll thrash him with my own hands."

The threat sounded awful, but did not alarm Jo, for she knew the irascible old man would never lift a finger against his grandson, whatever he might say to the contrary. She obediently obeyed, and made as light of the prank as she could without betraying Meg or forgetting the truth.

"Hum! ha! well, if the boy held his tongue because he'd promised, and not from obstinacy, I'll forgive him. He's a stubborn fellow, and hard to manage," said Mr. Laurence, rubbing up his hair till it looked as if he'd been out in a gale, and smoothing the frown from his brow with an air of relief.

"So am I; but a kind word will govern me when all the king's horses and all the king's men couldn't," said Jo, trying to say a kind word for her friend, who seemed to get into one scrape only to fall into another.

"You think I'm not kind to him, hey?" was the sharp answer.

"Oh, dear, no, sir; you are rather too kind sometimes, and then just a trifle hasty when he tries your patience. Don't you think you are?"

Jo was determined to have it out now, and tried to look quite placid, though she quaked a little after her bold speech. To her great relief and surprise, the old gentleman only threw his spectacles on to the table with a rattle, and exclaimed, frankly—

"You're right, I am! I love the boy, but he tries my patience past bearing, and I don't know how it will end, if we go on so."

"I'll tell you—he'll run away." Jo was sorry for that speech the minute it was made; she meant to warn him that Laurie would not bear much restraint, and hoped he would be more forbearing with the lad.

Mr. Laurence's ruddy face changed suddenly, and he sat down with a troubled glance at the picture of a handsome man, which hung over his table. It was Laurie's father, who *had* run away in his youth, and married against the imperious old man's will. Jo fancied he remembered and regretted the past, and she wished she had held her tongue.

"He won't do it, unless he is very much worried, and only threatens it sometimes, when he gets tired of studying. I often think I should like to, especially since my hair was cut ; so if you ever miss us, you may advertise for two boys, and look among the ships bound for India."

She laughed as she spoke, and Mr. Laurence looked relieved, evidently taking the whole as a joke.

"You hussy, how dare you talk in that way ? where's your respect for me, and your proper bring-ing up ? Bless the boys and girls ! what torments they are ; yet we can't do without them," he said, pinching her cheeks, good-humouredly.

"Go and bring that boy down to his dinner, tell him it's all right, and advise him not to put on tragedy airs with his grandfather ; I won't bear it."

"He won't come, sir ; he feels badly because you didn't believe him when he said he couldn't tell. I think the shaking hurt his feelings very much."

Jo tried to look pathetic, but must have failed,

for Mr. Laurence began to laugh, and she knew the day was won.

"I'm sorry for that, and ought to thank him for not shaking *me*, I suppose. What the dickens does the fellow expect?" and the old gentleman looked a trifle ashamed of his own testiness.

"If I was you, I'd write him an apology, sir. He says he won't come down till he has one; and talks about Washington, and goes on in an absurd way. A formal apology will make him see how foolish he is, and bring him down quite amiable. Try it; he likes fun, and this way is better than talking. I'll carry it up, and teach him his duty."

Mr. Laurence gave her a sharp look, and put on his spectacles, saying slowly, "You're a sly puss! but I don't mind being managed by you and Beth. Here, give me a bit of paper, and let us have done with this nonsense."

The note was written in the terms which one gentleman would use to another after offering some deep insult. Jo dropped a kiss on the top of Mr. Laurence's bald head, and ran up to slip the apology under Laurie's door, advising him, through the keyhole, to be submissive, decorous, and a few other agreeable impossibilities. Finding the door locked again, she left the note to do its work, and was going quietly away, when the young gentleman slid down the banisters, and waited for her at the bottom, saying, with his most virtuous expression of countenance, "What a good fellow you are, Jo! Did you get blown up?" he added, laughing.

"No; he was pretty clever, on the whole."

" Ah ! I got it all round ! even you cast me off over there, and I felt just ready to go to the deuce," he began, apologetically.

" Don't talk in that way ; turn over a new leaf and begin again, Teddy, my son."

" I keep turning over new leaves, and spoiling them, as I used to spoil my copy-books ; and I make so many beginnings there never will be an end," he said, dolefully.

" Go and eat your dinner ; you'll feel better after it. Men always croak when they are hungry," and Jo whisked out at the front door after that.

" That's a ' libel ' on my ' sect,' " answered Laurie, quoting Amy, as he went to partake of humble-pie dutifully with his grandfather, who was quite saintly in temper, and overwhelmingly respectful in manner, all the rest of the day.

Everyone thought the matter ended, and the little cloud blown over ; but the mischief was done, for, though others forgot it, Meg remembered. She never alluded to a certain person, but she thought of him a good deal, dreamed dreams more than ever ; and, once, Jo, rummaging her sister's desk for stamps, found a bit of paper scribbled over with the words, " Mrs. John Brooke ; " whereat she groaned tragically, and cast it into the fire, feeling that Laurie's prank had hastened the evil day for her.

CHAPTER XXII.

PLEASANT MEADOWS.

LIKE sunshine after storm were the peaceful weeks which followed. The invalids improved rapidly, and Mr. March began to talk of returning early in the new year. Beth was soon able to lie on the study sofa all day, amusing herself with her well-beloved cats, at first, and in time, with doll's sewing, which had fallen sadly behindhand. Her once active limbs were so stiff and feeble that Jo took her a daily airing about the house, in her strong arms. Meg cheerfully blackened and burnt her white hands cooking delicate messes for " the dear " ; while Amy, a loyal slave of the ring, celebrated her return by giving away as many of her treasures as she could prevail on her sisters to accept.

As Christmas approached, the usual mysteries began to haunt the house, and Jo frequently convulsed the family by proposing utterly impossible, or magnificently absurd ceremonies, in honour of this unusually merry Christmas. Laurie was equally impracticable, and would have had bonfires, sky-rockets, and triumphal arches, if he had had his own way.

Several days of unusually mild weather fitly

ushered in a splendid Christmas day. Hannah "felt in her bones that it was going to be an uncommonly plummy day," and she proved herself a true prophetess, for everybody and everything seemed bound to produce a grand success. To begin with : Mr. March wrote that he should soon be with them ; then Beth felt uncommonly well that morning, and, being dressed in her mother's gift,—a soft crimson merino wrapper,—was borne in triumph to the window, to behold the offering of Jo and Laurie. The Unquenchables had done their best to be worthy of the name, for, like elves, they had worked by night, and conjured up a comical surprise. Out in the garden stood a stately snow-maiden, crowned with holly, bearing a basket of fruit and flowers in one hand, and a great roll of new music in the other, a perfect rainbow of an Afghan round her chilly shoulders, and a Christmas carol issuing from her lips, on a pink paper streamer :—

"THE JUNGFRAU TO BETH.

" God bless you, dear Queen Bess !
    May nothing you dismay ;
But health, and peace, and happiness,
    Be yours, this Christmas-day.

" Here's fruit to feed our busy bee,
    And flowers for her nose ;
Here's music for her pianee,—
    An Afghan for her toes.

" A portrait of Joanna, see,
    By Raphael No. 2,
Who laboured with great industry,
    To make it fair and true.

> " Accept a ribbon red I beg,
>   For Madam Purrer's tail ;
> And ice cream made by lovely Peg,—
>   A Mont Blanc in a pail.
>
> " Their dearest love my makers laid
>   Within my breast of snow,
> Accept it, and the Alpine maid,
>   From Laurie and from Jo."

How Beth laughed when she saw it ! how Laurie ran up and down to bring in the gifts, and what ridiculous speeches Jo made as she presented them !

" I'm so full of happiness, that, if father was only here, I couldn't hold one drop more," said Beth, quite sighing with contentment as Jo carried her off to the study to rest after the excitement, and to refresh herself with the delicious grapes the "Jungfrau " sent her.

" So am I," added Jo, slapping her pocket wherein reposed the long-desired Undine and Sintram.

" I'm sure I am," echoed Amy, poring over the engraved copy of the Madonna and Child, which her mother had given her, in a pretty frame.

" Of course I am," cried Meg, smoothing the silvery folds of her first silk dress ; for Mr. Laurence had insisted on giving it.

" How can *I* be otherwise ! " said Mrs. March, gratefully, as her eyes went from her husband's letter to Beth's smiling face, and her hand caressed the brooch made of grey and golden, chestnut and dark brown hair, which the girls had just fastened on her breast.

Soon after every one had said they were so happy they could only hold one drop more, the drop came. Laurie opened the parlour door, and popped his head in; his face was so full of suppressed excitement, and his voice so treacherously joyful, that every one jumped up, though he only said, " Here's another Christmas present for the March family."

Before the words were well out of his mouth, he was whisked away somehow, and in his place appeared a tall man, muffled up to the eyes, leaning on the arm of another tall man, who tried to say something and couldn't. Of course there was a general stampede; and for several minutes everybody seemed to lose their wits, for the strangest things were done, and no one said a word. Mr. March became invisible in the embrace of four pairs of loving arms; Jo disgraced herself by nearly fainting away, and had to be doctored by Laurie in the china closet; Mr. Brooke kissed Meg entirely by mistake, as she somewhat incoherently explained; and Amy, the dignified, tumbled over a stool, and, never stopping to get up, hugged and cried over her father's boots in the most touching manner. Mrs. March was the first to recover herself, and held up her hand with a warning, " Hush! remember Beth!"

But it was too late; the study door flew open— the little red wrapper appeared on the threshold— joy put strength into the feeble limbs—and Beth ran straight into her father's arms.

It was not at all romantic, but a hearty laugh set everybody straight again—for Hannah was discovered behind the door, sobbing over the fat turkey, which she had forgotten to put down when she rushed up from the kitchen. As the laugh subsided, Mrs. March began to thank Mr. Brooke for his faithful care of her husband, at which Mr. Brooke suddenly remembered that Mr. March needed rest, and, seizing Laurie, he precipitately retired. Then the two invalids were ordered to repose, which they did, by both sitting in one big chair, and talking hard.

Mr. March told how he had longed to surprise them, and how, when the fine weather came, he had been allowed by his doctor to take advantage of it ; how devoted Brooke had been, and how he was altogether a most estimable and upright young man. Why Mr. March paused a minute just there, and, after a glance at Meg, who was violently poking the fire, looked at his wife with an inquiring lift of the eyebrows, I leave you to imagine ; also why Mrs. March gently nodded her head, and asked, rather abruptly, if he wouldn't have something to eat. Jo saw and understood the look, and she stalked grimly away, to get wine and beef tea.

There never *was* such a Christmas dinner as they had that day. The fat turkey was a sight to behold when Hannah sent him up, stuffed, browned and decorated. So was the plum-pudding, which quite melted in one's mouth ; likewise the jellies, in which Amy revelled like a fly in a honey-pot.

Mr. Laurence and his grandson dined with them ; also Mr. Brooke,—at whom Jo glowered darkly, to Laurie's infinite amusement. Two easy-chairs stood side by side at the head of the table, in which sat Beth and her father, feasting, modestly, on chicken and a little fruit. They drank healths, told stories, sung songs, " reminisced," as the old folks say, and had a thoroughly good time. The guests departed early, and as twilight gathered, the happy family sat together round the fire.

" Just a year ago we were groaning over the dismal Christmas we expected to have. Do you remember ? " asked Jo, breaking a short pause, which had followed a long conversation.

" Rather a pleasant year on the whole ! " said Meg, smiling at the fire, and congratulating herself on having treated Mr. Brooke with dignity.

" I'm glad it's over, because we've got you back," whispered Beth, who sat on her father's knee.

" Rather a rough road for you to travel, my little pilgrims, especially the latter part of it. But you have got on bravely ; and I think the burdens are in a fair way to tumble off very soon," said Mr. March, looking, with fatherly satisfaction, at the four young faces gathered round him.

" How do you know ? Did mother tell you ? " asked Jo.

" Not much ; straws show which way the wind blows ; and I've made several discoveries to-day."

" Oh, tell us what they are ! " cried Meg, who sat beside him.

" Here is one ! " and taking up the hand which lay on the arm of his chair, he pointed to a little roughened forefinger, a burn on the back, and two or three little hard spots on the palm. " I remember a time when this hand was white and smooth, and your first care was to keep it so. It was very pretty then, but to me it is much prettier now,— for in these seeming blemishes I read a little history. A burntoffering has been made of vanity ; this hardened palm has earned something better than blisters, and I'm sure the sewing done by these pricked fingers will last a long time, so much good-will went into the stitches. Meg, my dear, I value the womanly skill which keeps home happy more than white hands or fashionable accomplishments ; I'm proud to shake this good, industrious little hand, and hope I shall not soon be asked to give it away."

If Meg had wanted a reward for hours of patient labour, she received it in the hearty pressure of her father's hand, and the approving smile he gave her.

" What about Jo ? Please say something nice ; for she has tried so hard, and been so very, very good to me," said Beth, in her father's ear.

He laughed, and looked across at the tall girl who sat opposite, with an unusually mild expression in her brown face.

" In spite of the curly crop, I don't see the ' son Jo ' whom I left a year ago," said Mr. March. " I see a young lady who pins her collar straight, laces her boots neatly, and neither whistles, talks slang, nor lies on the rug, as she used to do. Her face is rather thin and pale just now, with watching and anxiety ; but I like to look at it, for it has grown gentler, and her voice is lower ; she doesn't bounce, but moves quietly, and takes care of a certain little person in a motherly way which delights me. I rather miss my wild girl; but if I get a strong, helpful, tender-hearted woman in her place, I shall feel quite satisfied. I don't know whether the shearing sobered our black sheep, but I do know that in all Washington I couldn't find anything beautiful enough to be bought with the five-and-twenty dollars which my good girl sent me."

Jo's keen eyes were rather dim for a minute, and her thin face grew rosy in the firelight, as she received her father's praise, feeling that she did deserve a portion of it.

"Now, Beth," said Amy, longing for her turn, but ready to wait.

"There's so little of her I'm afraid to say much, for fear she will slip away altogether, though she is not so shy as she used to be," began their father cheerfully; but recollecting how nearly he *had* lost her, he held her close, saying, tenderly, with her cheek against his own, "I've got you safe, my Beth, and I'll keep you so, please God."

After a minute's silence, he looked down at Amy, who sat at his feet, and said, with a caress of the shining hair—

"I observed that Amy took drumsticks at dinner, ran errands for her mother all the afternoon, gave Meg her place to-night, and has waited on every one with patience and good humour. I also observe that she does not fret much, nor prink at the glass, and has not even mentioned a very pretty ring that she wears; so I conclude that she has learned to think of other people more, and of herself less, and has decided to try and mould her character

as carefully as she moulds her little clay figures.
I am glad of this ; for although I should be very
proud of a graceful statue made by her, I shall be
infinitely prouder of a lovable daughter, with a
talent for making life beautiful to herself and
others."

"What are you thinking of, Beth ? " asked Jo,
when Amy had thanked her father and told about
her ring.

"I read in ' Pilgrim's Progress ' to-day, how,
after many troubles, Christian and Hopeful came
to a pleasant green meadow, where lilies bloomed
all the year round, and there they rested happily,
as we do now, before they went on to their journey's
end," answered Beth ; adding, as she slipped out
of her father's arms, and went slowly to the instrument, "It's singing time now, and I want to be in
my old place. I'll try to sing the song of the
shepherd boy which the pilgrims heard. I made
the music for father, because he likes the verses."

So, sitting at the dear little piano, Beth softly
touched the keys, and, in the sweet voice they had
never thought to hear again, sung, to her own
accompaniment, the quaint hymn, which was a
singularly fitting song for her :—

> " He that is down need fear no fall ;
>   He that is low no pride ;
> He that is humble ever shall
>   Have God to be his guide.

> " I am content with what I have,
>   Little be it or much ;
> And, Lord ! contentment still I crave,
>   Because thou savest such.

Fulness to them a burden is,
That go on Pilgrimage ;
Here little, and hereafter bliss
Is best from age to age ! "

CHAPTER XXIII.

AUNT MARCH SETTLES THE QUESTION.

LIKE bees swarming after their queen, mother and
daughters hovered about Mr. March the next day,
neglecting everything to look at, wait upon, and
listen to, the new invalid, who was in a fair way to
be killed by kindness. As he sat propped up in
the big chair by Beth's sofa, with the other three
close by, and Hannah popping in her head now and
then, " to peek at the dear man," nothing seemed
needed to complete their happiness. But something
was needed, and the elder ones felt it, though none
confessed the fact. Mr. and Mrs. March looked
at one another with an anxious expression, as their
eyes followed Meg. Jo had sudden fits of sobriety,
and was seen to shake her fist at Mr. Brooke's
umbrella, which had been left in the hall ; Meg
was absent-minded, shy and silent, started when
the bell rang, and coloured when John's name was
mentioned ; Amy said, " Every one seemed waiting for something, and couldn't settle down, which
was queer, since father was safe at home," and
Beth innocently wondered why their neighbours
didn't run over as usual.

Laurie went by in the afternoon, and, seeing

Meg at the window, seemed suddenly possessed with a melodramatic fit, for he fell down upon one knee in the snow, beat his breast, tore his hair, and clasped his hands imploringly, as if begging some boon ; and when Meg told him to behave himself, and go away, he wrung imaginary tears out of his handkerchief, and staggered round the corner as if in utter despair.

" What does the goose mean ? " said Meg, laughing, and trying to look unconscious.

" He's showing you how your John will go on by and by. Touching, isn't it ? " answered Jo, scornfully.

" Don't say *my John* ; it isn't proper or true " ; but Meg's voice lingered over the words as if they sounded pleasant to her. " Please don't plague me, Jo ; I've told you I don't care *much* about him, and there isn't to be anything said, but we are al to be friendly, and go on as before."

" We can't, for something *has* been said, and Laurie's mischief has spoilt you for me. I see it, and so does mother ; you are not like your old self a bit, and seem ever so far away from me. I don't mean to plague you, and will bear it like a man, but I do wish it was all settled. I hate to wait ; so if you mean ever to do it, make haste, and have it over quick," said Jo, pettishly.

" *I* can't say or do anything till he speaks, and he won't, because father said I was too young," began Meg, bending over her work with a queer little smile, which suggested that she did not quite agree with her father on that point.

" If he did speak, you wouldn't know what to

say, but would cry or blush, or let him have his own way, instead of giving a good, decided No."

"I'm not so silly and weak as you think. I know what I should say, for I've planned it all, so I needn't be taken unawares; there's no knowing what may happen, and I wished to be prepared."

Jo couldn't help smiling at the important air which Meg had unconsciously assumed, and which was as becoming as the pretty colour varying in her cheeks.

"Would you mind telling me what you'd say?" asked Jo, more respectfully.

"Not at all; you are sixteen now, quite old enough to be my confidant, and my experience will be useful to you by and by, perhaps, in your own affairs of this sort."

"Don't mean to have any; it's fun to watch other people philander, but I should feel like a fool doing it myself," said Jo, looking alarmed at the thought.

"I guess not, if you liked any one very much, and he liked you." Meg spoke as if to herself, and glanced out at the lane where she had often seen lovers walking together in the summer twilight.

"I thought you were going to tell your speech to that man," said Jo, rudely shortening her sister's little reverie.

"Oh, I should merely say, quite calmly and decidedly, 'Thank you, Mr. Brooke, you are very kind, but I agree with father, that I am too young to enter into any engagement at present; so please say no more, but let us be friends as we were.'

"Hum! that's stiff and cool enough. I don't believe you'll ever say it, and I know he won't be satisfied if you do. If he goes on like the rejected lovers in books, you'll give in rather than hurt his feelings."

"No! I won't! I shall tell him I've made up my mind, and shall walk out of the room with dignity."

Meg rose as she spoke, and was just going to rehearse the dignified exit, when a step in the hall made her fly into her seat, and begin to sew as if her life depended on finishing that particular seam in a given time. Jo smothered a laugh at the sudden change, and, when some one gave a modest tap, opened the door with a grim aspect, which was anything but hospitable.

"Good afternoon, I came to get my umbrella —that is, to see how your father finds himself to-day," said Mr. Brooke, getting a trifle confused, as his eye went from one tell-tale face to the other.

"It's very well, he's in the rack, I'll get him, and tell it you are here," and having jumbled her father and the umbrella well together in her reply, Jo slipped out of the room to give Meg a chance to make her speech, and air her dignity. But the instant she vanished Meg began to sidle toward the door, murmuring—

"Mother will like to see you, pray sit down, I'll call her."

"Don't go; you are afraid of me, Margaret?" and Mr. Brooke looked so hurt, that Meg thought she must have done something very rude. She

blushed up to the little curls on her forehead, for
he had never called her Margaret before, and she
was surprised to find how natural and sweet it
seemed to hear him say it. Anxious to appear
friendly and at her ease, she put out her hand with
a confiding gesture, and said, gratefully—

"How can I be afraid when you have been so
kind to father? I only wish I could thank you
for it."

"Shall I tell you how?" asked Mr. Brooke,
holding the small hand fast in both his big ones,
and looking down at Meg with so much love in
the brown eyes, that her heart began to flutter,
and she both longed to run away and to stop and
listen.

"Oh no, please don't—I'd rather not," she said,
trying to withdraw her hand, and looking frightened in spite of her denial.

"I won't trouble you, I only want to know if
you care for me a little, Meg, I love you so much,
dear," added Mr. Brooke, tenderly.

This was the moment for the calm, proper speech,
but Meg didn't make it, she forgot every word of
it, hung her head, and answered, "I don't know,"
so softly, that John had to stoop down to catch
the foolish little reply.

He seemed to think it was worth the trouble,
for he smiled to himself as if quite satisfied, pressed
the plump hand gratefully, and said, in his most
persuasive tone, "Will you try and find out? I
want to know so much; for I can't go to work
with any heart until I learn whether I am to have
my reward in the end or not."

" I'm too young," faltered Meg, wondering why she was so fluttered, yet rather enjoying it.

" I'll wait ; and, in the meantime, you could be learning to like me. Would it be a very hard lesson, dear ? "

" Not if I chose to learn it, but——"

" Please choose to learn, Meg. I love to teach, and this is easier than German," broke in John, getting possession of the other hand, so that she had no way of hiding her face, as he bent to look into it.

His tone was properly beseeching ; but, stealing a shy look at him, Meg saw that his eyes were merry as well as tender, and that he wore the satisfied smile of one who had no doubt of his success. This nettled her ; Annie Moffat's foolish lessons in coquetry came into her mind, and the love of power, which sleeps in the bosoms of the best of little women, woke up all of a sudden, and took possession of her. She felt excited and strange, and, not knowing what else to do, followed a capricious impulse, and, withdrawing her hands, said, petulantly, " I *don't* choose ; please go away, and let me be ! "

Poor Mr. Brooke looked as if his lovely castle in the air was tumbling about his ears, for he had never seen Meg in such a mood before, and it rather bewildered him.

" Do you really mean that ? " he asked, anxiously, following her as she walked away.

" Yes, I do ; I don't want to be worried about such things. Father says I needn't ; it's too soon, and I'd rather not."

"Mayn't I hope you'll change your mind by and by? I'll wait, and say nothing till you have had more time. Don't play with me, Meg. I didn't think that of you."

"Don't think of me at all. I'd rather you wouldn't," said Meg, taking a naughty satisfaction in trying her lover's patience and her own power.

He was grave and pale now, and looked decidedly more like the novel heroes whom she admired; but he neither slapped his forehead nor tramped about the room, as they did; he just stood looking at her so wistfully, so tenderly, that she found her heart relenting in spite of her. What would have happened next I cannot say, if Aunt March had not come hobbling in at this interesting minute.

The old lady couldn't resist her longing to see her nephew; for she had met Laurie as she took her airing, and, hearing of Mr. March's arrival drove straight out to see him. The family were all busy in the back part of the house, and she had made her way quietly in, hoping to surprise them. She did surprise two of them so much, that Meg started as if she had seen a ghost, and Mr. Brooke vanished into the study.

"Bless me! what's all this?" cried the old lady with a rap of her cane, as she glanced from the pale young gentleman to the scarlet young lady.

"It's father's friend. I'm *so* surprised to see you!" stammered Meg, feeling that she was in for a lecture now.

"That's evident," returned Aunt March, sitting down. "But what is father's friend saying, to make you look like a peony? There's mischief going on, and I insist upon knowing what it is!" with another rap.

"We were merely talking. Mr. Brooke came for his umbrella," began Meg, wishing that Mr. Brooke and the umbrella were safely out of the house.

"Brooke? That boy's tutor? Ah! I understand now. I know all about it. Jo blundered into a wrong message in one of your pa's letters, and I made her tell me. You haven't gone and accepted him, child?" cried Aunt March, looking scandalized.

"Hush! he'll hear! Shan't I call mother?" said Meg, much troubled.

"Not yet. I've something to say to you, and I must free my mind at once. Tell me, do you mean to marry this Cook? If you do, not one penny of my money ever goes to you. Remember that, and be a sensible girl," said the old lady, impressively.

Now Aunt March possessed in perfection the art of rousing the spirit of opposition in the gentlest people, and enjoyed doing it. The best of us have a spice of perversity in us, especially when we are young and in love. If Aunt March had begged Meg to accept John Brooke, she would probably have declared that she couldn't think of it; but, as she was peremptorily ordered *not* to like him, she immediately made up her mind that she would. Inclination as well as perversity made the decision easy, and, being already much excited, Meg opposed the old lady with unusual spirit.

"I shall marry whom I please, Aunt March, and you can leave your money to any one you like," she said, nodding her head with a resolute air.

Highty tighty! Is that the way you take my advice, miss? You'll be sorry for it by and by when you've tried love in a cottage, and found it a failure."

"It can't be a worse one than some people find in big houses," retorted Meg.

Aunt March put on her glasses and took a look at the girl,—for she did not know her in this new mood. Meg hardly knew herself, she felt so brave and independent,—so glad to defend John, and assert her right to love him, if she liked. Aunt March saw that she had begun wrong, and, after a little pause, made a fresh start, saying, as mildly as she could, "Now, Meg, my dear, be reasonable, and take my advice. I mean it kindly, and don't want you to spoil your whole life by making a mistake at the beginning. You ought to marry well, and help your family; it's your duty to make a rich match, and it ought to be impressed upon you."

"Father and mother don't think so; they like John, though he *is* poor."

"Your pa and ma, my dear, have no more worldly wisdom than two babies."

"I'm glad of it," cried Meg, stoutly.

Aunt March took no notice, but went on with her lecture, "This Rook is poor, and hasn't got any rich relations, has he?"

"No; but he has many warm friends."

"You can't live on friends; try it and see how

cool they'll grow. He hasn't any business, has he ? "

" Not yet ; Mr. Laurence is going to help him."

" That won't last long. James Laurence is a crotchety old fellow, and not to be depended on. So you intend to marry a man without money, position, or business, and go on working harder than you do now, when you might be comfortable all your days by minding me, and doing better ? I thought you had more sense, Meg."

" I couldn't do better if I waited half my life ! John is good and wise ; he's got heaps of talent ; he's willing to work, and sure to get on, he's so energetic and brave. Every one likes and respects him, and I'm proud to think he cares for me, though I'm so poor, and young, and silly," said Meg, looking prettier than ever in her earnestness.

" He knows *you* have got rich relations, child ; that's the secret of his liking, I suspect."

" Aunt March, how dare you say such a thing ? John is above such meanness, and I won't listen to you a minute if you talk so," cried Meg, indignantly, forgetting everything but the injustice of the old lady's suspicions. " My John wouldn't marry for money, any more than I would. We are willing to work, and we mean to wait. I'm not afraid of being poor, for I've been happy so far, and I know I shall be with him, because he loves me, and I——"

Meg stopped there, remembering, all of a sudden, that she hadn't made up her mind ; that she had told " her John " to go away, and that he might be overhearing her inconsistent remarks.

Aunt March was very angry, for she had set her heart on having her pretty niece make a fine match, and something in the girl's happy young face made the lonely old woman feel both sad and sour.

"Well; I wash my hands of the whole affair! You are a wilful child, and you've lost more than you know by this piece of folly. No, I won't stop; I'm disappointed in you, and haven't spirits to see your pa now. Don't expect anything from me when you are married; your Mr. Brooke's friends must take care of you. I'm done with you for ever."

And, slamming the door in Meg's face, Aunt March drove off in high dudgeon. She seemed to take all the girl's courage with her; for, when left alone, Meg stood a moment undecided whether to laugh or cry. Before she could make up her mind, she was taken possession of by Mr. Brooke, who said, all in one breath, "I couldn't help hearing, Meg. Thank you for defending me, and Aunt March for proving that you *do* care for me a little bit."

"I didn't know how much, till she abused you," began Meg.

"And I needn't go away, but stay and be happy —may I, dear?"

Here was another fine chance to make the crushing speech and the stately exit, but Meg never thought of doing either, and disgraced herself for ever in Jo's eyes, by meekly whispering, "Yes, John," and hiding her face on Mr. Brooke's waistcoat.

Fifteen minutes after Aunt March's departure, Jo came softly downstairs, paused an instant at the parlour door, and, hearing no sound within, nodded and smiled, with a satisfied expression, saying to herself, " She has sent him away as we planned, and that affair is settled. I'll go and hear the fun, and have a good laugh over it."

But poor Jo never got her laugh, for she was transfixed upon the threshold by the spectacle which held her there, staring with her mouth nearly as wide open as her eyes. Going in to exult over a fallen enemy, and to praise a strong-minded sister for the banishment of an objectionable lover, it certainly *was* a shock to behold the aforesaid enemy serenely sitting on the sofa, with the strong-minded sister enthroned upon his knee, and wearing an expression of the most abject submission. Jo gave a sort of gasp, as if a cold shower-bath had suddenly fallen upon her,—for such an unexpected turning of the tables actually took her breath away. At the odd sound the lovers turned and saw her. Meg jumped up, looking both proud and shy ; but " that man," as Jo called him, actually laughed, and said, coolly, as he kissed the astonished new comer, " Sister Jo, congratulate us ! "

That was adding insult to injury ! it was altogether too much ! and, making some wild demonstrations with her hands, Jo vanished without a word. Rushing upstairs, she startled the invalids by exclaiming, as she burst into the room, " Oh, *do* somebody go down quick ! John Brooke is acting dreadfully, and Meg likes it ! "

Mr. and Mrs. March left the room with speed ;

and, casting herself upon the bed, Jo cried and scolded tempestuously as she told the awful news to Beth and Amy. The little girls, however, considered it a most agreeable and interesting event, and Jo got little comfort from them ; so she went up to her refuge in the garret, and confided her troubles to the rats.

Nobody ever knew what went on in the parlour that afternoon ; but a great deal of talking was done, and quiet Mr. Brooke astonished his friends by the eloquence and spirit with which he pleaded his suit, told his plans, and persuaded them to arrange everything just as he wanted it.

The tea-bell rang before he had finished describing the paradise which he meant to earn for Meg, and he proudly took her in to supper, both looking so happy, that Jo hadn't the heart to be jealous or dismal. Amy was very much impressed by John's devotion and Meg's dignity. Beth beamed at them from a distance, while Mr. and Mrs. March surveyed the young couple with such tender satisfaction, that it was perfectly evident that Aunt March was right in calling them as " unworldly as a pair of babies." No one ate much, but every one looked very happy, and the old room brightened up amazingly when the first romance of the family began there.

" You can't say 'nothing pleasant ever happens now,' can you, Meg ? " said Amy, trying to decide how she would group the lovers in the sketch she was planning to make.

" No, I'm sure I can't. How much has happened since I said that ! It seems a year ago," answered

Meg, in a blissful dream, lifted far above such common things as an ordinary cup of tea and bread and butter.

"The joys come close upon the sorrows this time, and I rather think the changes have begun, said Mrs. March. "In most families there comes, now and then, a year full of events; this has been such an one, but it ends well, after all."

"Hope the next will end better," muttered Jo, who found it very hard to see Meg absorbed in a stranger before her face; for Jo loved a few persons very dearly, and dreaded to have their affection lost or lessened in any way.

"I hope the third year from this *will* end better; I mean it shall, if I live to work out my plans," said Mr. Brooke, smiling at Meg, as if everything had become possible to him now.

"Doesn't it seem very long to wait?" asked Amy, who was in a hurry for the wedding.

"I've got so much to learn before I shall be ready, it seems such a short time to me," answered Meg, with a sweet gravity in her face, never seen there before.

"You have only to wait. *I* am to do the work," said John, beginning his labours by picking up Meg's napkin, with an expression which caused Jo to shake her head, and then say to herself, with an air of relief, as the front door banged, " Here comes Laurie; now we shall have a little sensible conversation."

But Jo was mistaken; for Laurie came prancing in, overflowing with spirits, bearing a great bridal-looking bouquet for "Mrs. John Brooke," and evidently labouring under the delusion that the whole affair had been brought about by his excellent management.

" I knew Brooke would have it all his own way,— he always does ; for when he makes up his mind to accomplish anything, it's done, though the sky falls," said Laurie, when he had presented his offering and his congratulations.

" Much obliged for that recommendation. I take it as a good omen for the future, and invite you to my wedding on the spot," answered Mr. Brooke, who felt at peace with all mankind, even his mischievous pupil.

" I'll come if I'm at the ends of the earth ; for the sight of Jo's face alone, on that occasion, would be worth a long journey. You don't festive, ma'am ; what's the matter ? " asked Laurie, following her into a corner of the parlour, whither all adjourned to greet Mr. Laurence.

" I don't approve of the match, but I've made up my mind to bear it, and shall not say a word against it," said Jo, solemnly. " You can't know how hard it is for me to give up Meg," she continued, with a little quiver in her voice.

" You don't give her up. You only go halves," said Laurie consolingly.

" It can never be the same again. I've lost my dearest friend," sighed Jo.

" You've got me, anyhow. I'm not good for much, I know ; but I'll stand by you, Jo, all the days of my life ; upon my word I will ! " and Laurie meant what he said.

" I know you will, and I'm ever so much obliged ;

you are always a great comfort to me, Teddy," returned Jo, gratefully shaking hands.

"Well, now, don't be dismal, there's a good fellow. It's all right, you see. Meg is happy; Brooke will fly round and get settled immediately; grandpa will attend to him, and it will be very jolly to see Meg in her own little house. We'll have capital times after she is gone, for I shall be through college before long, and then we'll go abroad, or some nice trip or other. Wouldn't that console you?"

"I rather think it would; but there's no knowing what may happen in three years," said Jo, thoughtfully.

"That's true! Don't you wish you could take a look forward, and see where we shall be then? I do," returned Laurie.

"I think not, for I might see something sad; and every one looks so happy now, I don't believe they could be much improved," and Jo's eyes went slowly round the room, brightening as they looked, for the prospect was a pleasant one.

Father and mother sat together quietly re-living the first chapter of the romance which for them began some twenty years ago. Amy was drawing the lovers, who sat apart in a beautiful world of their own, the light of which touched their faces with a grace the little artist could not copy. Beth lay on her sofa talking cheerily with her old friend, who held her little hand as if he felt that it possessed the power to lead him along the peaceful ways she walked. Jo lounged in her favourite low seat, with the grave, quiet look which best became her; and Laurie, leaning on the back of her chair, his chin on a level with her curly head, smiled with his friendliest aspect, and nodded at her in the long glass which reflected them both.

So grouped the curtain falls upon Meg, Jo, Beth and Amy. Whether it ever rises again, depends upon the reception given to the first act of the domestic drama, called " LITTLE WOMEN."

